For Courtney and the late Harry Crews.
Also for Arian Asllani: *Ju jeni të bukur, vëlla*

CONNOR DeBRULER

THE MOUNTAIN DEVILS

MONTAG

And I saw the woman drunken with the blood of the saints, and with the blood of the martyrs of Jesus: and when I saw her, I wondered with great admiration.

—*Revelation 17:6*

To die daily implies be born daily.

—*Diane Cluck*

CONNOR DE BRULER

THE MOUNTAIN DEVILS

THERE IS A KILLER STALKING THE apple orchards of East Tennessee. The killer drives a stolen vehicle when he takes a victim. It is always a pickup-truck or an SUV which he later abandons in a gulch or the weedy parking lot of a derelict grocery store. The bodies turn up at dawn. Some are mauled beyond recognition. He only kills at night. He kills the immigrant workers of the farm markets and pick-your-own apple and blueberry orchards. They are all third-generation Mexican journeymen from the iron-belt or day-laborers from the Southwest in search of fixed work. Their community lives in fear.

At dusk, the women walk from the orchards and open fields along the dirt roads with their arms locked, unprotected except for a few switchblades and farm implements. The men keep handguns in the glove boxes of their trucks, but the women refuse to ride with them, worried the truck they choose will be the next to go missing. Some fear the killer is an orchard worker, one of their own.

The police cannot catch him. The killer strikes without pattern. The state police are involved and the North Carolina departments just over the border have been alerted, but there are no leads. No one alive has seen him.

When the season is finished, he stops killing. People aren't missing and trucks aren't being discovered in parking lots. The immigrants are now working in pumpkin patches, corn mazes, slaughterhouses and turkey farms. But the community still lives in fear. A month goes by. Rumors spread of similar crimes in Missouri. A suspect is caught. A tall white man from the Northwest has been killing women in the wake of a tornado. He is thought to be the same killer. The pandemonium subsides.

Another season comes to an end. The women aren't afraid to ride with the men any longer. They take their time walking home. They finish the harvest and begin sawing and wrapping evergreens. They mull wine and tie wreathes.

The killer strikes again with the first snow. Two children have gone missing. A woman's body is discovered on the edge of a goat farm and, not even half a mile away, a police cruiser sits in the grass covered in ice and the officer lies dead in the middle of the two-lane road. He is decapitated. His head, along with the two children, cannot be found. The latest stolen vehicle is found at a gas-station. It is the first chance the police have to see the killer on a surveillance camera. They watch in awe as the stolen truck pulls in beside a gas pump. The face is blurred by the DVR static.

The killer is a teenage girl.

PART ONE

1.

The steppe, spilling over from the green of the Urals, collided with the desolate outskirts of the Hindu Kush, dividing the tribal territories from the Himalayas. The barren topography of desert and steep crags was home only to small pockets of families. Clusters of box-like huts, known as *kolbas,* haunted the mountaintops on foundations of loose stone. The ridges grinned like jagged teeth.

Erik unfastened his pack and set it against the wall of the empty kolba. He felt colder inside than he did in the icy wind. The incessant gusts lead to long intervals of heavy rain. His Velcro nameplate was worn, falling off his uniform. His name, stark black letters jammed together to conserve space, read "VANDEROER." He pressed the nameplate to his breast, keeping the fibers hooked to his beige combat suit. Through the glassless window, Erik watched the herd of goats negotiating the sharp rocks on the ridge overlooking the old heroin field. The poppies were all chopped down and the soil had been chemically sabotaged. The goats hobbled in circles, bumping into one another, bleating in their nasal tone.

The sergeant kicked open the wooden door and shuffled into the kolba. "Jesus Christ, it's freezing in here."

Erik forced a smile.

"Sniper training in Alaska did y'all a whole lot of good when there are bushes and trees a plenty. Out here all we've got is high mountains, nothing, and higher mountains. Godammit, and if them Afghans didn't look like plain-as-day white folks when they wear blue jeans and t-shirts on the base, I'd be at a loss as to who to shoot. Remember the guy in Kabul with the blue eyes and red hair selling Chinese DVDS?"

"I don't think it was red," Erik said. "I remember it being lighter brown."

The sergeant looked out the window hole and scratched his scalp through his grey hair. "Want a smoke. Get out of this here shack. Got keep an eye on those fuckin' goats."

Erik stood up and followed his superior onto the ridge.

"The tides are changin' for us." He pointed to Erik's double chevron insignia. "When members of the United States military are reduced to watching after a goat herd. No, sir. Men like you and I. We're better 'an that."

"It's a sign of good faith," Erik said.

"What they don't tell you is these people will turn on you like a rabid, junkyard dog for nothing. And what kind of farmer needs soldiers to look after his goats. It ain't like guns are in short supply up in these hills." He spat into the ground.

"Are you gonna break out the cigarettes?" Erik said, tossing a rock down the ridge.

"You sound like a German man brought up in Australia, Erik. Everybody talk like that in South Africa?"

"Pretty much."

Erik van der Roer had moved to the United States while facing conscription to an Afrikaans military. He settled in Knoxville, Tennessee and, after a fruitless search for under-the-table employment, signed the dotted line to join the U.S. Marine Corps. The irony of which was lost on him.

"'Pretty much' he says. Out here in a war zone without a care in the world. I envy you."

"Just waiting for the smoke. Not here to be interviewed."

The sergeant pulled a pack of cigarettes from his shoulder pocket and handed one to Erik before setting one in his mouth. He flicked a metallic wick lighter like a switchblade and lit both cigarettes.

Erik thanked him for the smoke.

"Don't forget who you're talkin' to," the sergeant said.

"No, sir. Sorry, sir," Erik said.

The Sergeant inhaled and exhaled slowly.

"Now, all we need is cold beer. They got good beer down in South Africa?"

"Yeah, but I'm partial to a red wine and coke mix."

"Now that just sounds like a bad hangover."

Erik smiled more genuinely. "It's the *worst* hangover."

They both laughed. The sergeant shook his head. "I don't doubt it. Not for a second." He paused for a moment and took a deep drag on the cigarette's filter, then carried it in the side of his teeth the way fighter pilots chewed on their American Spirits. Erik observed him.

"So how about it, Africa? Why the USMC?"

"Fast track to citizenship."

"That it is. We're not always as privileged to get a man like you in our midst. Mostly we just got Mexicans and Costa Ricans trying to go legit, and Russians running the show. Can you believe it? Fucking Russians in the USMC. As if we're supposed to trust our lives with them, spying as they are for the ex-KGB. I don't buy it—not for one second."

"So citizenship, huh? What are you going to do with it then?"

"Work."

"It is always a good thing to work. I bet you can't guess what I did before this?"

"What?"

"I was a welder. MIG welder. I worked in a factory in Johnson City, Tennessee. It was an honest living."

Erik listened to the sergeant ramble on, straining to keep his palms steady as he felt the lightness of his carbine. He had emptied the magazine at gunpoint twenty minutes prior. Suddenly to his left, just behind the boulder, he saw a short man with a white polo shirt holding the teen shepherd girl's mouth closed. He pressed a long Bowie knife to her throat with his trembling hand. Below Erik and the sergeant, just behind the herd of goats, lay an enemy sniper. The goats had been trained to congregate in clusters.

A single bead of sweat dropped down his face as his Sergeant droned on stabbing at the sky with his forefinger. He wiped his forehead casually, trying not to attract attention.

"Now tell me something and don't judge a man for being ignorant, son. Do ya'll speak English in South Africa?"

"Sure," he said.

"What?"

"Well, yes and no. We speak English in the Cape, but there are eleven languages across the country."

"Which one is the official language?"

"They all are."

"The fuck?"

He looked at the belt feeder of the sergeant's M240 still filled with pointed bullets like brass spikes. He heard a muffled sound from behind the boulder. It was the girl choking for air in the assassin's hand. The sergeant noticed it too.

"The hell was that?" he said, spinning around to look.

"I didn't hear anything," Erik lied.

"Just as well," he said as he sat beside Erik and finished his cigarette.

The distant bleat of a goat broke the silence. One of the goats had wandered away from the group and trotted down the ridge toward the field.

"Damn goat. I knew that was going to happen," the sergeant said, stubbing his cigarette out on a rock. "Well, I guess I'm gonna have to go and get it?"

Erik tossed the smoldering yellow filter away. "I'll go get it."

"Don't bother. Have another cigarette. I have to drain the weasel anyway." He gave Erik the pack and the lighter and, leaving his machine gun behind, walked back up to the kolba and started urinating on the ground, his back to Erik. Erik stared at the herd of goats. He could almost see the sniper. In one panicked motion, he tossed his empty carbine aside and dove forward for the machine gun. Fire burst out of the muzzle as shells sprayed into the air like a stream of water. The belt feeder whipped up and down. The goats' bodies exploded. The living ones dragged their entrails behind them. The sniper's body lay face down in the loose rocks.

"What the hell is wrong with you, boy?" the sergeant said, running back to Erik. The man behind the boulder saw his opportunity. He jumped down, losing his grip on the girl, but slit the sergeant's throat before Erik was able to turn the gun their way, disintegrating both of their bodies in the machine gun fire.

The surviving goats ran alongside the girl through the old heroin field. Erik called out to her in Dari, asking her to come back. He threw the smoking gun to the ground and ran after her down the ridge.

2.

The official report described Erik's descent into field and his attempts to calm the girl. It even the described the wounded goats hobbling past him, but it failed to mention the claymores that had been planted by the U.S. military several months before the incident. According to the report, the girl had triggered an improvised explosive device left by tribal forces. It also clearly stated that he had killed two Taliban insurgents when, in fact, they where Uzbek drug runners. The girl, who spoke Urdu not Dari, triggered an explosion with the arch of her foot. There was nothing left of her or her goats. Erik was rushed to the military hospital. According to the report, Erik as unharmed in the blast and was discharged a day later.

When his unit returned to Germany, Erik deserted the base. He chose to live in Bavaria under a false identity. There, he did his best to forget about the war and the military, riding his bicycle in the European summertime along man-made lakes. Careless and drunk off the wine from his meals, he would reach out with his hand and graze the bulrush and birch trees growing on the mossy banks as he rode. He took his bicycle everywhere, drifting for hours across the menagerie of miniscule hamlets. The lakes stretched for miles and were often drained once the seasonal carp had been harvested, creating craters of desert wasteland punched into the otherwise lush, grassy countryside. After eight months AWOL, he received a lukewarm honorable discharge. When he was free to leave, he flew back to New York and took an Amtrak to Tennessee. Most members of the old unit were either from Colorado, California, or Eastern Tennessee. His friend Fillmore, a field medic, suggested that if he ever got to Tennessee, he should make a town called Bishop's Pasture his home. There, in the midst of Appalachia, Erik started his new life trekking the chipped sidewalks with his military duffel bag in toe, looking for work.

3.

Lady Godiva's, one of the town's only strip clubs, looked more like a garage than a topless bar: a windowless, rectangular structure of colorless, corrugated steel. Stowed away from the churches and fast-food restaurants of the main road, Godiva's had been built on a bald hillock of red clay and hidden from the nearest thoroughfare by a protracted gravel path blazed in the wild bamboo. Erik walked up the path, his duffel bag slung over his shoulder, a cheap cigarette hanging from his bearded lip. He stared at the marquee for some time, smoking his cigarette. A gust of cold wind broke through the brittle canopy to the left of the metal building and a murder of crows glided into the gray horizon. He watched the black birds and sucked on the tip of the filter with his pinched thumb and index finger, casting the smoldering butt into the clay. He set his bag by the eave, seeing that no one else was around. The bag made him look like a desperate vagabond and he knew it.

It was cool and dark inside. The smell of draft beer and Lysol mingled in the ether. The light was dim and orange like the house lights of an old theater. A short man in a black t-shirt sat in a tall stool at the entrance, reading a glossy magazine. A young woman in a G-string lay on the hood of a green Cadillac on its cover. He set the magazine aside and jumped off the stool to approach Erik. His triceps flared out from his arms like wings and his chest puffed outward, pigeon-like. He looked uncomfortable in his own skin.

"Cover charge is five dollars during the day," he said.

"I'm looking for the manager, actually," Erik said.

"Ace?"

"Yes, sir," Erik said, nodding.

The bouncer flinched and leaned his head back into the darkness toward the bar.

"Carla!" he yelled in a rasped voice.

Erik looked past the vacant platform with the dark brass pole and saw a tall woman in a blue track suit, spinning childishly on a bar stool.

"Carla! Fetch Ace."

She stood up and disappeared through the wooden door with the words 'employee's only' in the center. The message struck Erik as ineffective in the dim lighting.

The bouncer turned to him.

"You can sit at the bar while you wait."

Erik thanked him and took a seat at the far end. He felt the breast pocket of his flannel shirt for the ballpoint pen a few times.

The bouncer returned to his magazine.

A plump woman emerged from the beaded doorway

behind the bar. She wore nothing but a pink bikini bottom. Erik studied the soft girth of her stomach and the rose tattoo below her right breast.

"What can I get you, honey?" she asked.

"I'm waiting on the manager," he said. "I'm alright for now."

She nodded and continued cleaning the counter.

Erik bit into his thumbnail when a stocky man in a white button-up shirt patted him on the back as if they had been friends for years, pulling up a seat beside him at the bar.

"I'm Ace," he said.

Erik shook his hand firmly.

"Erik van de Roer," he said.

Ace moved his upper lip, wrinkling the outline of his mouth and blonde mustache.

"I don't need to know your name," he said, removing an envelope from his side pocket. "You just tell the Reverend that I'm keepin' it comin' so long the share is solid. Now we can start doing this month to month, but he seems to forget I got property costs and a liquor license to keep up."

Erik paused for a moment, staring at the envelope. He shifted his gaze to the muscular bouncer at the entrance, then to the empty platform. There was no work here.

He took the envelope from the owner and discreetly opened it under the bar top. It was thick with hundred dollar bills. He folded it and stuffed it into his pocket next to the ballpoint pen.

"I'll remind the Reverend of the expenses," he said.

"They gonna send you again?"

"Probably not," he said.

Ace flattened his palm on the bar top.

"Tell the next guy to ask for Carla. She'll have the payment. We done here?"

Erik nodded in silence.

Ace stood up and locked eyes with the topless bartender.

"Rosie, you get this man a drink on the house, you hear? One drink. Anything he wants."

She smiled, revealing a gold tooth.

"Thanks, Ace," Erik said.

He didn't bother looking back and pushed through the swinging door across from the bar.

"So that's why you was okay," she said, grinning at Erik. "You knew you wasn't gonna be payin' for nothing."

Erik reflected on his dumb luck.

"Watchya need?"

"I'm still deciding," he said.

"You from England?"

"South Africa."

"Africa?"

"Yep."

"Hell, you're whiter than an apple's half."

"There's a lot of white people in Africa."

"No, shit?"

"Yeah. I mean, we don't belong there, but we're there.

She laughed.

"So what do you want to drink?"

Erik scanned the bar behind the naked woman. All liquor and no wine.

"Do you have any red wine?"

"Nope," she said, automatically.

"I didn't think so," he said. "I'll just have a beer."

"Miller Lite?"

"Sure."

She cracked open the beer and handed it to him. He sucked on it from the side of his lip, never taking his eyes off the bartender's breasts.

"How long have you worked for the Reverend?"

He didn't know who the Reverend was, but he clearly had some pull across town. It was his money in his pocket.

"Not long," he lied

"Well, say 'Hi' to Fillmore for me."

Erik paused and raised an eyebrow.

"Fillmore Davies?"

"Only Fillmore I know of," she said.

"Yeah," he said, working things out in his mind, deducing whose money he had stolen. "I'll tell him as soon as I can. He comes here a lot?"

"Most every week or thereabouts."

He nodded.

"Small world."

"You met him in the Corps?"

"I did."

"I didn't even know Africa was fighting over there."

"I joined the USMC. I fought for America."

She smiled gently, hiding her gold tooth now that she thought he had noticed it.

"God bless you, then," she said.

Erik looked at her and sucked on the beer. He noticed the wrinkles in her face and the freckles on her breasts.

"Maybe, I'll come back and see you, Rosie."

"Maybe you should."

He stood up, finished the beer, and gave her twenty-dollars.

"I have a misunderstanding to go clear up," he said. "You don't happen to know whose hiring around here do you?"

"There's not much legit work 'round here, but I did see a couple of hiring posters on Main Street. Restaurants mostly."

4.

A rental car made its way down the Southern highway, speeding along on the winding road, heading for the next "ville" or "ton" or "berg" beside the interstate. The driver tossed a burning cigarette filter out of the window. Since being picked up at the airport, the fat Korean tires had seen little of the big city boulevards, leaving the tread full of the small town grit. The car drove off the exit ramp and past a narrow precession of evergreens. It continued to coast until, somewhere across the cow pastures, in the early morning light, the driver spotted a glistening shack with the sign above spelling out the word "EATS." It wasn't the best looking stop-and-go, but, for Cassandra Jimenez, it would do.

Cassandra parked her car in the gravel lot of the diner. In the adjacent field there were two Ford Mustangs propped up by cinder blocks; concrete squares submerged halfway in red mud. It had been raining all day in short windy bursts. North Carolina's winters were substantial, and she was not fully prepared for the cold days on the interstate highway with a Daewoo rental car only fit for the light chill of a Brownsville night. Her skin was dry and itchy and she applied lotion in giant handfuls. Empty lip balm tubes rolled across the rental car's floor like shotgun shells.

Approaching the age of fifty, she still possessed a youthful demeanor despite her constant smoking. She liked to smoke while she drank coffee in the hot morning sun beneath the colorful umbrellas of the upscale cafes near the center of Mexico City where she lived. In the United States, she was forced to smoke outside the Waffle House parking lots littering the interstate. Aside from smoking, she also liked to drink one hefty beer at the end of the day, every day. It was her relaxation ritual, and on her trip it had been hard to coordinate on which days the stores didn't sell beer in the drier counties north of Asheville.

People said she didn't look Mexican, at least, not to Americans. Her light complexion was complimented by clear blue eyes and light brown hair, which she always cut into short bangs and a small ponytail. She recently found some gray hairs and, instead of letting it go silver, she dyed her hair a burnt red.

Under the neon lights of 'EATS', Cassandra stepped out of the car, lit a cigarette, smoked it halfway, and tossed it on the ground where it smoldered like a lit fuse as she walked into the diner. An old man in a white apron was wiping the tables quietly. A small boy, darker than the old man, probably a Cherokee, bounded around the lunch counter and rushed her a menu.

"Here you go Ma'am."

"Shgee," she said: thanks in the Kituwa dialect.

He asked her if she spoke Cherokee.

"A little."

The boy gave her a second look before returning to the kitchen through the swinging door. As she looked at men, the old man in the apron approached her and asked her if she was an Indian.

"No, I'm from Mexico."

She took a seat in the corner of the diner.

The old man returned to his cleaning. She took off her glasses, rendering her face incomplete, and stared at the menu in her hand. She decided that she wanted a spicy breakfast and a creamy, weak coffee to cool her tongue. As she waited to order, she watched the old man finish cleaning and then, like the boy, disappear behind the swinging door. She pulled out her road map. Places that she needed to visit were dotted with markers. She was especially keen on getting to Tennessee. Tennessee, she remembered, was the Cherokee word for bending river. She took a pen from her purse and circled a short expanse of mountains directly north off the freeway exit.

As she studied her map, a short woman about Cassandra's age waited for her to finish, standing over her table. Startled, Cassandra apologized and ordered a café latte and the breakfast burrito—spicy if possible.

As she sat waited for her food, she jotted down a few notes on the pages of her journal then grimaced at them and started on a new page.

Cassandra Jimenez wrote haunted travelogues. It wasn't what she had planned to do with her life but it afforded her time to travel, and the money that she made was enough for a small apartment in Mexico City. For her first book, she had visited *La isla de las muñecas:* a small island in the canals outside Mexico City where a mysterious man named Don Pedro had tied more than 600 porcelain and plastic dolls to the trees and rooftops of the island in order to appease the vengeful spirit of a little girl who had drowned there in last turn of the century. Legend said that she could animate any of the dolls to do her bidding. Villagers who rowed by in the canal reported seeing baby dolls walking around conversing with the feeble old man. Cassandra had also written about the hundreds of unsolved murders in Juarez as well as the death cult started by the Texas University students in Matamoros. Shorter chapters in her Mexico guide explored the witches in the Puebla sewer system, the ghost bus in the deserts of Sonora, and a haunted waterfall and cave in the Yucatan. *Encrucijada mexicana* was a big success for a novelty travel guide. She had cashed in on the popularity of the dubbed American paranormal television shows which had captivated a superstitious Mexican audience. Regardless of her own beliefs, she was content to be a successful travel guide author even if her work no longer had the potential to change the world. The title—*Encrucijada mexicana*— spanned a third of the cover in bold, blood red letters, above a burning road map and her pseudonym in a textured white font: Auxilo Flores. She published under a pseudonym because Cassandra Jimenez had been a journalist, but an unfounded libel case had destroyed her promising career. An oligarchy of corrupt municipal officials and members of the judicial police pressured the newspaper to fire her, or run the risk of being shut down.

After a disappointing end to her career as a judicious and devoted investigative journalist, Cassandra Jimenez started anew. She was no longer an inspiring go-getter, climbing the endless ladder toward a corner office and a permanent column. She had to keep herself afloat. Her only other job besides the crime beat and the city columns had been a short stint as a cocktail waitress in Knoxville, Tennessee just before returning to Mexico for college. She had only been 17 then.

After she was found guilty of libel, she cried for two weeks until she was offered a gig by a friend who wrote for a UFO conspiracy magazine. That project led her to work on *Encrucijada*. By the time she was 47, she had camped at the base of Mount Fuji in the suicide forest, slept nights in Irish dungeons, searched for clown-faced serial killers in cursed whorehouse mirrors, shared meals with witch-doctors in Haiti, and published six volumes of her *Encrucijada* series. Now, she was 48 and working on her seventh title, *Encrucijada* del sur: a guide to the scariest places in the American South. Her publisher, Omar Castro, wasn't sold.

"What about New England?" he had said to her over a lunch of grilled chicken and beer in the open air restaurant on the edge of Zócalo. "People like the mystique of the Yankee ghost hotels and haunted harbors. You know like holding a candelabrum up the creaky stairs to a Victorian-style room. It's the country of Stephen King, and it will sell more copies. Maybe even the most!"

"New England is old news. It's been done again and again. And this is Mexico; we're still preoccupied with Fuentes and Paz. Think about it. The American South. Plantation homes. The specters of African slaves. The genocide of the Indians. Ghosts along the Mississippi. Voodoo in New Orleans. Bloody Shiloh from the Civil War. I was reading the other day about a Tennessee woman that claimed a six-foot-four bat was breastfeeding an infant that had been missing for two weeks in this little town called Bishop's Pasture. I cross-referenced the story and a baby had gone missing earlier this year from a young woman's home nearby. There are stories of pillars near some of the mountain churches, giant cross-shaped stacks of wood fitted with shackles and sodden with little bits of flesh–"

"Where are you going with this?" Omar said, grinding his teeth.

"Some say that say many of the people in the hills of Appalachia tie ostracized men, women, and children with a rare case of photodermatitis to these pillars in the dead of night and wait for the sun to come up to watch their skin peel off in bloody rashes. It started in the coal mining days and has continued since. If these stories are true, then they're gold, and I'd be the first to write about it"

"Why do they do that? Because they have a skin disease?"

"They think they're vampires."

"Didn't you used to live in Tennessee?" he had asked taking a swig of his Bohemia.

Cassandra, thinking on her feet, had admitted to living there once.

"It's another reason I can do this book. I know the region and I know the language."

By the end of the month she was driving through Brownsville headed for New Orleans.

The waitress brought her something not unlike a café latte and, much more to her liking, a piping hot breakfast burrito with extra jalapeño sauce. She stopped writing to eat.

As she wrote, a tall man in a beige highway patrol uniform stepped into the diner. The waitress acknowledged him with a brief smile. He turned to Cassandra. She looked at him, thinking that he was giving her a lecherous look, but he just smiled back a, friendly smile that echoed the Southern chivalry she had known as a 17-year-old. She returned the smiled before sipping her coffee.

"Howdy," he said.

"Hello."

The officer sat down at the lunch counter. The old man gave him a black cup of coffee. Cassandra heard the old man address the officer in an unusual language. The vowels were all bent and hacked off at the ends. The officer replied in the same language. Their tongues glided over Latin and Germanic cognates. Appalachia was an older world. Cherokee, Portuguese, German, and Irish Gaelic were still spoken by various mountain communities isolated by poverty and the endless forests. The police officer was speaking Gaelic with the old man. Feeling her eyes on him, the officer turned back to Cassandra.

"Willy here don't speak English too good. He's always talkin' Irish."

"I see."

"Don't pay him no mind, Ma'am. How's that breakfast burrito?"

"It's good, spicy," she said.

"Say, you from France?"

"Mexico."

"Mexico? What brings you north of Asheville?"

She hesitated. "Visiting family."

"You've got folks in town?"

"No. In Tennessee. I'm just passing through."

"Oh, lovely. I've got kin in Knoxville. You're English is wonderful."

"Thanks."

A waft of stale ammonia extended from the kitchen. She took another bite of her burrito just to have something to do. The Cherokee boy burst out of the kitchen and made his way out the door with a fishing pole in hand. She watched him disappear into a windblown thicket across the road. The two men returned to their Gaelic conversation. As they spoke, the old man stared directly at her while the police officer took short, coy glances. She felt pressure in the top of her head and heat accruing in her cheeks. Noticing how the young cop drank his coffee in heavy gulps, she finished her own coffee as quickly as possible and took the last bites of her burrito. She left the tip on the lunch counter and said goodbye to the police officer, then quickly headed back to her car and drove away.

In Mexico, she was often recognized. People even remembered her from her days as a journalist. Regardless of the region, the locals would tell her every legend and horrific story they could. She was even escorted to certain places by elders or the local youth who would always promise to protect her. In the United States, she was not so lucky.

The police officers and the old man at the diner had intimidated her. Leaving, she felt alone on the road. On her European travels she had been so much freer on the crowded buses and trains speeding along the countryside.

In South Carolina, she realized that the locals spoke a dialect of English that she could not understand. She'd ask a question, they'd answer, and she couldn't get a single word on the page. If she asked the question again, they'd get agitated. Within the cities she could understand the people, but they had nothing to say. They lived in a world removed from folklore and spirits. By the time she had gotten to North Carolina, she was alone in her rental car, a world of silence, driving northward, hoping for some friendly contact.

As she drove out along the road, she passed a small pond and saw the little Cherokee boy fishing and, as if traffic was such a seldom occurrence, he dropped his fishing rod, jumped up and waved to her with both arms. She took one hand off the steering wheel and waved back. Then she punched the radio on and headed further north for Tennessee.

5.

Cassandra Jimenez turned onto the exit ramp and slowed the Daewoo as she merged into the mild traffic of Bishop's Pasture. The clock had meaning again. There were things to write, e-mails to send, her stomach needed food, the cigarettes were running low, and the music—all the music that had gotten her from point Brownsville to point Bishop's Pasture—seemed louder, unnecessary, and distracting. Nothing was familiar. Thirty years ago, when she was here last, this road had been empty and the music better. She passed a few lesser chain hotels before pulling into the parking lot of a Holiday Inn. She rolled her suitcase across a parking lot that matched the dullness of the sky, and opened two sets of glass doors into the warm light of the marbled lobby. A thin Mexican teen with dark hair manned the check-in counter. The novelty of meeting other expatriates in the U.S. had worn off after the great migration in the 1980s. Now, Mexicans and other Latin Americans just switched languages to acknowledge each other. The girl at the checked her in in English.

When Cassandra got to the room, she flopped on the mattress and stared at the mini-bar before taking a shower, scrubbing herself down with the single bar of complimentary aloe vera soap, but used her own shampoo. She put on fresh clothes and headed back toward the parking lot. There was a family in the lobby placating a barking Schnauzer. They were also Mexican. In Spanish, Cassandra asked the girl behind the counter if there was a restaurant within walking distance.

"There's an Applebee's across the street," the teen replied in English.

She thanked her, crossed the street, and smoked a cigarette outside before entering the dark of the restaurant. Everything inside screamed 'family' except for an old-time saloon located just beside the upholstered double doors to the kitchen. The kitchen staff kept looking out through the round portholes. She set her purse on the bar and sat unmoving for the first time in hours, the ground still beneath her feet. As she sat, Erik van de Roer, the new fry cook, walked out of the kitchen. His face was shrouded by a trim red beard and dark red hair confined by a hairnet. He was pulling off his greasy kitchen apron when Cassandra caught his eye.

"Aye, miss? You been helped?"

"No, not yet."

"You need a drink?"

"Yeah."

"In the market for something a little strange?"

"Sure," she said, smiling.

He pulled off his hairnet, went behind the bar, and grabbed a bottle of cabaret sauvignon from the mini-fridge beneath the fresh glasses. After scooping shaved ice into a martini shaker, he poured the red wine into the frosted metal cup and, injected the Coca-Cola from the soda fountain gun. He shook it quickly with one hand then poured the dark fizzing drink into two scotch glasses. He handed her the drink and said, "I'm Erik. I saw you smoking outside. I'll buy you this drink if you'd grant me a cigarette."

She pulled out her pack of L&Ms and handed him one. He set it behind his ear. The bartender showed up just they finished drinking.

"Two red wine and cokes," he told her and paid with a five-dollar bill.

Cassandra noticed the young woman's expression, and then focused on Erik's face. He couldn't have been older than his late 20s; however, something had aged his hands and eyes beyond his youth. They seemed withered and wrinkled, the first sign of a fast-approaching old age.

Sitting in one of the dining room booths, Cassandra ate a cheeseburger and drank two beers after she had finished her second coke and wine. Erik wasn't tempted by her plate of food, but kept talking instead. He talked a lot when he discovered where she was from. They discussed the war, the Cartels, and life in the United States. She didn't say very much about herself.

When she finished eating, they went outside to smoke.

Erik refused her lighter, striking a match book to light the cigarette she had given him.

"Here, allow me," he said.

She leaned in with the cigarette between her lips.

The match hissed the life as she inhaled and quickly died in the wind.

"Thanks," she said.

"So where are you staying?" he asked, boldly.

"I'm 48 years old," she said.

"Are you married?"

She shook her head, exhaling smoke from the side of her lip.

"Then what's the problem?" he asked.

"The problem is that you're very young. And I'm not sure I can trust you."

"That's fair," he said. "It's no fun if you're not comfortable."

"No, it's not."

He shrugged and tossed the rest of the cigarette into the sand-filled ashtray.

"It was nice talking to you, Cassandra."

"It was nice talking to you too, Erik."

He started down the sidewalk when she called back to him.

"Erik,"

He turned around to look at her.

"I'm in the Holiday Inn across the street. If you want to keep talking, I'd like that."

"Yeah, that would nice," he said.

She stared up toward the ceiling, sprawled on her back across the hotel bed, a hand over her heart as if the adrenaline would cause it to burst from her chest. He didn't seem to care that she had a scarred belly or large hips. She tried to keep her glasses on but he took them off to see her face. He leaned over kissed her neck. She hadn't been kissed in a long time.

6.

Arráncame la vida was on TV. Framed by the Holiday Inn wardrobe, the picture lacked the same depth since Cassandra had last seen it at the cinema. She was reclining on the queen-sized bed, drinking her bottle of Corona for the night. She briefly thought about what it would be like to get married to the naked man beside her but soon gave up and stared at the textured stucco ceiling. Her lover was asleep beside her and still cradling her left arm. She set the beer bottle on the side table and turned off the lamp before running her hand through his reddish, brown hair. He was probably born a blonde child and, just like her, slowly lost the cornflower hue with time. The credits were scrolling across the television screen when Erik awoke and caressed her belly.

"Does this make me a cougar?"

"No, it makes you a human being."

"Are you spending the night?"

"May I?"

"Yeah, that'd be nice." She changed the channel to a Western. Two masked gunmen passed beyond the threshold of a hacienda, pistols in hand. She held onto Erik's torso and nuzzled her head in his chest.

"You're very fit," she said.

"Thanks."

"I'm not."

"You're fine," he said.

"For an old woman."

They lay beside each another for a few moments of silence. She thought he looked flushed.

"You're blushing."

"No, I'm not."

"Where you spying on me before you came out of the kitchen?"

"I was."

"Why are you so honest all the time?"

"I was once lied to."

"Was it painful?"

"It was. Very much so."

"Do you speak any other languages?"

"I speak Afrikaans and German."

"Impressive."

"What about you?"

"I'm teaching myself Cherokee. Maybe I should learn to speak Irish too after today."

"How come?"

"These two guys—one of them was a cop—were speaking Irish at the diner today."

"A lot of Irish in Appalachia."

"A lot of *indios* too."

Erik smiled.

"Your English is spotless."

"English isn't an achievement. I used to live here."

"You lived in Bishops Pasture?"

"I worked in Bishops Pasture when I was young, before college. I followed my boyfriend up here, hoping to do the American thing—get married, get a green card, find work, start a family. He hit a few times so I left him and then...well...something else happened. Something I wasn't sure I could come back from. I went back to Mexico and finished schooling. I became journalist."

"I never went to school."

"Afrikaans? So you're from Zimbabwe?"

"South Africa."

"Then why do you live here?"

"This place? It's where I got my footing. I know how to live here. I work here."

"I understand that."

He continued to caress her stomach, tickling her belly button. She squealed and rolled away from him. He sighed and gave her a sober look. Her own expression became curious. He decided not to speak. Cassandra clearly had a scar from a c-section on her stomach. She had already professed to him—as well as lamented—that she had never been married. But there was a child, or, at one point, there had been a child. He balked from the tough subject and said: "I'm 29. I'll be 30 next month."

"Is age an issue for you?"

"No, I just thought you'd want to know my age."

"I already knew you weren't a kid."

"It's the beard."

"The beard definitely adds age."

She reached for the floor to grab her laptop. She was halfway through her new chapter on Tennessee.

"What's that?"

"My work," she said, reading over the paragraphs...

Beneath the chalk-white sliver of a crescent moon, a pair of hands rise from the loosened soil of a treeless valley, blindly grasping for a lowered branch, a tombstone, anything to pull the remainder of the body from the aphotic tomb of the underground. The soil bends inward as withered, compressed arms grab at the clods of black dirt. The yellowed nails bend backward, peeling from the leathery fingers, as bony shoulder blades strain to free the indented torso. A sallow dirt-covered face contorts upward to take in a deep, painful breath. Dust bellows from the body's unused lungs, a plume of smoke in the pale moonlight. A grotesque husk of a girl exhumes her own legs from the depressed mound of earth and staggers to the top of a barren hill. The sunken pits which still hold jaundiced, flattened eyes that stare directly into the blurred radiance of the ancient symbol above her. The crescent moon held significance to her in life. Her heart pumps once, forcing the clotted blood through desiccated arteries. She stares at the land under the sky and immediately knows this place is not home. This place was not where she died. She is plagued by visions of her killers, flashes of undeserved prosperity and happiness. Laughter from every corner of the valley permeates his grit-filled ear canals. She screams with a rasped, animalistic growl, dropping to her brittle collapsed knees, overpowered by a relentless thirst for human blood.

She is The Bardha.

Cassandra closed the laptop.

"What times is it?" Erik asked

She grabbed her phone from her purse and glanced at it.

"10:30 pm."

"Well, do you want to go get Denny's? The owner's a Namibian, he knows me."

"I don't understand."

"It's a diner. We can go get something to eat. They're open 24 hours."

"Oh, no. I don't want to go anywhere." She squeezed his chest. "Just lay her with me."

"Okay."

In the middle of the night, Cassandra got out of bed and walked to the bathroom naked. She chagrined when she turned the light on and saw her body, knowing Erik had seen the scar. She bit her upper lip and stepped into the shower. Wrapped in a white bathrobe with a turban for her wet hair, she emerged from the moist tiles of the bathroom onto the cool hotel carpet. There was the young man in her bed: a stranger. He groggily lifted his eyelids.

"You took a shower."

"I just needed to feel clean."

"What time is it?"

"4 o'clock in the morning," she said.

"Fokken poes."

"What does that mean?"

"Puta madre."

She went back into the bathroom to blow-dry her hair.

7.

Erik stared at the rainy day beyond the glass window; a plate of broccoli smothered in bourbon sauce and fried rice piled before him on the table. The Chinese restaurant was the last place in town that allowed smoking indoors. They also sold beer and sake without a license. Cassandra was comfortable in the puffy red booths, smoking and tapping her ash over the crystal tray, nibbling on a simple chicken dish.

"Thanks for lunch."

"I'm a gentleman."

"Do you have a girlfriend?"

"No," he said, taking a large bite of broccoli.

"You don't have a ton of South African girls waiting for

you back home?"

"No, do you have a bunch of Latin men waiting for you in Mexico?"

"A few."

"Good."

She smoked her cigarette and stubbed it out in the ashtray. It was difficult to read the complacent expression on Erik's face. They both knew she'd have to shuffle off along the Tennessee road soon. And when she did, they probably wouldn't see each other again. He was more than willing to pay for her lunch and kiss her goodbye with a smile on his face.

"Are all your relationships hit-and-run?" she said, seeing his jaded, wry smile for the first time.

"Well, it's sometimes safer. I've seen enough people blown up to know life is short. Very short."

"You've seen people get blown up?"

"Yeah,"

"And you're telling me this now? In war?"

He nodded.

"Who did you see blow up?"

"A little Afghan girl."

"Oh my God."

He took another bite of his broccoli. "On a lighter note, South African girls are almost universally beautiful. I mean, supermodel beautiful. South African girls are also almost universally racist pigs."

"I'm still thinking about the little girl."

"It is a bit heavy I'll admit."

"A bit heavy? You'll admit?"

8.

Erik walked her to her car. They hugged once more and kissed. She thanked him. He squeezed her breast. They laughed. After a few awkward seconds, she got into her car and drove away. The sound of the tiny Daewoo engine and the windshield wipers drowned out the radio she had forgotten to turn off. She watched Erik stuff his hands into his pockets and walk down the crumbling sidewalk in the rear view mirror, and then she quickly checked her purse to make sure he hadn't stolen anything. He hadn't. She spent the remainder of the afternoon on the road thinking about the scar on her stomach while his smell clung to her clothes.

9.

When Erik was fifteen, he worked at a small grocery in the Johannesburg suburbs. He lasted three weeks until he was fired for assaulting a customer. The customer, a bearded white man with a theatrical Boer accent, wouldn't stop harassing the Xhosa girl about his special order for a fifty pound bag of jasmine rice. The flustered girl checked the back stocking room for the order, but, as usual, the delivery truck hadn't brought the rice. Her job wasn't even stocking. That was Erik's responsibility, but the intimidating white man had locked on to the tiny black girl as his servant for the day. Mr. Leblanc, also an Afrikaner, remained in his office consistently exercising his hands-off style of management, closing the blinds on his indoor window, choosing not to do anything.

The screaming customer refused to interact with Erik when he intervened and instead pointed to a pile of fallen grapes in the produce section.

"Boy, go sweep that up," he said.

Erik stood his ground and told the man that produce wasn't his department. Ignoring Erik, the man continued bullying the cashier girl.

With a firm hand, he pressed him aside and asked him to leave the grocery.

"You, boy, cannot talk to an elder like that. You're committing a sin. I am your elder and I have the right to deal with this matter. It is of no concern to you and I won't tolerate it," the Boer said. The power in his voice harkened back to a conservative time, a time mantled in razor wire, a time without foreign news or television that wasn't run by the state.

Erik nodded and walked away. He could feel his hands shaking as he inched toward a display of pickle jars. He held the heavy jar in his hand and stepped back toward the yelling man. Again he politely tapped him on the shoulder.

"Is this what you were looking for, Sir?"

As soon as the old Boer turned around, Erik smashed the jar across his face. The girl screamed and ran to the manager's office. The Boer was on the ground cursing him in Afrikaans. Erik, picking up a jagged shard of glass dripping with blood and vinegar, slashed the man's face and sliced open his cheek to expose his teeth. When he thought back on it, he assumed the man would have a mangled face for the rest of his life. Erik didn't regret it.

When he was twenty, Erik quit school and left the country. He admired Dave Matthews and J. M. Coetzee for becoming citizens abroad, both in the U.S. and Australia. His first foreign experience was in Sierra Leone on the Gold Coast, then to Amsterdam where he was rejected for political asylum. He bummed around Paris for a year drunk on wine and stoned on marijuana where he washed dishes in a bistro in the Algerian ghetto. He arrived in Tennessee on a whim where he joined the military. He came back with a Purple Heart and word that Eugene Terre'Blanche, head of the white supremacist AWB, had been beaten to death with pipes and pangas while napping in his bed. The world seemed lighter. One less Boer on the face of the Earth. He despised his Boerness and, above all things, identity itself.

10.

The outline of a Stetson, dripping with rain, blurred by distance and darkness, appeared on the far end of the ridge. Jeremy and Fillmore watched the figure come trudging up the rock quarry, recognizing Erik's green poncho, which he slung across his shoulders like a cape, before they could scramble into the night as they always planned if the law were to come down on them. The Reverend sat wrapped in a Mexican blanket near the cooling tank at the edge of the dugout beside the copper still.

Jeremy wiped his wet hair back. "You just about scared us to death, god damn it."

"Nobody's coming this way. It should hail tonight," Erik said.

Fillmore spat into the mud. "And we're out here in this shit."

"Making money," Erik added. He pulled a bottle of bourbon from his pocket and unfastened it. They came in handy when he needed to push back brambles or handle the propane burners. He took a swig then passed it to the

Reverend who grabbed the bottle and downed a third in one swallow.

On the mountain north of Bishop's Pasture, the ones that hung over the town like a title wave, the old mining company grounds had been shut down. Erik and his partners from the Baptist church had built the still in a dugout on the side of a ridge where the noise and the glow of the propane burners couldn't be detected from town. They cleaned out old cat litter buckets with cheap vodka and dish soap and collected their barley shine from the copper vat and dunked it all in a cooling tank. There, the Reverend would bottle it in old wine jugs and punch the tops with his re-sealer. The scotch was sold on the church basketball court on Saturday nights. "We gonna age this in ah apple barrel one day and we gonna make thousands on the ol' Johnnie brand," the Reverend once said.

"You're sure there ain't nobody on the perimeter?" Fillmore said to Erik as he grabbed the bourbon and took a short pull.

"Not a soul."

"Good."

The second batch started to pour down the copper tube. The golden liquid trickled through a funnel lined with a t-shirt and two handfuls of cheesecloth before spattering into the bucket.

"Ain't that a beautiful site," Fillmore said as he handed the bourbon back to Erik.

The Reverend stood up

"I think we're fixing to catch pneumonia out here."

"The still's giving off enough heat for all of us," Jeremy said.

"Dangerous proposition to turn up those Rhino tanks."

"Turn'em up?" Fillmore chewed on a wet cigarette. "Ya'll seem to have forgotten we're making fine whiska out here. You gonna scorch it you turn up the damn heaters. You want top-dollar licker you have to suffer a bit. What's comin' out there is liquid gold. You don't mess with a good thing." He shifted the tarpaulin hanging over the spout.

Erik sat down and covered his body with the green poncho. "I used to moonshine in Sierra Leone."

"You don't moonshine. You make moonshine. It ain't no verb," Fillmore said.

"In Sierra Leone it is."

"That in Italy?" The Reverend was curious.

"No, West Africa."

"Africa?"

"We'd have the still connected to the back of the Jeep. A bunch of Spanish kids and a couple white trackers and poachers. Rough people. By night, we'd make a run across the fields our jugs dangling off our shadows. We were shot at once. We didn't know by whom. Probably other moonshiners. One of my jugs shattered. Cold liquor pouring down my back as I'm running as fast as I can to get behind some trees."

"You're a seasoned runner then," the Reverend said. "You make it out okay?"

"Oh, yeah. I disappeared into the bush and they gave up. Nobody follows me into the darkness. And nobody's crossing that border into Liberia."

"Liberia. Ain't that where the pirates come from. Muslim terrorists?"

"No, that's Somalia. I'm talking about the worst failed state crisis in Africa. Liberia is the wild west out there."

"You sure rattle off some talk," Jeremy said.

"You calling me a liar?"

"Just sayin'. You know how to tell a good story, but can you walk the walk?"

"He's knows what he's doing," the Reverend said. "I know a liar when I see one."

The men stood silence.

Fillmore spit in the mud.

"I heard you went home with a woman from Applebee's, Erik," the Reverend said.

"Yeah,"

Jeremy produced a buck knife and started whittling under his finger nails. "So how bout it then. She something special?"

"Just a passing fancy."

"You talk British you know that?" Jeremy said, blowing the end of the knife.

"She was a writer," Erik said, ignoring Jeremy's question. "She writes about all the haunted legends across the world. She's working on a Tennessee chapter."

The Reverend looked fixedly at Erik and said, "Well hell, you know the only legend worth reading about in Tennessee is Jackdaw. You don't think she's headed up that way do you?"

Erik paused.

The four men, alone in the rain, heard the moonshine bucket overflowing.

"Shit!" Fillmore ran over to the bucket and dumped it in the cooling tank. "Let's not let that happen again."

Erik sipped the scotch from the cooling tank ladle. He nodded his head in approval and started humming the African street songs. *"Gaan kak op jou ma se poes! Poes julle!"*

"My favorite"—the Reverend commented—"is the one about the monkey. How'd it go?"

"Buttfuck the monkey's like you and me/ Buttfuck the monkey has HIV."

Jeremy stared whittling on a wet stick. He finished a notch in the wood and said, "Remember the rhyme about Jackdaw? *And I gotta be strong and I gotta be careful/ I gotta keep up when the wife is awareful/ No time to give up/No time to look down/ The whole world spinning into the ground/ There's no clown in the mirror/No boogeyman neither/ She knows not to speak/Her eyes do deceive her."*

Jeremy sheathed the blade and leaned in closer. "How about it? Let's have it then?"

"What?" Erik said.

"You know, about Jackdaw, Tennessee."

Erik shook his head. "I don't ken, mate."

"Let's have it, Reverend, tell us the story 'bout that there Jackdaw city up on the mountain low." He looked at Fillmore than at the Reverend. "Boys? We listening?"

The Reverend took another tug of Erik's bourbon.

"Splendid," he said in a slurred warble. "Here we go. Twenty years ago, things were different here. We had us some Klan just outside of town. But not anymore, cause of Pedro Jones. Jones was a big young, black fella taller than his daddy or any other man in town. He played a fierce game of football and mangled up some people bad. He was feared, and he wasn't afraid of nothin', especially not the Klan. But he had one weakness: girls. He found himself with a beautiful white daughter, Amy Sue…"

"The girl in your last story was Amy Sue," Erik said.

"It's a common name around here. Anywho, him and Amy Sue was with each other near every night. He got to loving this girl bad and invested a considerable amount of his feelings in her. Her daddy, the farmer, caught wind of this after nearly catching'em in act, and he went looking for the Klan. The Klan though, they can't ever be trusted. They weren't into right-violence, the playground toughness, protecting your kin and such. They were cowards who didn't give a damn who they hurt, as long as blacks got the hurt in the end. Only thing set them off more than a black was a white girl who slept with blacks. They thought all the black men would take up all their white women and there wouldn't be nothing left for'em.

"The farmer asked them to help him, but it was all wrong. The clan was afraid of Jones. He could've broken any of their necks if he wanted to. And there was a rumor he wasn't a bad shot either. The Klan was angrier at Amy Sue, since it was known that most of the younger Johns in town had their eye on her. They decided it was more important to get at her and make Jones hurt in his mind. They dragged her off the street and slashed her face up good with a razor before they raped her.

"She hanged herself in her daddy's barn, writing a letter to Jones before she did it," he said. "But you see the Klan was wrong when they thought they could break Jones. Jones was just set off by what they had done. So that night, he went out into the kudzu and asked to see the devil. Old Scratch come up from the depths and asked him what he wanted. Jones told him what he planned to do, and he told the devil he needed to be exempt from death for a few days. So the devil agreed and in exchange for promising him exempt, he took Jones' heart out and put in a coffee tin and buried it in the dirt for safe keeping. Then he filled Jones with the powers of hell and watched as Jones went and killed Amy's daddy and every last Klan member he could find, feasting on their souls one by one. But Jones lived the rest of his life cursed, cause he couldn't find his heart in that coffee tin anywhere. Some even say that the devil tricked him and never buried it, but slipped it in his pocket and buried a rock instead, winning another soul in the deal."

"None of that bullspit's true, right?" Jeremy said as he dumped the hooch into the cooling tank.

"No, none of that's true. There was no Sue Ann or Amy Sue, and no big roundup of the Klans. But I can tell you what is true, and that is that the locals who lost the 84 lumber mill are robbing German tourists on Cherokee tours. Rounding'em up like cattle, collecting wallets and taking off into the woods."

"Hell, who are we kidding? Those are our customers, hillbilly-biker-hippie-methhead-monkey wrench gang-eco-terrorists-Eric Rudolph and the mother fuckin' Sasquatch. They'll all strip yer pockets bare if you're dumb enough to run into them," Fillmore said.

Erik paused again.

"Do you really think she's going up there?"

"Up to that voodoo place? I think she's likely headed smack dab for that famous bed and breakfast."

"Not the one that—"

The Reverend cut him off and said, "If she's going to write about Jackdaw then she's probably going to try and find Pedro's heart in the woods."

"*The* woods."

"Yep."

"A lot of hillfolk in those woods. It ain't a good place for hikers all alone."

"Reckon she'll get a rude awakening."

"Not if I can help it," Erik said.

"You gonna drive up there?"

"Do I have a choice?"

"How you gonna do that exactly?" Jeremy asked. "Last I saw, you ain't got no wheels."

The Reverend tossed Erik the keys to the van. "The tank is full. Be safe."

"You're just gonna give him the fucking keys like that?" Fillmore said, minding the moonshine dribbling into the new bucket.

"Yeah, I get the fokken keys," Erik said as he started to walk down the ridge.

"What about the perimeter? Aren't you still workin' for us?"

"Let him go," the Reverend said. "He's done his job for tonight."

Fillmore sank his knees into the mud. "Am I the only guy that gives a fuck about making moonshine?" he yelled.

Fillmore's voice faded away as Erik ran toward the van in the church parking lot down the road.

11.

The boys were still gathering twigs when the sun finally set behind the western half of the mountain and the glow of distant porch lights and window screens peppered the landscape like fireflies in the summertime. The cold of the night had set in and the air, once scentless and crisp, grew thick with chimney smoke. The boys, both of them cousins living under the same roof, searched the field for kindling, wrapping bundles in twine, stacking them in the Radio Flyer. Their gloveless hands numb in the frigid air, and their nostrils dripped with mucus.

The taller boy, a year younger than his cousin, wiped his nose on his jacket sleeve.

"There are no clouds," he said.

"Yeah, I can see."

"Know what that means?"

"The stars are out."

"It's gonna get real cold tonight. We should ask pa to make us hot water bottles."

"I'll just sleep with my pants on," the other said.

They returned to their work. The field grew darker. Their shoes became one with the brittle ground. The tall boy looked east at the white oak on the opposite end of the straw field.

"Let's go and get more fagots," he said, pointing to the tree.

"You ain't supposed to say that word." "A pile of sticks is a fagot. I learned that in school. Let's go over there."

"Ma said we can't go out that far," the shorter boy said.

The taller boy held his palm flat over the Radio Flyer, measuring the amount of bundles they would need complete their task.

"We ain't near finished. You wanna get whipped, or stay out in the dark forever?"

The boy hesitated.

"Okay, but we have to go fast."

"There'll be more twigs under the tree."

They dragged the squeaking wagon across the dark field, looking back, in short intervals, toward the house to make sure they weren't missed. Smoke rose up from the stone chimney, touching the last blue strip of sky before rising up into total darkness. The last of the kindling in the shed was already burning.

"Pa started without us."

"We'll have good fagots for him."

"Don't say that word."

"Fuck you."

"Fuck you too."

"Straying out by the tree'll have to be our secret. You can keep a secret can't you?"

The shorter boy nodded.

"Good."

Twigs snapped beneath their shoes with each step when they reached the edge of the field. They bent over, collecting great handfuls of kindling, fighting over the twine. The stacks in the Radio Flyer grew quickly.

The taller boy wiped his nose on his sleeve and licked his upper lip. The taste was metallic.

"Am I bleeding?"

The other boy stared at him, squinting to make out the strip of black blood leaking from his nostril.

"I reckon so," he said in a whisper, squeamish at even the thought of blood.

"Damn."

"Don't swear."

"You swore just now."

The kindling stacks had reached two feet by the time they chose to head back across the field. They could see the porch lights flicker to life in the distance. Their time was nearly up. The boys raced across the field. Four of the bundles toppled over and rolled away through the straw.

"I'll go back and get 'em. You go ahead," the taller boy said.

His cousin ran off toward the house. He watched

him and slowly retraced his steps through the darkness, spotting the twigs in what little light he was afforded. He parted the straw, searching for the last of the fallen bundles, when he saw a figure standing in the straw like a scarecrow: a teenage girl with porcelain-white skin. She was nude. She was steady, unshivering, and silent. Her eyes looked into his.

"You'll die out here if you don't have any clothes," he said. "What happened to you?"

Fear and excitement overwhelmed him, confusing him.

"You're gonna die in the cold like that," he said.

She moved toward him.

He trembled, paralyzed by fear.

She reached out with her slender hand and wiped the blood from his nostril with her thumb.

The shorter boy waited by the porch afraid to tell his aunt and uncle where they had been. His bladder was full and his hands were numb. He waited for his cousin to emerge from the night with the stray bundles, but he never came. He couldn't call out to him, or else his aunt would hear. The boy took a deep breath and ran into the straw, whispering his cousin's name. He searched for an eternity, aimlessly wandering through the dark until he tripped over a small pile of sticks. He touched the piles and felt the coarse twine.

He whispered his cousin's name again and began to whimper. A low noise came from the opposite side of the straw. He stood, crying, pissing in his pants.

The straw parted behind him. He had no time to

scream.

12.

She had driven to Jackdaw, Tennessee where she found the Kiowa Inn. The only vacancies available to her were room 303, 501, and 204. She didn't care since they were all smoking room so she let the clerk pick. The young man gave her the magnetic card to room 303. She wheeled her bag to the room and sat down on the bed with the door slightly ajar, hoping that no one on her hall would think anything of it. The window offered an opulent, smoky panorama of Appalachia, pockets of snow visible on the mountaintops. She pulled out her legal pad and wrote down "303=6." Her memory lagged. She tried to remember the other two available room numbers but couldn't. One of them had a king-sized bed, that much she could remember. She let it go and turned on the television, so she could have something to listen to while she wrote. She hated writing alone in empty rooms like Horacio Quiroga, Edgar Allan Poe, and Charles Baudelaire before her. This way the television was a chatty friend she could ignore while she worked. In college, she read more fiction than the newspapers and trade journals that her peers devoured and it showed. She wrote more like a novelist, even when she omitted the adjectives from the page. Perhaps that's why it had been easy to charge her with libel. The cartel funded city council, as some would allege, must have picked up on some of her more bizarre articles.

Flipping open her laptop, Cassandra proceeded to write.

Chapter 6: The Great Bending River of Riverbend

a.k.a Tennessee

Part Four: The Mountain Devil

The foreigner walks along the gravel in the early morning rain, past the light posts and telephone poles of splintered wood, to the lone house at the end of the road. He is tall even without his hair wrapped in a turban of dark green colored cloth. His boots are western. Along with his duffle bag and military-style camouflage pants and jacket, he keeps an Arkansas toothpick sheathed at his hip and a switchblade carefully wrapped in his turban as well.

The saint-soldier treads softly, noticing the field and the feral pony in the distance covered in shaggy, matted hair. Mocking birds fly through the trees mimicking the sounds of car alarms, stopping to perch on the electric cables between posts where man has left his mark on the landscape.

Gurveer Singh sets his right foot on the weathered stoop and fixes his boot laces. A boy, blowing on the lip of a Mountain Dew bottle, watches him heading down the pathway. The young boy's hand reaches out to touch the Sikh's graying beard. Gurveer lets him touch but only for a moment, before slapping the wrists away and asking, in a stinging British accent, for his father.

The boy stands and hollers for his father who his cleaning toothpaste stains from his khaki-colored sheriff's uniform. His wife peers her head into the open bathroom door.

"I told you not to brush your teeth with the uniform on, Rob."

"I know it," he says. "Why don't you seat Mr. Singh at the kitchen table and pour him a cup of that nice coffee."

"The Maxwell House?"

"No...the damn Godiva."

She pauses for a moment. "Can his people even drink coffee, Rob?"

"Yeah, they can drink coffee, Martha."

"Don't take that tone...just sayin'...that analyst from Utah couldn't drink coffee. How am I supposed to know these things?"

She walks to the rainy porch and pulls her son away from the tall Sikh, setting him aside like a piece of furniture. "Awful sorry, Jacob isn't good with strangers. It's isolated out here. We homeschool with a few local children, but..."

"Not a problem Mrs. Conway. He hasn't yet attempted to unravel the turban or steal my knife. Among American children, Jacob is a saint."

"Oh, I don't know about that." She pauses. "Your English is so...well spoken."

He smiles. "English is my first language. I was born in Punjab, but educated and raised in Britain and South Africa."

"Punjab? Robert told me you were from India."

He smiles again. "Ah yes, I see. Punjab is a province... eh...a state in India. Northward, near Pakistan."

"Well, I don't know if you're interested in any coffee. We have Dutch chocolate in the pantry," she offers.

Gurveer sets his duffle bag near the screen door frame. "I would like nothing more. And if I may be so bold as to ask if you have any bacon."

"Sure, sure thing. Let me take your bag."

"No, I'll take it in myself." He picks up the green canvas and tosses it in the shoe closet. The three of them walk to the kitchen.

Martha Conway, wife to the sheriff of a sleepy Appalachian community, keeps the foreigner in her peripheral vision as she sets the coffee in the mug and places the limp strips of bacon into the George Foreman grill, closing the top as if it *were a waffle iron. She watches him pull the long blade from his hip and offer the handle to Jacob. It looks like a sword in his tiny hands. Gurveer lets the boy touch the steel near the tip of the knife before returning it to its leather case. She watches him silently, recalling the magazine clippings her husband has shown her of the legendary mercenary and tracker: the rescues in the Outback and New Mexico, the expeditions through war-torn states in Africa, and the conservation efforts in Indonesia. A former member of the South African military, Gurveer Singh had become an embellished story in the finite world of adventurous men looking to prove themselves. An apocryphal story had been written in a British magazine that Singh had been trained by Gurkhas in Nepal. Gurveer never read it, but had sent a letter to the editor denying its veracity.*

He was now fifty-three years old, accepting jobs close to his home in the United States, unwilling to risk his life. He did not drink alcohol, refrained from cutting his hair in accordance to his Gurus' belief, and spent hours in a local gym in his home of Knoxville, Tennessee. There, very few people knew his name.

The sheriff walks down the creaky steps and sees his anticipated guest crunching through several pieces of his wife's bacon, reluctantly sipping the expensive coffee.

Gurveer turns his head. "You must be Sheriff Conway."

"Sure am," he says "Please finish your coffee and accompany me to the study." The sheriff is trying to come off more as an English gentleman, common in the Deep South. Tennessee is no exception.

Gurveer eats the bacon and follows the Sheriff. He closes the door behind him in the modest study. The air smells of clove. Conway stands at the center of the room behind his desk, looking out the large window.

"You know the reason the county hired you, correct?"

"Mr. Conway I've been chasing this beast since Nepal."
"Then you know what we want?"
"Yes."

Six weeks later this icon of modern adventure tales—a strong advocate for the revolutions in the Middle East—was said to be found in the middle of the Appalachian trail dead, torn limb from limb. The park service believed a large black bear had probably done it, but the Conway family insist to this day that an undiscovered ape creature they believe had been tormenting the town had attacked him. His mission was known throughout the small town of Bishop's Pasture, a secret kept for eight years. To this day, his case remains unsolved and open.

A large part of the United States believes in Bigfoot and almost every county has a Bigfoot story. The most prominent region for sightings is still the Pacific Northwest, but Tennessee and other southern states also lay claim to the legend.

Gurveer Singh was thought to have been brutally killed not far from the county line. His disappearance has never been solved.

Cassandra set the laptop aside and fell backwards, hitting the pillows on the bed. She lay there staring at the stuccoed ceiling. Ten minutes went by as she stared absently, then she pulled off her clothes and took a luke-warm shower.

Room 303 had no complementary bathrobes.

Sitting on the bed, still damp, wrapped in a short white towel, Cassandra watched an episode of *Family Guy* with Spanish closed captions. Outside her window, twilight spread down the hills over the town. Rain continued to fall in heavy waves, breaking downward across the glass of the hotel window. A mist formed over the creek. She changed the channel and saw the two little twin girls from *The Shining* holding hands at the edge of the hallway. She changed the channel again. Nothing but commercials. She switched to a rerun of *Ghosthunters*. The minibar was on the opposite side of the bed. She reached across the mattress, opened the door, and grabbed a couple miniature bottles of rum.

In her dream, she had a son: a little boy with blue eyes pulling on her sweater sleeve at the edge of the playground sandbox. A hand gun was kept in the cabinet of the frontier home. He played with it and shot himself. She woke up in a pool of her own sweat. Her chest hurt. The dream had been too vivid.

Now awake, her attention veered to the side of her room, looking at the bathroom door. She could hear the sound of running water. Something must have been wrong with the toilet tank. From then on, she couldn't sleep. She watched television with the lights on for the rest of the night.

In the morning, Cassandra decided to eat her continental breakfast in the tiny lobby beside the mounted cast-iron fireplace. She wore her new jogging outfit with the sleeve pocket designed for her new iPod; the one she bought in Polanco. Later in the day, after the big lunch, she went jogging along the nature trail the started behind the Kiowa. Her throbbing hangover from the bottles of rum steadily lifted as she began to sweat. Her thoughts drifted to the young South African she had met at the Applebee's, and the legend of Jackdaw. A cat dove across the gravel trail ahead of her, leaping into the dewy bulrush. A single false step and she would have tripped. Cassandra kept running.

After twenty-minutes, she ran back through the chilly forest and up the lacquered wooden steps of the rustic inn where she paused to catch her breath. A cool wind pushed a few leaves along the road as if it were just passing through town with no intention to stay. She felt a gentle tapping on her shoulder. She popped out the ear bud in her left ear and saw the little girl with pigtails standing behind her on the steps. She held a porcelain plate of strawberry slices with a shot glass full of brown sugar in the middle.

"Hello?"

"Hello, Miss, would you like a strawberry?"

"I'm sorry, no thank you."

"It's raw kitten meat," she said.

"What?"

The little girl promptly stood up and walked back inside the inn. What the girl said made no sense to her, but she wondered if it was a problem with the language. Perhaps the expression was local? Lost in translation, she reverted to thinking Spanish.

A truck sped down the main road at 50 miles per hour blaring a croaked version of Johnny Cash's *I Hung My Head*, weathered by the Doppler Effect as it went by. Still thinking in Spanish, she imagined a Paris ambulance scooting past the Rue Erlanger as the song played: *"The horsy kept ridin'/ the Rider was dead/ I hung my head/ I hung my head."*

After the truck had gone, she walked into the lobby. There was a pale girl behind the front desk. Her name tag read, "Michelle."

"Can I help you?" she said.

"No," she hesitated, trying to remember what she needed. "Yes, sorry…I just came back from jogging. Can I have the key to my room, 303?"

Without speaking, the girl named Michelle handed Cassandra the key-card. As she took the key a sudden burst of confidence came over her and she asked the pale girl if she knew the legend of Jackdaw. The girl told her the story of Pedro Jones' heart in the coffee tin. The legend was macabre.

"You can't be serious," Cassandra said.

"That's what I've heard. That's the legend. Some say he's still out there in the mountains looking for his heart."

She stood in silence.

"His heart in a tin?" she asked again.

"In a big red Folgers coffee tin. People have seen him searching for it out by the Haverton woods."

"Haverton woods? Just a couple of miles up the road?"

"Yeah, but be careful. This is Appalachia. People went missing up there last winter."

"Thanks," she said, shaking the pale girl's hand.

"I could tell stories all day," the girl said, staring into Cassandra's eyes.

Their handshake wasn't ending.

"Okay," she said. "I'm going up to my room now."

"Okay," the girl said, finally letting go.

13.

The woods where Pedro Jones searched for his heart was a well-maintained state park. Cassandra hadn't counted on paying a $2.00 visitor's fee. The bored-looking ranger in the tollbooth gave her a park service decal, which she hung on her rear-view mirror. After parking at the small welcome center, she took a quick glance at the trailhead map carved into a wooden board beneath a chipping wood-shingle roof, the kind she had seen on worn-out bird houses. Key parts of the map were defaced by graffiti. A heart with an arrow read, "Jimbob loves Leah TL4ever." She chose the steep and aptly titled Pedro Jones Trail. It took effort to scale the wooden steps built into the muddy ridge. She was already tired from jogging. Her camera dangled from the woven strap around her neck. She watched her balance and minded her grip as she remembered cutting her hand on sharp edge rocks in Transylvania. She had trekked that forest for the vampire chapter of her European book. The terrain here was no different. Everything was wet and muddy and steep. She came from a flat geography, where moisture, even sweat, evaporated in the Mexican desert like rings of smoky vapor before a single drop could accumulate. The razed earth and sparse vegetation of her homeland dried out in the day and cracked at the first sign of the cold night. The slick earth here appeared unfinished and waterlogged as if it were melting despite the frigid air and gray winter clouds. Some of the locals had told her that they enjoyed the rainy weather only because of the long, humid summers which choked the region in a palpable layer of nausea. Her shoulders quivered as she made her way up the steps.

To Cassandra, Appalachia was the tortured, wrinkled

backbone dividing old America from the new America. Those who lived on the crooked, exposed spine had long been forgotten, lost to the mountains, and lost to the sky.

As she climbed, she heard youthful voices emanating from the plateau above her. She sat down on one of the steps and pulled the lens cap off the camera to take a few pictures of the shadowy leafless trees. What was a ghost book without pictures of possible ghosts? A picture above the tree line would look better. She saw the trees standing as a sea of skeletal hands in the gray murk of winter. A photo like that could be her cover, she thought. She staggered to the end of the steps, crawling onto the plateau with the camera in one hand.

Four young men sat on the outcrop, shirtless in spite of the cold, drinking Miller High Life from a plastic ice chest. Their flat stomachs twitched as they spoke.

"You takin' pictures? Take pictures of us?"

She nodded as the one of the boys waived trying to get her attention. She took a better look at his face. It was freckled. His nose was crushed. Just to be friendly, she waived back. All four boys were waving at her now, but only the one approached her. His freckled face was in front of her before she could shy away down the trail. Now she would be forced to converse the young stranger.

"My name Gimphy," he said.

"You're name is most certainly not Gimphy."

"Tim," he said extending his hand. "But you can call me Gimphy."

"What are you doing in the woods?"

"I'm documenting a legend for a book."

"You the writer?"

One of the other boys put his shirt back on and stood

up. He called to his friend, "Come on, leave the poor lady alone."

"Your friend needs you," she said. "You better take care of him."

He paid his friends no attention and continued to pester her with questions.

"You sound foreign."

She said nothing.

"Well…" He grabbed a nearby tree branch with his thick palm, leaning in her direction.

"Well what?"

"Aren't you gonna answer my question?"

"That wasn't a question."

"Where are you from?"

"Mexico!" she said, angrily.

"Don't bite my head off."

His friends asked him to leave again. He ignored them.

Cassandra tried to walk away through the shaggy evergreens but Tim continued to follow her.

"What do you write?" he asked.

She knew that she had to get away from him, recognizing the goading tone in which his friends had called to him and the subtle giveaways in his cadence and pauses. He spoke with levity and viciousness: an apple in one hand and a knife in the other, daring her to call him out. She was being taken for a ride and she knew it. Her own bravery and her adherence to social graces kept her from telling him to fuck off before running, as fast as she could, in the opposite direction. Instead, she stuck to her laconic mannerisms.

"Come on now. Leave the nice lady alone," another

said, handing a few more beers over to his friends. They didn't have any intention to leave after all.

"So you're a writer? What do you write?" She had already told him she was writing a book about a legend. He had followed her through the bushes toward a small creek that she was backing into trying to lose him.

"Poetry," she muttered, hiking up a pile of rocks to escape. Above her, one of the other boys swung along a leafless Empress of China branch and landed in front of her. He leaned into hug her, rubbing his cheek against hers.

"You sure do smell good."

She tried to push him out of her way but his grip around her waist was too strong. It was like being locked in a straight jacket. She looked down at his thick forearms and struggled to get free.

"Whoopsy daisy," she heard Tim say as he grabbed at her ankles. Her forehead came down hard on a slab of rock as she fell down into the cold mud on the bank of creek. The camera fell from her hand tumbled down the brushy slope. She tried to scream for help as she scrambled across the frigid creek water. As she did, the third boy, the thin, silent one, threw a large stone at her back, flattening her body in the ankle-deep creek bed. Tim casually stepped toward her with his heavy boots and stomped on her clenched fist, crushing it into the mossy silt. She opened her mouth but couldn't make a sound beyond a wheeze.

Tim sat on top of her and began to stroke her hair. "We're gonna have fun together. It's gonna be nice," he said.

She choked back a mouthful of frigid creek water, coughing it up as she tried to scream.

14.

Erik saw the girl standing idly under the harsh gas-station lights between the kerosene tank and the telephone kiosk. She wore her unwashed hair in pig-tails. She pulled in her shoulders as the wind blew.

At their elevation, by night, the temperature had plummeted down the length of the mountain range. She couldn't go inside because she didn't have any money, and the clerk would not allow her to use the bathroom more than once. Instead, she was waiting out in the cold, hoping for some lonely trucker to pay for another unsatisfying, foil-wrapped meal and a warm night in his musky cabin bed. She was from here. No one came to this part of the country on their own accord. A girl like her should have already trekked south this time of year, trying to make it toward Myrtle Beach or Daytona; close to the ocean where she might find an actual job, catching the frat boys on spring break or, at the very least, an easier time turning tricks, hoping some tourist would promise to take her home and get her out.

Erik headed up into the quickie mart, trying not to look interested. Whatever her age, she was too young for him.

But she didn't have time to wait for someone who was interested. She was cold and hungry. Erik didn't look like a nice guy heading home after a long day, nor did he look like a trucker, a seasoned man of the road who spoke its language and knew where to look and when. What he looked like was an enigma: a face she had seen flash across a news bulletin, or the cork board near a drink cooler filled with the faces of the forgotten and the missing. But he was the first person she had seen in hours. He could see her life written on her face, written on the rubber bands holding her magenta-dyed hair in place, on her scuffed white t-shirt, on her ripped jeans, on her hand-me-down sneakers caked with red clay. He could see all the stolen, half-smoked cigarettes that got her by when she didn't have dope, and every back-handed, unprovoked strike cataloged in the rawness of her cheeks like wind burn. He could see the unwanted hands of strangers groping every inch of her body. He saw a kindred spirit. She was on the run....just like him.

She approached him quietly, and asked if he wanted a good time.

"I don't need a good time," he said, averting his eyes.

Her shoulders sunk in and the leather shoulder bag, which she had slung over her bony shoulder, dropped to the crook of her elbow. She stood silently on the verge of tears.

"But if you need some food or something I'll get it for you," he said.

She sprang toward him. He could smell the wear and tear of the road on her clothes, and that she was bleeding.

"Do you need tampons?"

She nodded.

"Alright, let me go inside."

"You're an angel," she said. "You've been sent from heaven."

He turned around and gave her a stern look. "Don't say that. As long as you're with me you don't talk about anything like that. Got it?"

"Okay."

"Stay here. I'll be right back."

The fluorescent glow of the gas station burned into

the pavement like stadium lights: a harsh, false shine that only increased the surrounding country's blackness. The door jingled as he stepped inside.

An elderly clerk in his bright red and yellow uniform garbled a bright but tired 'howdy partner.' All he had to do was nod and the clerk disappeared into the stock room. He picked out a ginger ale for the girl. It was easier on the stomach than other sodas and her blood sugar was, in all likelihood, abysmally low. He knew street life. He grabbed a pouch of jerky from the shelf and a few bags of chips. He already had some trail mix and a few apples in the car. It was enough for tonight. He quickly stepped over to the toiletries and grabbed a box of generic tampons. He got himself a few beers and croissant sandwiches.

He walked back into the night and gave the girl her supplies. She had been crying.

"Try to get yourself together and get off the street, okay?"

"Are you English?" she asked.

"Yes, I'm from London," he lied.

Erik walked the loose gravel path from the gas station to the road. The plastic bag, stretched by the beer cans and sandwiches, swayed back and forth from the tangled plastic on his wrist. He ducked under a dying magnolia and walked up a short incline to Jackdaw's main street, continuing alone under the glow of the municipal street lamps. His motel was just down the road. A police cruiser, parked halfway up the sidewalk and flashing its lights, blocked his way. Flashing blue light burned into his dim pupils. Beyond the police car, a GMC Acadia was parked at an oblique angle. A pale, blonde-haired girl sat with the window open. She looked calm.

Erik stood on the dirty concrete sidewalk and studied the officer as he wrote some kind of warning, or ticket in his car. He looked back at the girls. She wasn't much older than her mid teens. Her face was childlike and familiar to him. He watched the officer get out of the cruiser, exchange a few words with the girls, then return and write more. Erik stepped across the asphalt to the mulched median. Keeping his distance as he passed, Erik asked the girl if the officer was bothering her. She smiled and said, "No, I', fine." She spoke with a hushed Eastern-European accent.

Erik saw the police officer approaching him in the corner of his eye.

"I'm conducting an investigation here, son," the officer said.

"Okay sorry," Erik said, rolling the double r.

He stuffed his hands in his overall pockets which were still caked with mud. When he got to the room he unfastened the holster to his .357 hidden by the jean overalls and set the beer into the mini-fridge. He pulled the paper off one of the breakfast sandwiches and took a bite. He rested the gun on the table adjacent the television.

He had been in Jackdaw for two nights searching for Cassandra. He had heard rumors from the locals in Johnson City and Bishop's Pasture. The rumors were hard to believe. 'A whole town of Irish gypsies robbing anyone who comes by. The police protect them in exchange for bits of pay.' 'Student backpackers from Europe and Australia found dead on the side of the road.' He wondered if Cassandra had taken a wrong road, or knocked on a wrong door. Surely she would know that any methlab would kill her on sight. How pushy was she for information? How much did she invent in her stories? How far would she go for the truth? His mind wandered back to the girl in the GMC. If a police officer stopped two blacks, Erik's father had once said, then he's doing his job, since blacks were always up to no good. But if a police officer stops two whites he's probably blind and needs to be corrected. In that situation, his father thought a white man could become his own lawmaker since the police no longer served the interest of the people. In his father's eyes there was only the Boer, the Platteland, and God. God, having created the universe, had also created fagots and queers, which he could not understand. He surmised that God created niggers and *coloureds* for hard labor, and people between those castes like the Indians and the Chinese for clerical work and record filing. "Everyone has their place", he used to say. "We've got to keep the north pure, but we have to be smart about it. I'm talking about inbreeding of course. It's becoming a startling problem. Instead, of simply refusing to mix with blacks, we must improve the race. I can foresee a system where we send for young women to be sailed from Europe to Pretoria. We need a flood of white women in the area to increase our numbers and rise up as a majority. The Irish did so in the 1960's. Why not here?"

Erik grabbed a beer from the mini-fridge, snapping it from its plastic holster, and drank it quickly, burping. He stared at his handgun on the table and thought of Andre Stander. Stander was the Johannesburg police captain who turned to bank robbery. He had been shot in Fort Lauderdale, Florida. His partner Allen Heyl who had escaped to Greece and then turned himself in once President Mandela was elected, had said that Andre Stander was the most vicious human he'd ever met. Heyl said that Stander despised apartheid and felt–in his strange manic state of logic–that the Africanization of whites was a step backward in their evolution. Whatever Stander believed, he wasn't easy to understand. His mood swings and mix-ups between English, Afrikaans, and Zulu made him almost impossible to understand. He was known to drink heavily and smoked dagga clandestinely as a police officer and eventual detective, then boldly and excessively as a criminal. After escaping to Florida, he ended up getting into a fight with a beat cop who killed him with a shotgun. Stander had died a free man on the pavement two blocks from his condo. Erik looked up to him and enjoyed the stories, the myths, and the mystique of South Africa's most nefarious white criminal.

After finishing another beer, he stood up and put the gun back in the holster before buttoning his overalls closed. He shut the door and locked the deadbolt. A he walked down the sidewalk of the small Tennessee hamlet, he thought about the police officer who had stopped the blonde girl in the SUV earlier that night. He also thought about aluminum baseball bats.

When he got back to the spot, the SUV was gone but the police cruiser remained on the sidewalk lights still flashing. Erik walked up to get a closer look. The driver's side window had been smashed. The policeman was slumped forward in his seat. Erik leaned into the window. The officers face was mangled, and his lower jaw missing, torn from his skull. His uniform was stained with the blood gushing from his aorta. When he looked closely, Erik saw that the officer's eyes were watching him. He was still alive, but barely. Erik started to walk away. He stopped to look at his watch and turned calmly down the street, checking for other police car, or the GMC. A gunshot sounded. The cartridge illuminated the car with a quick spurt of fire and the windshield was spattered with more blood. Erik didn't look back.

15.

The fiberglass insulation hung like Spanish moss from the ravaged ceiling of the secluded trailer. Tim pressed his switchblade into her fleshy hip as he led her inside. There was a narrow closet left of the kitchenette blemished by streaks of water damage. He pushed her inside the closet with surprising force. It smelled of cigarettes and fresh earth. She heard a possum scuttle across the roof, as she tried to wrestle her hands free from the layers of duct tape. Warm blood trickled down her leg. The door opened again and she felt the tread of a thick boot push her head down against the splintered edge of the closet, which was no bigger than a coffin. She couldn't turn her head to see who was pressing into her neck. An incandescent light bulb blinked to life and illuminated her cell a dim, nicotine yellow.

"A little light for ya," the boy said. "Wouldn't want ya lying here in the dark. We're no monsters."

The closet door slammed shut and she rolled back, sitting on her bound hands. She started to scream, but it didn't bother them. She guessed there wasn't another person for miles, but she still had to try something. Her feet were covered with mud. They had walked till dusk and she had gotten a slash across her shoulder the two times she had tried to run off. This was the end of the line.

She froze. An alien emotion overwhelmed her: desperation. She could feel an iguana slowly crawling up through her stomach, fighting to free itself. She could smell her father cracking eggs over his greasy stove in her kitchen. With her eyes closed, she could see him as he sliced his thumb off. The blood trickled over his *papas*.

When enough silence had passed, Cassandra opened her eyes and turned over in the closet, peeking out through the space between the hinges. They had reinforced the knob with a rusted steel rod.

The possum returned to the roof, nibbling on the sweet sun-baked tar paper and sooty black top. The branches of a wiry persimmon tree scratched against the roof.

Through the gap in the door Cassandra's could see that Tim was now holding longer a butterfly knife, flicking it open and closed with finesse. He was shirtless. His stomach, though thin, was unformed and doughy along with his childlike chest. His face, however, appeared haggard like a man's. The others were passing around a cheap cigar and drinking from a jar of grain liquor.

Tim spoke first: "Now, the important thing to remember is to never let the bitch bite you. There was this cocksucker a long time ago in Canada. Not a reasonable guy. I'm talkin' a total psycho. Sick as fuck, I'll tell you. In his early days, for one reason or another, a woman managed to bite a chunk out of his cock. So for the rest of his adult life as a drifter, he left bodies of women along the highway. When the cops found these bodies, sure enough, he'd have pulled their front teeth out with a pair of pliers. Nasty motherfucker was getting blood smoothie blow jobs, 7-Eleven cherry cock slurpies every fuckin' time." He grinned coyly at the others while they continued to listen.

She covered her mouth at the horror of the story, hyperventilating as she considered the amount of pain the Canadian women had endured. She could feel everything in a heightened sense of panic. Her jaw locked into place; bone grinding on bone. For a split second, she thought Tim had spotted her watching them through the door. She had no doubt that his gaze could have burned into her soul like a medieval iron brand. She couldn't be bothered to worry about xenophobia or biblical subtext because these people were in the dark ages: a culture of violent, young white men lost in a country that gave them everything that they wanted, and still they were unsatisfied.

As she lay on the musty floor, the world around her split as if a zipper had been sewn perfectly into the terrain. Mountains shifted. The earth rumbled. She'd hit the roulette wheel of bad luck. Ironically, it was America that had let her down and not crime-addled Mexico. It was always the kids with the candy who had the glass heart and laughed when the cat was run over.

"Fuck," she said to herself. "Fuck!"

The boys heard her and responded. "Yeah, fuck. That's right, lady. We're gonna fuck. Fuck you up at least. Fuck you up real bad. You wait and see."

"Fuck you!" she screamed in retaliation. "I'll bite your fingers off before you can get near my mouth with a pair of pliers. You hillbilly fuckers!"

Tim stood up and slowly walked over to her in the closet. Speaking through the gap between the door and the wall, he told her not to worry. There were other places where a pair of pliers could sting her something fierce.

"I'll kill you." She promised. "I'll kill each and every one of you. I'll show you no mercy."

Her threats helped arouse their attention. One of the boys handed Tim the cigar. He held the crooked roll between his fingers and inhaled it like a cigarette, then placed his lips next to the crack in the door and blew smoke in at Cassandra. She recognized the sweet odor of home-grown dope. She did her best to spit in his face. They laughed at her. Tim kicked the steel rod out from under the doorknob, grabbed her by the hair, and threw her onto the floor. He pulled a small golf ball from his pocket.

"We'd really hate for you to choke to death, Señora. That'd be a fuckin' shame."

He fed her the golf ball knocking the indented urethane plastic shell against the enamel of her teeth. Once the ball was inside her mouth, he wrapped a long strip of duct tape against her lips and around the back of her head a couple of times. They shoved her back inside the closet.

Once again…she had no voice.

16.

Palm wine demons danced in the veins of child soldiers who stood on the hill under the fat-leaf tree. Cocaine and heroin clouded eyes glowed in the darkness of every shrub and bush. Africa! Africa! Liberal intellectuals abroad tread on broken straw and, like a burning spinal cord, in one electric wave; they are dismissed from the human face of the earth. And the children leap over the bonfire; teeth sharpened ceremoniously. The tallest among them—most devote in his convictions—held the heart of a great general on the tip of his bayonet. They danced until a white adolescent among them made his presence known by jumping clear over the bonfire in one impressive bound. He could have been a German or a Scandinavian: a son of the Danish machine gun regiments from Biafra. The Afrikaner lifted the bottle and poured it into his mouth like Bacchus and spewed in all four sacred directions. One the boys fired a pistol in the air. Another blasted his AK-47 into a nearby stump. The bullets were slowed as if he had tossed them into the tree by hand.

Erik was approved of. He had earned his right to see General Butt-Naked's orphan shelter.

Africa! Africa! Southward the children screamed into the night. Fight night. Banana liquor. The kid soldiers ran up the gravel entrance path for the Jeeps and pickups. They entered a modern children's shelter. Some of the boys looked strange holding submachine guns around the children's books, bean-bag chairs and fresh finger-paint sets. One of the boys brewed a pot from the eggshell white, instant coffeemaker. A UNESCO sticker was peeling off the side. The murky creek water, stained with blackened grit and coco beans, bubbled and frothed as streaks of condensation bled down the edge of the glass. Erik, still ripped out of his mind, noticed the heart was missing from the tall one's bayonet. The boys took turns gulping steaming mouthfuls of coffee, spewing it on the walls of the shelter to resemble dried blood and rust. They whispered stories in a circle, stories of war when General Butt-Naked ate the hearts of daughters born of the descendants of returned American slaves, their enemies. The tribes, having kidnapped the girls and painted them white with cow feces and talcum powder, fed them till their stomachs bulged and they vomited. Delirious, drunk, and overfed, the girls were brought to the shaman's inner circle where the eleven-year-old general sat upon the dirt mound, handing the sacrificial blade to the spiritual guide. The stone blade, sharper than it appeared, easily sliced away the flesh of the girl's left shoulder. Her screams carried through the village and into the jungle. The crowd, praying for a safe year during the war while the soldiers, asking the gods to protect them from the bullets, lifted their hands to the screaming as if it were music. The elderly women walked through the crowd to wipe away the painted child's tears with their handkerchiefs as the shaman continued down her chest with stone blade to carve out her heart. He pulled out the heart with quick jerk like he as pulling fruit from a limp branch. The general on the mound took the first bite. With blood dribbling from the sides of his mouth, he yelled with his soldiers like dogs at the moon.

They spoke of old ceremonies before the white men outlawed them. Some of the boys looked at Erik, but none of them dared challenge him. The changed man, General Butt-Naked, eater of American hearts as a boy, now ran the orphan shelter. One of the boys spat on the ground and called for another war. They spoke of Monrovia and the churches on the outskirts. They spoke of priests who used welding equipment to dismantle the church gates for spears. The streets were full of shells and metallic spatter. The constant drum roll of machine gun fire. A pulse. A dying world. Nightmares of cyclical history.

Africa! Africa!

Erik spat onto the soiled rug, screaming about Charles Taylor and Sierra Leone. Moonshine dripped from the tear ducts of present ghosts. The tallest boy held the rotting human heart in his hand. He spoke: "We heya. Wi wu kā a long wey! We'em up to dis white boy, Erik. Damn with gun. Damn with violence. We animal!" One of the boys shot a bullet through the ceiling. They told more stories of atrocity and finished the coffee, then, without warning, warm for the night and jittery with caffeine, they ran naked into the jungle, gimpy and sore-footed, under the dismal canopies. The bonfire had subsided, the smoldering chassis of an automobile.

Sixteen years later, Erik could still smell the fire in his nostrils as he closed his eyes. He inhaled the mountain air and watched the sunset. He thought about Fillmore and Jeremy. He had told them his stories of Butt-Naked and Charles Taylor over drinks after his shift at Applebee's.

"That has got to be the most fucked up story I've ever heard," Fillmore had said. "I mean, that shit ain't right. He was an…"

"An eleven-year-old child soldier who ate human flesh daily during the Liberian Civil Wars," Erik finished his sentence.

"Ain't nothing civil about them wars. God!" Fillmore said as he held his cigarette close to his forehead as he massaged his temples. "What is it about Africa that just… fuck, man."

"The cradle of humanity. Even groups that don't belong there want a piece. Set up the frontier homestead and think about drinking and killing yourself."

"Leaving is easier than staying," Jeremy had said.

Erik sat on top of the rock as the sun finally went down. He looked down upon the dilapidated trailer and listened to Cassandra's screams.

"I'll kill you. I'll kill each and every one of you. I'll

show you no mercy." It was her alright. He'd followed her on her morning jog and later on her hike into the woods, out of sight, but keeping an obsessive eye on her at all times. Then those dumb boys showed up, he thought, the imbecile pricks who just had to have her. They could have done a lot better at any point last night with all the young strays he kept running into. The nerve of them to just take Cassandra. A woman like that deserved better. Of course, tonight was her lucky night, because all his stalking and obsessing would save her life. Let'em think they've got her. Let'em think tonight was their night.

He watched a raccoon run along the trailer roof. A tree shifted in the wind. Erik smiled to himself and waited. The jungle cat always waited for the perfect moment to strike. Patience is what makes them deadliest. Likewise, the python could wait for days before enjoying a distended stomach slowly filling up with acids in its coma of digestive bliss. He continued to reminisce. The bygone days of banana leaf beds and *welifidag'hanâga* were still vivid, locked within his unflinching, unforgiving memory.

17.

"Well, what are we waiting for boys?" one of them said blowing smoke from his nostrils and mouth as he spoke. "Let's get her done."

"This cabin sure ain't getting any warmer."

"It's a trailer, Jerry."

"You get it."

Tim set the 'shine back inside the cooler, which was now filled to the brim with cold water and a few stray Miller High Life bottles, then stretched his shoulders and started whistling. One of the other boys recognized the old folk tune and sang along: *"My name is Gurveer Singh and I sing all day long/ I never shear my hair for the lord says it is wrong/ I live in Punjab India where my heart clings so tight/ and I laugh like a jackal in the hot moonlit night/ Satan is my enemy to whom I wage all my war/ and I help all the hungry and build homes for the poor."*

Tim laughed at the short-lived tonal perfection they had achieved.

"Golden oldies."

"Yeah, something like that." Tim flicked his butterfly knife open and yanked the steel rod from the closet. Cassandra, bound and gagged, her mouth painfully extended by a golf ball, had been leaning against the flimsy door, exhausted, and fell to the floor. He knelt beside her and leaned in as close to her face as possible. She had been crying. He could see fresh streams of tears running down her cheeks, leaking into the firm strip of duct tape wrapped around her mouth. The golf ball he had jammed in her mouth ached her jaw. Tim leaned even closer and licked the tears from under her eyelids. After pulling himself from her face in one immediate report, he ripped off the duct tape strip. Cassandra gasped as the bloody golf ball rolled from her lips to the shabby floor. Against her will, Tim gave her a long passionate kiss. Her mouth was too weak to bite off his tongue. He finished by sucking on her lips and spitting her own saliva and blood back in her face. Blood was seeping through the gaps in her teeth. He finished their courtship by giving her a violent punch in the face. She could hear her own nose crack and feel the bridge, which now seemed to favor one side, throbbing as blood poured out her nostrils.

"Please don't kill me! I have children!"

Tim laughed. "If they're close, we'll probably fuck them to death too, bitch."

"Drag her!"

The other boys dragged her into the bathroom by her feet. She felt one them pull her pants down. Another successfully ripped off her underwear. She saw it: two handfuls of frayed-white cloth.

"No! Please, you can't do this!"

They crowded around her, laughing at the indelible c-section mark. One of the boy's faces changed. She thought, only for a panicked second, that she could see his eyes well up with fresh blood and his skin rid itself of the leftover summer tan. She began to pray: "Nuestra Señora de Guadalupe, la rosa mística, para interceder por la Santa Iglesia, protege al Soberano Pontífice, ayudar a todos los que te invocan en sus necesidades, y puesto que tú eres la siempre Virgen María y Madre de Dios, nos obtenga de tu santísima Hijo la gracia de mantener nuestra fe, dulce esperanza en medio de la amargura de la vida, la caridad ardiente y el precioso don de la perseverancia final. Amen."

Erik, clasping his revolver, appeared as if from thin air, kicking open the door to the bathroom. The boy's gave him an expressionless look.

"Oh, a good old-fashioned jackroll. Fantastic."

Tim flipped open the butterfly knife. Erik immediately shot him in the genitals. Cassandra could see his pant legs fill up with urine and blackened blood. The sides of his neck stretched as he strained them to scream. Never before had she heard someone scream as loud or as long as Tim. Erik, as if in slow motion, opened the .357 revolver and plucked out the smoky cartridge. He quickly reloaded and snapped the gun back together, pulling the hammer back as if he were resetting a mechanical watch. Tim kept screaming.

Erik pressed the gun against the next boy's chest, firing the bullet through his back. The barrel was hot enough to set his chest hair on fire and cauterize the entrance wound. He extended his hand and shot an ear-piercing three rounds, one after the other, into each of them. She could hear their bones splintering inside the skin and muscle.

Erik pulled out his buck knife and sliced off the tape binding her. Halfway through putting her pants back on, Cassandra realized she was covered in blood. She went wash her hands in the sink.

"What are you doing here?"

"I had a feeling you were heading to Jackdaw and I knew that it wasn't going to be safe. So I came to look for you."

She shook her head violently.

"No, I don't believe that for a second. You didn't find me you've been following me."

"Finding? Following? Does it matter? You're alive."

Tim raised of weak hand up from the bathtub where he had fallen. He was surrendering. Erik walked over to the bath and shot him in the side of his head, cracking his skull like an eggshell. Two streams of blood poured down the side of his face, forking at his right ear.

The boy with black hair, the last of the living, lay on the bathroom floor in a growing puddle of blood. Two of Erik's bullets were lodged inside of him: one in the stomach, and the other mashed and fragmented under the boy's mangled shin. He clenched his doughy, boyish stomach, trying to stop the bleeding, and begged for Erik to kill him.

Erik shuffled into the living room of the trailer and took one of the blunts from the ashtray and relit it with a book of matches lying next to it. He walked back into the bathroom and emptied his gun dropping the bullets on the floor.

"Sorry, kid. Looks like I'm all out."

"Please, there are coyotes."

"There's more than just coyotes. Sure, the coyotes'll come first. Nibble bits of your stomach wound there. But what most people don't think about are the wolves. The universities here have been reintroducing the red wolf for the deer population problems, and up here they've got a substantial population. Some people even recall seeing packs of timber wolves too."

The boy started crying and squeezed his gut harder.

"Yeah, the timber wolves migrated down here from the Midwest looking for a warmer climate. If they showed up here, they'd kill the coyotes first, they've got no time for'em, and then you might want to reach for that butterfly knife to defend yourself, because there's nothing worse than having a ravenous dog bite into you. The sheer power of their jaw alone backed up by a mouthful of teeth. They can fokken bite through you like an apple. Crisp. Cleanly. If you survive, I'll be sure to buy some silver bullets in case we meet again, but, in all honesty, you'll probably be torn to pieces." Erik carefully took Cassandra by the arm and led her out of the bathroom, tossing the blunt into the bloody tub. The boy screamed.

Outside, Erik sat Cassandra down on a cypress stump and offered her his shirt to wipe off the blood stains but she was lost to a state of numbness and turned down his offer.

"Fucker," she said.

18.

Erik punched the radio knob. A tune from bygone days filled the church van. Cassandra started to come back. The distance seemed further, an ever increasing horizon. Erik smiled and said something. It took her a few seconds to understand him.

"What?"

"Sam Cooke," he said.

"What about him?"

"Do you know him?"

"Of course I know who Sam Cooke is."

Erik wiped his nose and said, "My father wouldn't let us listen to a black man's music. I hid my records underneath the bed. A good buddie of mine in the suburbs had an old record player. We'd light up a spliff and listen to Rodriguez, Sly and Family Stone, N.W.A, and Sam Cooke."

"Rodriguez?" She pronounced it correctly.

"The singer Sixto Rodriguez."

"See-toh not Six-toe," she said correcting him.

"Seeto Rodreeegez."

Cassandra smiled. Erik noticed.

"Are you feeling better?"

She raised her right hand and wobbled it from side to side to signify her ambivalence, but in sarcasm there was healing, which Erik recognized.

He drove the church van through the thick forest. Two lights bursting from the vegetation. Beams of foggy mist. Wheels rolling along washboarded gravel. Pitch black.

"One of the boy's faces changed," she said under her

breath.

"They all changed. They went from living to dead."

"I thought I saw a demon's face."

"You were probably going into shock. The brain hallucinates when under horrific stress," he said, calmly.

She turned to him and studied his placid expression as he steered the wheel. He had just killed four people. The smell of gun smoke and death filled the van. The screams of the boy Erik didn't kill haunted her, ringing in her ears. The image of a wolf tearing into the boy's fleshy stomach tormented her. Erik didn't seem to mind at all. In fact, he appeared calmer than he did when she met him. Seducing a stranger must have been more traumatic for him than killing four young men.

"Are you a killer?" she asked.

"Well…technically…yes."

He changed the radio dial to a country station.

"How could you do something like that?"

He hesitated.

"You have a strange way of thanking me for rescuing you."

"You've been following me."

"Just to protect you. Jackdaw's a rough place compared to Bishop's Pasture. I had a couple days off work, so I thought I'd come up and make sure that all's well end's well. You can't deny that I was right."

"You shot four boys."

"Have you ever been raped before?" he asked, taking a serious tone.

"Yes, but not by four men half my age."

"I'm sorry," he said. "So you know how shattering it is?"

Subtlety, she reached under her shirt and felt the scar.

"It's the complication that makes things hardest. The trauma of the rape. And the floodgates that open up afterward."

"It breaks you," he said.

"Yeah," she agreed. "It breaks everything."

She took her hand off her stomach before Erik could notice. "But you killed four people in cold blood."

"And I honestly believe that running over a squirrel would bestow more suffering on the earth than killing those yahoos. Hopefully a coyote will come along and make that last fokker's final minutes his worst, or a swarm of rats...yeah...a fokken swam of rats can nibble his screaming ass to death. Fuck him to hell."

"Where are you taking me?"

"If you think you're okay to drive I can take you back to the parking lot, or I can go back to your hotel."

"Take me back to the Kiowa. We can get my car tomorrow."

"We?"

"Please, don't leave me alone now. I might collapse."

"Didn't think you'd want to see anymore of me," he said.

She looked out the window to watch the full moon as it stalked them just above the blacked out silhouette of the forest. The moon didn't have any medicine for her tonight, so she wouldn't be cracking an egg under her bed. The radio station played on and John Stewart was confessing that he had not been known as the Saint of San Joaquin, and then something about being drunk out of his mind. She couldn't understand the words, since she was barely listening. It was the bruised sky overhead that transfixed her, as if the earth was bleeding, bleeding with her on the inside. The scar on her stomach was merely a reverse wound bleeding inward from where her daughter had been ripped out.

"The boys gave you a happiness burn,"

"¿Qué?"

"You know a hickey. Burst blood vessel in the neck," he said. "Did they try to bite you?"

"No."

"They put their mouths on your throat though, right?"

"They didn't. Not that I remember. The vessels probably burst from fear. My hair must be white too."

She checked her hair in the side mirror, suddenly noticing the lights of the SUV behind them.

Erik took out his cell phone and handed it to Cassandra.

"I'm just watching out for you. There's strange shit up in the mountains.

"Why are those people driving so close behind us?"

"Which people?"

"The big car behind us."

Erik looked at the murky reflection of the SUV following them. He recognized the vehicle from the main street in Jackdaw. He thought of the police officer without his jaw killing himself alone in his car.

"Well," he said. "There's only one remedy for this."

Before Cassandra could say anything, Erik accelerated the van. The trees bled away on the margins of her periphery. She turned and looked out through the rear window to see the SUV speeding up behind them.

"They're still behind us," she said.

"I know, I know," Erik assured her. "I have a method to this. Don't worry." He swerved the van between two oak trunks, which appeared too narrow to pass through. She closed her eyes and clenched her teeth, but the crash she anticipated never came. Instead, the van slipped through, cruising along a bumpy, dirt road, heading deeper into the forest. The SUV didn't seem to make the turn. Cassandra looked behind them. It was gone.

"I think we lost them," Erik said. He had started to sing along to another John Stewart song on the radio as it ended. The uninterrupted marathon continued. *Gold* played through the speakers.

"Where are we going?"

"I've driven on these back roads before. Should be about now." He floored the gas pedal and launched the church van up an almost vertical incline. The back tires rotated in the silt, kicking up black and red mud. The van reached the top only to cruise down a long valley of tall grass and weeds.

"Are you sure?"

"I know what I'm doing."

His confidence surpassed recklessness and achieved a strange transcendence. Erik van de Roer was not of Cassandra's world filled with cold facts and hard truths. He bent his surroundings to what he saw fit. That included killing people.

"Where are we going, Erik?" she asked once more. Tall grass and weeds rose up to the rear windows of the van.

"Patience," he said.

"No, tell me where you're taking me right now."

"Back to your hotel."

"We're in the middle of nowhere!"

"You're saying you don't trust me?"

The opening chords of *Ohio* from Crosby, Stills, Nash and Young cranked through the radio behind a barrier of static. The noise of the screaming motor pierced her skull and she imagined her brain hemorrhaging from within. Erik's gun, sloppily jammed into the holster, was slowly wiggling out from beneath his overalls. Without thinking, she gripped the butt of the pistol and pressed the muzzle against his neck. It was a double action revolver but she pulled the hammer back just to be sure.

"I wouldn't play with that," he said.

"I'm not."

She pulled the trigger and heard the sharp metallic click. "I don't know if you can count, but I can and there's still one cartridge in here and I'll keep shooting until I hit it."

Erik smiled. "I can count just fine. And you are right; I did fire just five shots. But if you recall, I emptied the entire the barrel just to fuck with that kid who wanted the easy way out. That gun's empty, Cassie."

"My name is Cassandra!" she yelled as she spun the gun around, holding it by the barrel, and beat Erik's face with the butt. His nose cracked as hers had in the trailer. He yelled at her to stop while he attempted to keep the van on the dirt path. She knocked the side of his head with the top of the empty gun. The hammer stuck deep inside his skin. A bleeding gash appeared as she ripped the gun back out. Erik screamed from pain as he tried to stop the bleeding with one hand. Cassandra didn't notice the tall grass abruptly end, making way for a paved road bisecting the forest. Erik slammed the brake as the van lunged forward before stopping just before hitting a telephone poll on the side of the road.

"How's this for a happiness burn?" She said as he continued to beat him with the pistol.

"Stop it! Stop it! For God's sake. I told you the truth. This fokken road takes you right up to the Kiowa Inn. Stop hitting me!"

She kept beating him.

"Get out of the van!"

"This van doesn't belong to me!"

"Get out!"

He opened the driver's side door and stepped out of the van. She watched him walk down the road, panting from exhaustion. She punched the dashboard. The glove compartment door dropped open in her lap. Inside were a pack of Mavericks and three bullets.

She loaded the gun, opened the door, and stepped into the cold. The van was badly dented by the trees. One of the lights had been destroyed.

Erik was still walking away from her with his back to the van when she called to him.

He hesitantly turned around.

"Are you in a better mood now?" he asked.

She raised the pistol, aimed it at his chest, and pulled the trigger. Fire erupted from the barrel. The gunshot echoed through the woods like an explosion. Erik's face strained. He clasped his chest. She fired twice more. One of shots jolted his body backwards. The kickback sent the second bullet ricocheting off the asphalt, bouncing back to graze her leg. The pain was paralyzing like a deep cut from a red-hot iron. She screamed and took a few steps back toward the light of the van before the heat of the wound set in. The agony was perfect and empty. She realized what she had done.

She had killed him, gunning him down in the street. Her malice evaporated and all that was left was panic and guilt. She tossed the hot gun into the ditch beside the telephone poll. A chill rose up her spine. Erik lay face-up on the wet asphalt, expressionless, still. His eyes were wide open as he looked up at the purple sky. She staggered away, relying on her good leg to reach the van and shut off the engine, then moved back into her passenger seat, shifting the van with her weight. Her entire side stung as if her skin were peeling off as she sat down. The glove compartment was still open. She took out one of his cigarettes and lit it with her Bic. She smoked with the passenger door open, looking at the forest surrounding her like the parameters of a nightmare. The tobacco and paper crinkled as she smoked. A distant noise punctuated the lull: a grunt. She lowered the cigarette and looked toward Erik's body. It was moving. Her thoughts raced again. She froze. It felt like adrenaline was attacking her heart. She could feel tears streaming down her face as Erik sat up from the ground, coughing, trying to catch his breath. He pounded his chest with his fist.

"Jesus Christ," he said, standing up.

"But? I shot you," she whimpered.

"Yeah, you did."

He was walked back to the van.

Cassandra crossed herself as she tried to ask him how it was possible, but her words fell apart rendering her speech a gargled, panicked mess.

Erik sat back down in the driver's seat and picked the keys off the floor.

"How?"

"It's a long story," he said.

The first thing she saw, just before waking, was an endless black tunnel too small for a person to crawl through. She was in the middle of it. Sharp pain surrounded her arms and legs as she struggled through. Her skin was tearing off the muscle and bone. The tunnel was lined with teeth; viper fangs that stuck in her palm, shark teeth slicing off the fat around her hips, rodent tusks wedged into her elbows. The tunnel narrowed as she was juiced like a pulpy mass of fruit.

She awoke instantly bolting upright, catching her breath before having to lay back down. She wasn't back in her room at the Kiowa Inn, she was inside some kind of shack; a corrugated tin roof above her held up by clapboard slats and steel beams. Her wounds had been treated and thoroughly bandaged.

"Erik? Erik!" she called out.

A tall man with black hair and a dark complexion sat in a rotten chair at the foot of the gurney up on which she had been sleeping.

"Where am I? And where's Erik?"

"You're at the Bishop's Pasture First Baptist. Well, out back at least. Don't worry, your car keys are on the table near the old engine."

She looked over and saw her keys in an ashtray beside the gutted remains of several vehicles.

"He brought you back here 'cause you were bleeding out. Pretty bad too. I fixed you up."

"Who are you?" she asked.

"Name's Fillmore. Me and Erik were buddies in Afghanistan. I was a field medic." He stood up and changed his tone. "There's a gun just next the old gurney there. It's yours to keep, just in case you feel the need to shoot someone. I'd like you not to shoot me though. Unlike our boy Erik, I'll probably just stay dead."

"You know about him?"

"Of course, I've patched more wholes in him than… well…I guess I've run out of steam for the metaphor, but you get it. I watched a guy pump six shotgun rounds into his chest. It was routine village check; we were confiscating weapons and trying to find out who was selling'em. Erik opens up a wooden door to a kolba and all I saw after that was fire. Was a kid that shot him. Erik never hit the ground. He just held onto the door frame and took it."

"Why?"

"Well, the kid was scared and probably thought we were gonna be like the Russians and just…

"No, why can't Erik die?"

Fillmore started walking away, opening a slab of clapboard to exit the shack. He was shaking his head.

"Why can't he die?"

"Some things, like these for instance, are just better left alone." He paused. "You can leave anytime you want, or you can stay. It's no problem which. And no mention of Erik's differences to anyone else, 'specially to the Rev. He won't understand."

He disappeared into the daylight.

Cassandra leaned back in the gurney and looked up at the faded sun shining through the holes in the roof. She couldn't believe it. She was right back in Bishop's Pasture. All her things, her computer, her pills, her purse, every goddamned important document she had was back in Jackdaw. She was still paying for the room too. Adrift and angry, impotent with a wounded leg, part of her wanted everything of hers back and another part knew that in the wake of last night nothing would ever be the same and all those petty things were about to fall to the wayside. Then a far-flung notion of hope overwhelmed her, and she realized exactly who Erik was and why she was so lucky to have crossed his path. She was panicking, horrified and delighted at her own morbid ambition. The real reason she had cajoled the editors to come to Tennessee was surfacing in her mind: the sadness, the violence, the confusion, the wonder, the terror, and the most palpable loss anyone could have ever experienced.

She did her best to stand up and walk to the slat where she entered out into the first sunny day she had seen since arriving in the state. Fillmore was sitting atop the hood of an old Cadillac. An old man, the Reverend, sat sideways in the driver's seat of the van, tinkering with the inside of the door. He didn't seem to notice or care about the warped grille or the busted headlight.

"Sorry," she said. "That was me."

The Reverend didn't say anything. Neil Young was playing on the Cadillac radio.

"*After the Gold Rush,*" she mumbled under her breath.

"What?"

"That's the name of the song," she said. "American radio. It's all the stuff that we liked in college. Now they only play dance-hall music for us back home."

"What like Duke Ellington?"

"No, hip-hop and reggaeton, *'Me gusta la gasolina.'*"

Fillmore shook his head in confusion.

"It doesn't matter because I like this kind of stuff," she said.

"Crosby, Stills, Nash, and Young were one hell of a group. But me, you just can't beat that old forgotten guy. Who the fuck was it? Shit! I can't remember,"—he paused for a moment—"John Stewart. That was him. *Wake up sleepy Jean,* that motherfucker."

"July, You're a Woman."

"Fuck yeah. I know that song."

"What happened to those old songwriter types?" she asked, half-heartedly.

"There's still folks around writing good stuff, they've just taken a backseat to the niggers and their drum machines."

She wasn't about to argue with him just in case he "didn't take kindly" to Mexicans either. As a fan of e.e. cummings, she was also partial to Snoop Dogg but, considering the situation, she suppressed any notion of indignation.

"Where's Erik?"

The Reverend briefly looked up from his aimless tinkering to scowl at her. She returned the gesture. Fillmore noticed the exchange and ignored it.

"He's at Applebee's. Won't be back till 'round 9:30."

"I think I'll wait here then for him."

"That's what he figured you'd wanna do."

19.

The bustling dining room of the Spring Water Road Applebee's franchise, filled to the brim with fake smiles and false starts of people whose glass eyes lazily rolled up into their vacant sockets and burned into total darkness as bile flooded over the dismal evening spilling and dripping down the tinted windows. The world of greasy eggs and vinyl bench seats was an underexposed photograph, melting all features and dignity away at the first sign of light whenever the door opened. Vampires, Erik thought as he flipped two burgers on the crackling stove top, were really just photographs. They were forged in an alchemical incident existing only as the memories of the people they once were. And like a black and white still, they were paler and more eternal than humans. It was the sunlight they couldn't survive. But the sunlight didn't affect Erik, nor did he subsist on the hemoglobin and plasma of others. He tossed the burger into the air and smacked it back down with his spatula. His manager, who preferred a hands-on role in the kitchen having been fry cook for twelve years, approached him with two baskets filled liberally with French fries.

"Just two all day?"

"Sí, señor," he said, inflecting the Spanish words with an East Tennessee accent.

Erik cut a left-facing swastika into each of the patties and scooped them onto the buns.

"Why do you do that every time, Erik?"

"I'm honoring the cow."

"The cow was a Nazi?"

"No, the cow was Hindu."

"Oh, yeah. They don't beef in India do they?

"No, they certainly do not," Erik said.

"Have you been there?"

"No, but there have been Indians in South Africa since the beginning."

"Ah."

"Girijaa Shankara namah Shivaaya," he sang.

"You're a trip, Erik," the manager said before stepping through the swinging double doors. With only two burgers so far, the dinner rush dragged on uneventfully. Halfway into the night, without any order chits left to fill, Erik stepped out behind the dumpster to smoke a bowl. He leaned against the sooty green steel and packed the resin-filled indention in the glass pipe with a few pinches of flower and several flakes from the tip of a cigarette. Erik could withstand gunfire and emerge unscathed. He could drink gallons of liquor and the most that could happen was a mild hangover. But his favorite aspect of the unique condition was his ability to smoke dagga without getting red eye. He smoked alone behind the dumpster enjoying the separation between thought and action, watching the bile in the sky drip like vomit from a bearded chin.

He went back to the kitchen, pirouetted around a spilled bowl of Romaine Caesar salad, croutons, grated Romano cheese and creamy dressing splashed onto the floor, and staggered to the bathroom. He spent six minutes washing his hands. He left the bathroom and looked fixedly at a little girl alone in a booth in a tight soccer uniform. Overweight, hair the color of dirty dishwater, holding one of Erik's Nazi burgers in one hand and a copy of *The Clan of the Cave Bear* in the other, she had a look of despair not just written on her face but indelibly etched into the muscles permanently offsetting the color of her pupils. She couldn't have been more than ten years old and already she had the eyes of a prostitute, the eyes of an alcoholic, the eyes of a serial killer, the eyes of a small town news anchor, the eyes of a grandfather lost to a faceless warehouse with the rest of his generation, the eyes of a body pulled from an icy river. He approached the little girl quietly.

"Everything taste good?" he asked.

She nodded.

"You play soccer?"

"I don't like it," she said.

"Are you here with your parents?"

"My dad's up there." She pointed to the bar.

Erik saw a dark man drinking from a tall glass of beer, transfixed by the plasma screen tuned to Football on ESPN. It was his father.

"You're dad's just sitting there?"

She nodded.

"He doesn't even care you're sitting alone.'

She shook her head.

He looked at her book. "You're reading a big book. How old are you?"

"Eleven," she said.

"That's not so young," he said.

The girl appeared afraid of him.

"Look I'm gonna go back to the kitchen. Just let me figure something out here. You don't like soccer do you? That's why you're reading. You're a sensitive soul. But your father wants you to be good at sports because he tells you you're fat."

She nodded.

"Coming here was his idea, but he's mad because you lost the match. Right?"

"It wasn't even my fault. I didn't get to play. I sat on the bench the whole time."

"You're father's a terrible person isn't he?"

She nodded.

"So was mine. But I killed him and I've always been

glad I did it. I'm from Africa you see. My dad was a farmer. He used to beat me for speaking English or trying to learn Tswana. So I tied him to his favorite horse by the neck and it dragged him across the flatlands. I'm quite free now." He handed her a switchblade from his right pocket. "It's your choice, but you shouldn't wait until you're older. Then you will go to jail. But if you kill him now, nothing can happen to you. You'll get to meet doctors and councilors. It would be okay."

She took the contracted blade and nodded again.

"Ata girl."

He walked back to the kitchen and worked steadily for another hour, slicing more symbols into the burger patties that came in with the last orders, talking fast with the rest of the staff. He didn't think twice about encouraging a little girl to stab her father. Thirty-minutes before closing, he scraped off the stove top and filled up the mop bucket with sink water and pink sanitizer. The floor was screaming at him as he drowned it in a shallow layer of suds and began to mop.

Juan slammed another loud of plates into the dishwasher and parked himself at the edge of the kitchen, holding onto the door frame languidly, studying Erik as he mopped the floor. It took Erik a moment to notice.

"You like what you see, *cabron*?"

Juan gave him a condescending smile. "You don't think anyone can tell but we can all tell, Erik."

"Tell what?"

"We know you smoke weed on your breaks. You come back from the dumpster and you're just not a hundred percent anymore."

"Is it a problem?"

"It was with the last guy."

"I thought he drank."

"No he smoked weed."

Erik kept mopping.

"Why do you smoke weed?"

"I don't think there's anything wrong with intervals of horror, epiphany, and intensity in an otherwise simple mundane life. Significance is for everyone. Spread it around, you know. A little magic never hurt anyone."

"That's just what a high person would say."

20.

Cassandra cajoled Fillmore into giving up Erik's home address. She couldn't stand another minute of the Reverend staring at her like a suspicious old dog.

She had expected a cabin somewhere on an isolated road where voodoo dolls and African charms hung from the branches as sigils and omens, but Erik lived in an apartment complex for young professionals with a young couple from New York named Andrew and Linda as roommates. They were both well dressed and had a clean appearance despite the décor of the apartment which reminded her of a college dorm room. When they opened the door she asked for Erik. Andrew simply smiled and adjusted his glasses, not bothering to ask who she was, and, assuming she was a friend of Erik, let her inside.

Instead of trying to entertain her or offering her anything, Andrew and Linda just sat there and asked her questions: Who was she? Where was she from? What she was doing in Tennessee? As she answered their questions, she studied their faces. Linda's skin was dark and her hair was dyed magenta. Andrew's skin was more pallid. He had curly gray hair despite his young age and stark Germanic features. Halfway through Cassandra's explanation about her relationship to Erik, and just after Andrew and Linda's explained why they left Long Island. Andrew abruptly announced that he needed change into something more comfortable. When Andrew returned to the couch, he was wearing pajama pants and a t-shirt. Then Linda left the room and came back in a large tie-dye shirt that hung over her like a dress. They took out the cigar box beneath the coffee table. Politely, Cassandra pretended not to notice. She looked at the LP player and the vinyl collection beside the large flat screen television instead.

"Are those your records?" she asked.

"No, those are Erik's," Andrew said, rolling a joint.

Cassandra made her way over the crate of records, sitting Indian-style on the rug and thumbed through each one: Crimson King, Pink Floyd's *The Wall*, Rodriguez Cold Fact, St. Pepper's Lonely Hearts Club, Giant Owls, Handgun Kids, Bat out of Hell, The Bloody Masturbators, The Locust, Billie Holiday, Miles Davis, Dave Mathews, Monkey Dogs, Men at Work Greatest Hits, Toto, The Yeah Yeah Yeahs, Ag Pleez Deddy, and a final record which took her by surprise.

"He's got an Inti-Illimani record. *Viva Chile* all of all things."

"Put it on," Linda said, pointing to the record player.

"You think he wants me going through all of this stuff."

Andrew had the joint dangling from his lip as he spoke. "He never plays those records. They just sit there and collect dust. Play it."

"Okay, I guess…" Cassandra flipped the record onto the turntable and set the needle. Music filled the room.

Linda asked her if she'd been to Chile.

"No, the furthest south I've been is Colombia."

"Bogota?"

"Medellin."

They listened to the music for a few minutes. Linda pantomimed to Andrew asking where his lighter was or perhaps she had asked whether or not he was about to light another joint. Cassandra couldn't tell. Andrew turned to Cassandra and asked her she was okay with them smoking while she was there.

"Sure, it's your house," she replied.

Linda asked her if she wanted to smoke with them. Cassandra hesitated. Andrew offered her a beer instead. He told her that they had tons of beer in the fridge. She told Andrew and Linda that she hadn't smoked in years.

"This stuff isn't strong," Andrew said. "It's your standard Kentucky Skunk. Nothing but weed."

The three of them smoked as the record changed into a stranger, fuller sound. Andrew and Linda told Cassandra a story about smoking weed in front of a cinema and forgetting which film they had planned on seeing. In the midst of their laughter, the front door unlocked. The bolt retracted loudly as if it were a bank vault. Erik walked inside in his Applebee's uniform.

"This looks friendly," he said.

"We were just having a smoke with Cassandra," Andrew said. "Do you want me to role you up some dagga."

Erik laughed at his pronunciation. "No, you have to soften the g so it's more like a ch sound almost."

"Dagcha?"

"Almost like that."

Erik stepped into his bedroom and returned in fresh

pajama pants and a white under shirt. He stepped out onto the small concrete porch and lit a cigarette, watching the rain mist. It took Cassandra a few moments to stagger to her feet and follow him out. He gave her a cigarette which he had already lit, passing it from his mouth to the crook between her bony fingers.

"How did you find this place?"

"Fillmore told me."

"Ah, hah. Well, congratulations. It's not easy to get information out of Fillmore."

Cassandra paused then closed the door to the patio.

"Why were you just going to leave me with them?"

"I thought you'd be going back to Jackdaw after Fillmore patched you up. Didn't think you wanted to see me again."

"Why didn't you just take me to fucking hospital in Jackdaw?"

"You can't trust anyone up there."

"What are you?"

"I'm just a guy, Cassandra."

"And me?"

"A writer. A woman."

"What am I to you? Why do you care?"

He sucked on his cigarette and exhaled out his nose lost in thought. Cassandra listened to the falling rain, Inti-Illimani playing inside, and thought about her father cooking again. Unable to think about anything else, she tossed the cigarettes over the balcony and cursed Erik in Spanish.

"Chupe mantequilla de mi culo."

"Hey, don't do that."

"What?"

"Don't toss your cigarettes onto the lawn. There's a strict rubbish policy in this complex. You could get Andrew and Linda fined for that kind of shit."

"Why did you follow me to Jackdaw? Why did you stalk me and kill those kids?"

"Because I like you. You're one of those people that you see from afar and want to talk to but never do. Either the timing isn't right or you're too afraid. But I thought, fuck it, I need to talk with this woman. You were lonely and I was bored. I thought if I followed you I'd get another chance and maybe you'd like me more. But I got too close, and I made a mess of things didn't I."

She nodded.

"You mess it up, Erik. I'm already a mess. I don't know why I came to this horrible place. I could have gone anywhere else in the world to write the next book. My publisher told me to go to New England. I could have done that just as easy. But I thought I could handle coming back."

"Coming back?"

"I was pregnant when I lived in Knoxville a long time ago. I came back here because I thought I could face my thing alone, something that had been tearing me apart for years."

"You lost your child."

"She was taken from me."

Bored, Erik stubbed out his cigarette and stretched his arms above his head.

"I'm sorry about that."

"God, you piss me off," she said.

"If I piss you off so much why did you come here?"

"Because I need your help."

Erik stood up. "Come on, let's go inside. I'm starving.

Are you hungry?"

"We're talking. I just started to spill my guts for you."

"We'll talk more after you eat. I think you might just be hungry. Come inside with me."

"Pendejo! You are a pendejo. You know that right?"

"Besa mi culo."

Erik opened the door and they stepped back into the apartment. Linda had changed the record. Africa by Toto was riding on the turntable. Andrew and Linda hadn't been talking which led Cassandra to assume they had been eavesdropping on the two of them, but that might have been the paranoia she felt from smoking. If they had been listening to her, she was glad that Erik had cut her off before she said anything too personal. Maybe that's why he had done that. What did they think of her, a 48-year-old showing up to see Erik? Andrew seemed to be skeptical and even a little condescending, not that he let it show. On the other hand, it was ten o'clock at night and they were probably just tired. Andrew stood up from couch and walked into the kitchenette with Erik and grabbed another beer from the refrigerator. It was a micro-brew she had never seen before. Andrew was fit for a man who smoked so much pot and drank so much beer.

"Does anybody else want a beer?" he asked.

Erik shook his head.

"No thanks," Linda said.

"No thank you," Cassandra said.

Erik started making Cassandra a sandwich.

"I'm not really hungry."

"Have you eaten today?"

"No, but, seriously, I'm not very hungry at all."

"Really? You just smoked a bunch of pot. That's curious. You better eat just the same."

Erik van de Roer was a fry cook at Applebee's, a dec-
orated marine with extensive combat experience, and, after his military service, a naturalized U.S. citizen. He was
also a brutal murderer and an obsessive romantic. His bed
was elevated by concrete blocks and closed off by a white
chalk circle which he obsessively redrew every night in
case the Tokoloshe should come after him for a second
time. Cassandra sat down on the end with her pancetta
and tomato sandwich in hand.

"What's with the voodoo?" she asked.

Erik opened up his closet and grabbed a photo album
before sitting down beside Cassandra. "It's not voodoo. It's
just practical measures the way you'd use a mosquito net
or a security alarm system for a big house."

He held up the photo album.

"I was thinking about burning these. Lucky for you, I
still have them."

"What are they?"

"Pictures of my home."

He opened up the book and showed her an old Po-
laroid of tall man with red hair stuffed into a panama hat.

"This is my father, Kasper van de Roer. I killed him
when I was a child before I left for Sierra Leone."

"Why?"

"He was evil and he used to beat me, before I was
stronger than him of course."

"Did you shoot him?"

"No, I tied him to his favorite horse by the neck and
had the thing drag him toward Botswana. I thought it was

pretty creative at the time. He was gargling a lot, but I had the noose so tight he couldn't scream…"

"I don't want to know," she said, swallowing a bite of her sandwich.

He turned to the next page. She inspected it the pictures.

"Which of the kids are you?"

He pointed to a child on the far left of the photograph. "That coy little oukie there."

"Is this your grammar school class?"

"These are my brothers and sisters."

"All these children?"

"All of them."

Erik flipped past a few more photographs until he found the picture he was looking for. He covered it with his hand, hiding it from Cassandra and asked her to promise not to scream. She promised and he lowered his hand from the album for her.

"This is my mother," he said.

Cassandra stared at the picture. She wasn't sure what had been photographed at first, then, like the delay of an optical illusion, she suddenly saw the image for what it was: a pale, naked body of something inhumane with black eyes and an animal's snout. She saw nothing human in the photograph.

"That's your mother?"

"Not most photogenic woman in the world," he said grinning.

He put the closed the album.

"How?"

"My father was a little touched in the head. He could feel the tides turning in South Africa and wished desperately to change them. He became obsessed with eugenics and Nazi-era science and started planting rune stones across the farm. He discovered a genetic outcome of cross-breeding vampires and humans."

"A what?"

"A dhampir."

"You're a dhampir."

"All of my siblings are. My father was trying to improve the race. He wanted to perfect a race of superhuman Afrikaaner separatists."

"How did he meet your mother?"

"He caught her. He traveled all the way to Europe to find her."

"Bulgaria? Romania?"

"Somewhere ancient. He never told us. We kept her in the basement and…we'd often kidnap people from the cities and bring them back to feed her."

"How could you…"

"I had no choice. She was my mother and I loved her. But that's not the only thing my father had us do."

"Where is she now? Your mother."

"I released her after I killed my father. She's somewhere in the flatlands. Maybe she made her way to the Serengeti. Wouldn't that be something?"

"How did he have sex with her?"

"Vampires can take many forms. At their weakest they look like us."

"But how did he—"

"Probably rape."

Cassandra stared at the pancetta and tomato sandwich in her hand. Eating it didn't make sense.

"You better try to eat that," he told her.

She forced herself to take another bite.

"Now that you know more about me, what's this about you needing my help?"

21.

August heat. Oppressive sunshine bleaching the stop signs. Sun-faded fliers stapled to splintered wood. Have you seen this cat? Have you seen this girl? Please help. Endless telephone poles like ski lifts leading to nowhere. Kudzu waves overtaking the gulches and fields, draping the chain link mimicking lace. Creek beds babbling...

Sirens...syncopating with one another. Epileptic, metallic blue flashing of two police cruisers, zooming along chipped asphalt, turning onto a dirt road, racing, side by side, tall thistles whipping against the side mirrors all in the wake of a cryptic 911 call.

No words. Just screaming.

The cruisers screeched to a halt in front of the decrepit ranch. David Llewellyn, a local big shot back in the 1960s used to raise horses here but it's been empty almost ten years now. The station was surprised that the telephone line still worked, reigniting their suspicion that an illegal enterprise has been operating here.

What do you make of it Sheriff?

The sheriff strokes his jaw as it had been numbing with panic. I don't think anything. I just do what needs to be done.

Ah hell.

Draw your pistol now.

The two men entered of the house. Creaking floor amid dead silence. Darkness.

Check your corners! Sorry Sheriff.

Then each the room...

Horror...

F carved into wall.

Jesus, this is fresh. They just cut that into the wall. They move through the narrow hallway. Sunshine bleaching the earth. Inside pure darkness. The sheriff grabs a flashlight. God eats a monkey. Out the corner of the deputy's eye. Does he see it? No. Adrenaline flows. Turn. Turn again. No room goes unchecked.

Hey! Put your hands up! Sheriff's Department!

A tall pale figure. Dressed in ubiquitous beige pants. Suspenders. White shirt stained in red clay and black dirt.

I said put your hands up!

The figure doesn't move. A heavy clank. A bloody pair of scissors fall to the floor. The man is so pale he's blue. Shimmering. Ethereally blue.

He dropped his weapon. Now put your hands up!

No movement. Before they can think of how to approach the suspect, they hear screaming. Look up. Look behind the darkness of the room. Past the couch draped in a white sheet. A woman. Screaming she grabs the deputy's ankle. She bleeds on the floor. Her stomach. The gash. The opening. Her trembling hand. She screams and frantically speaks. (the scissors pierced from the top down on her bulging stomach curving slightly as if to imitate a legitimate surgical procedure but she has been cut with unending pain with long metal spikes that are also dull are extremely rusted smattered with congealed motor oil she can feel it tearing through the flesh rather than cutting through her belly she can feel the blade inside her she can feel everything she can feel the baby kick one last time she can feel her spine folding backwards she can feel the foreign hands enter the wound in her stomach and pull out the child)

The sheriff. Stands above the man who rests on his knees handcuffed behind the back.

A crash like thunder.

The sheriff's hand twisted and dislocated, dangling from his joints. His gun falls to the floor. The albino rises. His handcuff's separate into wristbands. He snaps the sheriff's neck. The deputy shoots him three times propelling his body against the wall. The Mexican girl is still lying on the floor holding onto his ankle.

Grab her you dipshit! the sheriff says from beyond the grave.

Ok I'll do it!

That's it hold her like that. Don't tear the damn gash deeper into her stomach, son! She's bleedin' out. Kick the fuckin door open. Gettir towa dam hospital!

He gets her to the car. Blood everywhere. She bleeds onto the back seat. He shuts the door.

His head cracks on the side of the cruiser as he…

Falls…

Gunshot.

In the back.

The albino man stands in the doorway. Teeth jagged and overlapped. Hideous. She strains and holds her gushing stomach.

Tienes que hacer algo, Cassandra, she thinks.

22.

"I don't know how I did it. Maybe all the pain and shock numbed me somehow, or perhaps it was the prospect of living to see another day outside. Either way, I crawled around and into the front seat and drove myself to the hospital. He never followed me." She took the last bite of her sandwich and gave Erik the second half. He ate it quickly.

"They really did that? They cut your baby out of you."

"The girl ate my unborn daughter, Erik. I watched everything."

Erik went silent.

"I want to find her again, Erik. She's the one who lead me to the house. I want to find her and I want to understand her and then I want to kill her. I want vengeance. That's what I want most of all, Erik. I want vengeance. They tore my daughter out of my womb and they ate her. You can kill them better than anyone else. I saw how you killed those teenagers. Help me again. I want to kill these vampires the same way you killed those boys. That's really why I'm here. Please help me, Erik."

"You don't want vengeance. You don't know what you want. You don't even know what brought you here to Tennessee. You're searching for something, but you're not sure what it is. Everything that happened to you happened to you 20 years ago and before your run in with the local boys, it didn't appear to be dogging you when we first met. You went to college and have lived a full life since then. You're even going through your second career. Why get revenge now? You don't even know if they're still alive. I only killed those kids to get you out of harm's way. I won't help you go looking for trouble. You have to let it go."

"Have you let go of South Africa."

"Yes, I have. I've even let go of Afghanistan."

She lowered her head. "There were seven of them. The worst of them was the girl, the very young girl. She was the one who lured me to that house."

Erik stood up and paced back and forth.

"I can't do it. I can't help you. I'm sorry."

23.

Past the highway where the trucks sandwiched the sedans like sheep amid a herd of cattle moving down the long road in a sea of red lights; across the still, opaque river in the desolation of full dark where, in the spring, the muskrats skimmed the reflective top and retreated like the pitted jaws of a striking copperhead; through the black paper silhouette of the tree line barely visible from the road harboring devil-horned, nighttime owls and fork-tongued leaf burrowers in deep hibernation; along a warn dirt road where asphalt had been forgotten and weeds hung low like hooks reaching out to the pathway; in the very middle of an abandoned farm field rested the corpse of a milk cow. Its limbs where gnarled and stiff with rigor mortis and its stomach distended with foreign inhabitants. Under a pale sheen of moonlight, a girl crawled from the warmth inside the cow's abdomen into the cold night air, dragging her naked body through the grass with the listless motion of an alligator, wiping herself clean of the cow's innards and rotting tissue. The girl wore a necklace. The police officer's jaw served as the pedant, which she had thrown across her shoulder as she pulled herself through the grass, allowing each muscle to stretch out and realign itself. She crawled until she reached the edge of the river and began to bathe, using the lower jaw, still blemished with dangling flesh, as a tool to scrape off lingering entrails from the inside of the ruminant.

The stolen SUV was hidden behind the elephant

grass on the edge of the river. She pulled open the back and put on their clothes, stolen clothes, acceptable clothes unblemished by dried blood and dirt, clothes taken from another girl lying dead behind the gas station, face down in a drainage culvert. Once she was clean and dressed, she drove up through the narrow path in the forest, crunching over badger holes, loose rocks, and layers of dead leaves, toward the smaller back roads just off the highway. She thought in an arcane dialect from the Balkans and noticed the great horned owl gliding above past the moon as if it were the specter of the impundulu. The memory of the iron-toothed asanbosaam dangling from the tree branches with a murderous amphetamine gaze might have remained lodged in the superstitions of the Tennesseans whose long, tortured heritage lead them back to the age of the American shackle and the shores of West Africa. But no one would lock their doors and board the windows for a young girl. Harmless in her appearance, the ancient shroud eater was able to lure almost anyone. Children playing alone disappeared from playgrounds and schoolhouse yards in the evening. Old men went missing from their front porches at dusk.

She had survived for hundreds of years. In the First World War, they searched the trenches and battlefields for living men. Soldier's heard the screaming in the dead of night. She only had vague memories of the beginning, the days before they were relegated to scavenging in the night. Her parents, the inbred royalty of Kruja Castle, were killed in a peasant revolt. Her father, a hemophiliac, was bled like a hog in the town square and finally struck through the heart with a silver-plated spike. Their mother was tied to a cross and mounted at the top of the castle wall by torchlight. She hung there until the sun rose when her skin reddened into a raw pink hide and large puss-filled boils began to form, popping and bleeding. At first the sun burned gaps in her cheeks exposing her teeth and her eyelids melted over her blinded pupils. Her skin turned to a thick brown leather and chipped off in flakes fluttering down the mountain onto the town like ash leaving her to slowly bleed to death. Her fangs were finally exposed as her jaw muscles wore away. It was rumored by the villagers that a surviving daughter was taken south and drowned on the bank of the Ishëm River. In reality she had survived with others in forgotten catacombs beneath the city. They surfaced through the sewers pulling children and the sick and the elderly back down for sustenance.

Years went by. She was forced to flee upland from the shores of the Adriatic into the endless darkness of Poland. War shaped the terrain and war changed the direction of the wind. In the rubble from the first Great War, they found themselves blending in with the refugees in the Warsaw sewer system. The Wehrmacht had her rounded up and had thrown her onto a crowded train heading nowhere but further into the desolate Polish flatlands where, years before, she had learned how to hide inside the carcasses of the oxen and cows as cover from the daylight. She huddled in the corner of the train car. The rest of the people on the ground and those standing up, some standing atop others avoiding their pleas to get off, others stabbing the Achilles tendons of fellow victims just to have a place to stand, dead bodies piled atop living people, others slowly starving to death in the corners or suffocating underfoot, all of them in their tattered coats and threadbare, striped uniforms their shivering, bony flesh blocked out the few precious rays of the sunlight. She survived. At night, when nothing, even the plains beyond the railroad tracks, could be seen by the human eye, she would feed on the living. An old man who had somehow endured the train and the girl's massacre for six days and six nights, half-insane, a Sephardi Jew from the ancient communities in the Balkans, raised in the traditions of vampirism and folklore, broke his silence one night and stood before the girls in the pile of rotting cadavers and spoke to them in their language, her dialect of old-world Albanian. He asked them if the Nazi's had planted them on the train to devour the Jews. She didn't respond.

"Of course," he said to the remaining members of the train cart. "They rounded you up in the night with the rest of us unaware you are the true Christian." he said "No, you're not Christian, you are not a follower of Christ, you're the head of the beast, the true disciple of Christ without even knowing it. You are a shroud eater from the Albania. I've killed your kind before. Remove the head or remove the heart. But the best way, of course, is to leave you to die in the sunshine. I've watched you here every night feeding off the blood of the Jews. Drinker of the blood! A true disciple of Christ, not the Christian doctrine. Nosferatu, the undead, he is risen. For whatever it is worth now as we talk here in the depths of Hell, I'll tell you of the truth of Jesus of Nazareth. Do you not see that Jesus was a vampire, the dead one, the Dybbuk? He was gathered with his disciples, those who he spread the disease to and whom he asked to further spread the disease. He said take, drink, this is my blood which is given for you. Do this in remembrance of me. The translation is wrong.

The blood offers no remission of sins. It offers eternal life! Eternal life as the damned! The eating of flesh and blood was not a metaphor. His blood was infected. That night he made more vampires, inhuman creatures sent out to destroy the Jewish people. Modern science is undeniable. On the third day, he rose again not as the son of God, but the son of a God. He was the son of the Dragon Demigod. Jesus they say. Savior they say! What blasphemy is this! Jesus Christ himself was none other than Dracula, the fallen Count of Romania, slain by none other than Abraham Van Helsing, a former rabbinical student and man of modern science! And you two here sit before me, my tormenters, my murderer, a daughter of Christ, the devil herself, here to kill in the end times as the Jewish people are no more, carted off like cattle in these trains, in these camps. Do your worst."

The entire speech had been lost on the remaining Jews who could not speak Albanian. The train car went silent. The old man fell backwards and broke out in violent spasms. He clutched his chest and died a few moments later. She hadn't laid a finger on him. After eating the last living inhabitants of the train car, she hid from the inspection beneath the enormous deluge of bodies. The SS guard fired a machine gun into the pile as they came spilling out from the side, and then threw the bodies into a pit. She was able to crawl out into the snowy tundra before the pile was set on fire, lighting her way to a Nazi-run cattle farm before the sun came up.

She spent six more years in Poland. The insignias on the tanks changed several times over, but nothing changed for her.

Her SUV rolled down the steep incline as she drove

deeper into the rural mountain communities on the fringes of Jackdaw. Once she had inadvertently rammed an illiterate preacher from the local radio station in his Ford pickup. She had been driving a stolen Jeep from a liquor store parking lot. Both cars were totaled. The preacher was still alive and she was still able to suck his jugular and femoral artery dry. From the warped opening of the trunk slithered dozens of Eastern Diamondback rattlesnakes. They were used in the sermons he had given.

She slammed on the break. The lights of the van briefly flashed from behind a wall of trees. She sped back in reverse, searching for a road out. There was nothing. Eventually, she maneuvered the vehicle perpendicular to the partially effaced dividing lines and used the headlights to find the beginnings of the dirt road. This night, like every other night before it, would be filled with victories and failures. Using a car was the safest method. Home invasions were surprisingly unfruitful. Farmers and Appalachian folk were crack shots not unlike their northern brethren in the hills of Kentucky. Gunfire wasn't enough to kill her but still left her fazed, especially when she was shot in the head. The pain was unbearable and the bullets would remain lodged in her brain for weeks before her body's advanced immune system finished dissolving the metal. She could have a deer slug in her thigh, or kneecap, or skull for months before the healing process began.

The most vulnerable people were people in transit.

Never before in the girl's protracted life, and never again since, had she ever feasted the way she had in the nooks of the Paris subway system in the 1960s.

In the distance, just beyond the pines and angled shadows cast by headlights, a dim orange gas light burned like a torch marking the outlines of a mobile home. She pulled up through the treeless patch of brush and then rolled around the giant dead oak to the loose patch of gravel. She parked and stepped out of the SUV. She saw fresh tire tracks in the gravel. The front door was left wide open. She entered the creaky trailer. Cigarette butts and liquor bottles littered the floor. Oppressive wafts of gunpowder, blood, and sweat mingled with the lingering stench of tobacco and marijuana. She stepped inside the closet. Her nostrils flared as she sniffed the plywood sides. Someone had been here and they had been panicking. She sniffed once more, then reached up and turned on the single incandescent light bulb hanging above. There was electricity after all. She followed the smell of blood to the bathroom. The door swung open with a gentle push. She peered inside. The sight of dead bodies was like looking at a platter of spoiled meat. One of the boys had taken longer to die. The skin of his face had been eaten away exposing his teeth and muscles. She could smell the lingering musk of a wolf. It wasn't far. Her presence had driven it away. Taking her time, she harvested each corpse and tore off the hips and glutei then peeled back the skin for the fat, which she smeared on the filthy walls. She ripped out the fattier organs from the stomachs squashed them into the rug. She made a pile of kindling by tearing the cabinets and inner wall of the closet asunder. While snapping the cabinet doors in half, she smelled alcohol in the fridge and later splashed the jar of white lightening on the walls which dripped with gore and human fat. She broke the first gas lamp across the funeral pyre, but it took another to start the blaze. The walls ignited in a short burst of blue flame. Heat and smoke filled the trailer as she returned to the SUV.

24.

Jeremy rested his grass-stained shoes on the truck's dashboard.

Fillmore shot him a stern look before returning his eyes to the blackened road ahead.

"Get your goddamned feet off my dash," he said.

Jeremy slowly bent his legs inward. Placing his feet on the floor, he left bits of hayseed and lawn trimmings on the black vinyl.

"Sorry," he said.

"Thinkin' you can do whatever the hell you want in my truck. Just light a cigarette, stub it out on the dash and take a piss in the back, man."

"Come on now, I didn't mean no disrespect. When I'm riding in the car, I like to put my feet up. It's just more comfortable."

"Well, I don't give a fuck what you do to your shit. You get your shit all smoky, all green and beat up and dust-covered. I like to keep my shit nice. Especially my Chevy."

"And I can respect that, which is why my feet are on the floor now."

"Good."

"Good," Jeremy said. "Although, I gotta say, Fillmore, I really thought of you as more of a Ford man."

"A Ford? Hellfire, I'd rather walk down the street with a Chevy hubcap taped to my bare ass than drive a Ford."

Neither of them spoke for some time.

Jeremy turned to look out at the thick forest beyond the road. The short field separated the edge of the woodland from the back road like a dark lake, pristine and void of life. The Chevrolet turned left and climbed the dirt incline through the open gate beside the sugarberry and cottonwood trees, before giving way to an endless sea of hickory and pine. They were deep in no man's land. The outline of a night bird coasted past the white glow of the moon like an unstrung kite.

"What are we doing out here, Fillmore?"

"Collecting," he answered. "Collecting for unpaid shine deliveries."

"It's those motherfuckin' kids isn't it? The ones in the trailer."

Fillmore nodded.

"I gotta whip somebody?" Jeremy asked.

Fillmore shrugged.

"You might," he said.

Jeremy sighed.

"I probably will. That kid what calls himself Gimphy is half crazy."

"Ain't much more crazy than Erik," Fillmore said.

"Yeah, that's somethin' I don't mind mentioning. You think Erik's a psycho?"

Fillmore thought before he spoke.

"Sometimes I think he's disloyal. But a psycho...Naw, not him. He can't be much more crazy than the Rev."

Jeremy laughed.

"If it weren't for the Rev., I'd be living in a shoebox."

"How's the landscaping thing going for ya?"

"Not as good as the shine money, I'll tell you that. Tennessee, man. Shit get's weird here in good ways and bad ways. Sometimes I can't tell the difference."

Fillmore raised an eyebrow.

"I thought you was from here," Fillmore said.

"Hell no, I'm from Jacksonville, North Carolina."

"No shit?"

"What? Are you from there?"

"Naw, I was stationed there in the Corps. at Camp Lajeune."

"Oh, yeah. There's a base that way. Small world. Whereabouts are you from?"

"Catawba country," Fillmore said.

"Indian?"

"Yep."

"Mm."

A light broke through the darkness, silhouetting the surrounding pines. Fillmore turned onto an even cruder dirt path, headed for an orange glow in the distance. The two of stared out the windshield as the truck's suspension undulated over rocks and clods of winter-hardened clay.

"You got any protection?" Jeremy asked. "Shit might get rough."

"I got a Ruger P.90 in the glove compartment there."

"Are you serious?"

"Yeah, that's my gun."

Jeremy opened the glove compartment and took a quick look at the giant pistol in the compartment light.

"Goddamn, Fillmore! You plannin' to blow them kids clean in half?"

"Well, what've you got on ya?" Fillmore asked.

"My knife."

"You ain't got a gun?"

"I got my Browning with the deer slugs at home."

"Bring it out next time."

"If you say so," Jeremy said.

Smoke wafted through the air vents. Weightless

sheets of red hot carbon drifted through the underbrush carried by a burst of yellow sparks like a fountain of fire-flies released from a chamber at once. The trailer, caught in a blaze of demonic fire, was beyond saving. It's interior already hollowed by the flames. A black SUV pulled away from the scene.

"They're haulin' ass! You think it's them?" Jeremy asked.

Fillmore floored the gas pedal, chasing after the SUV.

"I ain't got time to wonder," Fillmore said. "Tell me you're a good shot."

"I'm a crackshot," Jeremy said. "You want me to shoot at them."

"Shoot at the tires."

"Then get close enough that I can see' em with the headlights."

"I'll do what I can," Fillmore said, racing through the underbrush.

Tree trunks flashed by their headlights as they sped, gaining on the SUV ahead of them. The road leads to an-other steep incline where the SUV dropped from their view as if it had driven off a cliff. Fillmore drove further speeding down the slope. He pressed the break and slid to the side, avoiding the SUV's bumper.

"We're close enough now. Take' em out."

Jeremy leveled the Ruger and rolled down the window. He unbuckled his seat belt and leaned out the window, aiming at the tires.

The SUV was already driving away.

"Go, on. Hit' em."

"Drive up closer. I can't get a shot."

Fillmore floored the pedal again. The Chevrolet skidded in the dirt and, with a sudden jolt, took off down the road like a rocket. Jeremy nearly fell from the window. He held onto the frame aiming the Ruger.

"Don't shoot the windshield in back. Shoot out the tires!"

"I heard ya the first time," he said, aiming for the rear left tire before firing off a shot.

The gun sounded off like a snapped tree branch, and the tire, a rippling shadow, in the glare of the headlights, compressed and disappeared. The SUV swerved violently, colliding into the trunk of a white oak. Its headlights exploded upon impact as the angular front wrapped around the trunk. Smoke arose from the U-shaped engine.

Fillmore and Jeremy sat in the car, staring at the wreckage.

"You see anybody moving?" Jeremy asked.

Fillmore shook his head and shut off the engine, leaving the battery running to keep the headlights on. They stepped out of the Chevrolet and into the cold night. The air was still thick with smoke.

Jeremy handed the Ruger to Fillmore, who grasped it without looking, keeping the barrel pointed toward the earth at an oblique angle. He went ahead of Jeremy and inspected the totaled vehicle. The black paint was cracked where the metal wrinkled in the collision. Smoke rose up from the engine, bellowing sideways in the wind. No passenger and no driver. Half of the steering wheel had broken off, and the windshield had shattered completely.

Jeremy opened the rear passenger door and checked the back seat. A headless raccoon carcass lay in a giant scab of coagulated blood on the gray carpet. He turned over the carcass with his buck knife and looked at the burst stomach squirming to life with maggots.

"Jesus," he said. "Them boys are crazy."

Fillmore prodded a few shards of thick glass from the windshield frame with the butt of his gun.

"Whoever was doing the driving burst clean out of the window here."

"They can't have been thrown too far," Jeremy said.

"So what do you wanna do? Search the woods for him?"

"Let's at least look around."

Fillmore followed Jeremy through the underbrush, kicking over dead branches and decomposing leaves. They had already lost the light from the Chevrolet a few yards out, and the stars overhead did nothing to brighten the winter landscape.

"Fuck this shit," Fillmore said. "My hand's startin' to stick to the gun."

Jeremy kicked through more detritus and spit.

"Come on, now. I wanna go home," Fillmore said.

"Not but five seconds ago, you were all on about getting your money, about *collecting*."

"Well, it don't look like I'm getting my money now does it? Come on, I ain't got time to fuck around in the woods. I got a bad feelin'."

An ethereal hiss, like a leak from a spigot, punctuated their conversation. Both men scanned the underbrush for its source. The hissing had transformed into a horrible gasping when they finally saw the blonde girl lying in the patch of dried blackberry brambles. The bloody muscle fibers lining her skinned arms and face turned pink. A new layer of porcelain-white flesh spread across her body like a layer of fungus. It was raw and pristine as if she had never been touched. The process appeared painful. The girl writhed and convulsed as her skin grew back and steam rose off her emaciated body. Thorns tore long incisions into her skin as she moved; fading away like ripples in water. The regeneration was violent, rapid, grotesque and organic.

The two men stared at the ageless creature.

"Is that—?"

"It is," Fillmore said. "Go get the rope from the truck bed."

"How come?"

"The Rev's gonna want to know about this."

"You sure? Just shoot the thing."

"Not this one," Fillmore said. "This one's special."

"How do you know?"

"You don't recognize her? She's wanted across the state. But, I bet you a million the cops don't know what she is. No, they can't find her because they don't know what it is they're looking for. The Rev will know what to do with her. Come on, go get the fucking rope."

"Shit," Jeremy wheezed, running back toward the light. He turned back and watched Fillmore take a knee beside the girl. He said something that Jeremy couldn't hear.

Part Two

1.

Summer was the wet season in Mexico City. It rained almost every day. Sporadic torrents pierced the smog that lingered over the basin to transform the streets into shallow canals and sequester droves of hapless tourists under bus stop eaves, tourists who had been preparing for dry heat and abundant sunshine. In the summer, Cassandra pushed her queen-sized bed against the far window of her small Coyoácan apartment to listen to the rain each night as she slept, pretending she lived somewhere else like London or Auckland. Dead dogs and duck fetuses flowed through coal slurry marring her nightmares while memories of working at the newspaper and the image of her father filled her dreams. In the mornings, she lingered in bed and cracked the window open, extending her hand out to catch the rain. Cool droplets spattered against the sill and wet her cheeks and pillow. Summer was also the season of kidnappings. Rainy, gray days on the crowded streets under anonymous umbrellas made good cover for kidnappers. Before returning to Tennessee, whenever she walked the streets, she had carried a can of mace in her purse, a knife in her pocket, and a rape whistle on her key chain. Now she had the unregistered revolver that Fillmore had given her. On her long drive back to Mexico, she stopped on a deserted road in Louisiana and fired it empty into the marsh. Later, she found an antique store north of the federal district that carried the right bullets.

While the owners sympathized with a single woman's dilemma in modern Mexico, he wanted her to be sure about what she was getting *(Now these bullets here you won't find anywhere else in the world. The maker was a small company in Transylvania, if you can believe it. Lotta nonsense up in those parts what with communism and all coming down hard and all the people flooding out of the place. But these bullets, they'as the last bullets made by this distributor. That gun you got there something else completely. I don't know where you found it, but ain't no bullets gonna fit an old thing like that lest you wanna blow the damn thing off in your hand. These'll do though. These are special. Powder's good in' em. Everything should work).*

By the time the summer rains rolled in, *Encrucijada del sur* had been available in bookshops and discount racks at tourist's junctures for a month. The new book made her some money but not much. The title baffled readers. Mexicans didn't usually think of the U.S. as the South. The few reviewers that she was close to wrote that it was the weakest in the series. But the book's failure didn't bother her after a windfall of cash came her way when a prime time television show, *Algo Paranormal,* asked her to be a commentator. The new program was based on a successful show from Colombia, which, in turn, had been a rip-off of a short-lived American show: Fact or Faked: Paranormal Files. The producers wanted her to talk about the witches in the Puebla sewer system and the infamous Zone of Silence in Chihuahua. A representative of the show explained that her comments would increase the programs authenticity. She accepted, knowing what they really needed was more talking heads for filler and creative editing. The station sent a driver to the edge of her apartment complex to chauffeur her to and from the studio. She expected an old man behind the wheel of a limo, but instead a kid, listlessly cranking the stick shift to the van, pulled up on the side walk before getting out to open the side door for her.

"After you, Miss," he said.

"Oh, thanks. I'm Cassandra Jimenez," she said, shaking his hand.

"Pleased to meet you, I'm Juan." He didn't say his last name. When he got back into the front seat he whistled in a manner she was only used to hearing from American Southerners. "Damn, you live out here in Coyoácan. That's some upscale living. You must be pretty rich."

"I live in a small barrio twelve blocks from here," she lied.

"I bet you're being modest," he said, starting the van up.

"Trust me, Coyoácan is no Zona Rosa."

"Well who wants to live out there with all the fagots and trannies?

"That's one way to look at it," she said, placing a cigarette between her lips.

"Oh, sorry. You can't smoke in here. Company rules."

 She pushed the cigarette back into the soft pack.

"Don't get me wrong. I love a good smoke. Tobacco, among other things."

 There was a brief moment of silence. Cassandra was looking out the window, but the kid thought she was shunning his drug reference.

"Didn't mean to be offensive. It's a joke."

"You're fine. I smoke weed from time to time. Actually, if it's not against your morals or too much of a hassle, you wouldn't by any chance have some weed I could smoke later?"

"I don't. But I can give you the number of a guy in Tepito. He's pretty reliable. Just tell him you know me and you'll be fine."

"I don't think he'd like that. People tend to think I'm a cop."

"Maybe we'll go buy some another time?" he said smiling at her in the rear view mirror.

"Where exactly is this guy in Tepito?"

"You know Barrio Bravo?"

"I'm not going to Bravo just for some weed."

"Yeah, I guess you could always snag some off a tranny or a coked-up executive in Zona Rosa, huh?" he laughed. "Leave the rough parts to us Indians."

The television studio provided her with a free meal and some cheap beer. She smoked her cigarette in the green room with the sweaty glass of beer dripping onto its paper coaster. Wide-eyed girls from an inane game show passed through the costume department in their busy carnival outfits. She did enjoy getting her makeup done and talking to various workers that helped her get ready for her time on set. At one point, while they were styling her hair, she felt so pampered that she almost forgot she was supposed to present on television. Luckily the camera didn't intimidate her and she could tell a good story on the fly. Once she got on set, she wore a tweed jacket and sat in front of a bookshelf background filled with fake books. When she finally watched the episodes, she cringed as they mentioned not only her book series but her previous career as an investigative journalist in a short montage that she hadn't approved. She had wanted to lay that part of her life to rest. That's why she wrote the travelogues under a pseudonym: Auxilo Flores. Her publisher, Omar Castro, called her while the show aired, promising her that he hadn't told the producers about her work with the newspaper.

Still, it's a good day to be a pseudo-intellectual, she thought.

As a concession, or at least what Cassandra assumed to be a concession, Omar Castro offered to take her out to dinner at his favorite a Korean barbecue hut the following weekend. Knowing Castro, she prepared herself to talk business throughout the dinner. It was inevitable. As soon as she sat down they discussed a new book, one about the ghost ships in the sea of Cortez and the phantom truck stops in Baja California del Sur, while Castro's new boyfriend, who had tagged along uninvited, stared off into the distance. Eventually, he mentioned the things he did like about Encrucijada del sur, which made her feel worse than she had before they had started discussing the terrible sales numbers and how far Castro was from recouping his advance that he paid her.

"The Sikh tracker, Guru Singh..."

"Gurveer Sigh," she said. "He wasn't a guru."

"Yeah, that was a fine chapter. Did you make that one up or was he real?"

"He was a real person. In fact, the Americans have folk songs about him because the story was so popular."

As she recounted what she knew about the songs, she felt like she was back in the trailer listening to the boys singing the song. Her face reddened and she began to sweat.

"He was hired to kill Bigfoot and never seen again?"

"It was a local legend of a bear hybrid creature. Not really Bigfoot." She collected herself and took another bite of the beef and a sip of her Perrier.

Castro's lover, the young man in the black turtleneck with faintly blonde hair oddly coupled with stark indigenous features, suddenly found the conversation interesting and stared at her from across the table. It was first time she noticed his dark blue eyes.

"You researched the Sasquatch?" he asked.

"Not in this book, but I have. Sure."

"I love everything about Sasquatch. That's almost all I watch on television. I don't believe in ghosts and goblins, curses and vampires, or anything like that."

Cassandra cringed at the last reference.

He continued. "Nothing paranormal convinces me. Psychics. What garbage. But cryptozoology, it fascinates me. It is the only thing that makes sense to me. For God's sake, we didn't discover the mountain gorilla until the 1940s. I was actually reading an article a year ago where Jane Goodall visited the Pacific Northwest and she said she believed in the Sasquatch."

Castro was awed at his lover's comments.

"What the hell is the Sasquatch?"

"Bigfoot is the Sasquatch," Cassandra told him.

"Ah hah!"

"For me, cryptozoology is the perfect window into the perception of man, or the limited ethnocentric perception of human kind."

"What do you mean by that?" Cassandra asked.

"Well, think about the latest discoveries of animals thought to be extinct. What was that fish in Africa? That ancient fish that looks all messed up and gross?"

"The coelacanth."

"That's the one. The fisherman in the region knew it existed; they just never made a big deal out it because they knew that fish tasted like shit. But it wasn't accepted as a scientific discovery until some old gringo with a title and a degree proclaimed its existence. Most scientists don't go after the folklore of the regions they're in because they're racists. But who would know the land better? Who would know if a dinosaur or a hairy primate stalked the jungle? I think if the anthropologists would just listen to the Indians in the Pacific Northwest, they'd find the Sasquatch."

"How do you know so much about this stuff?" Castro asked him.

"I watch TV."

He turned back to Cassandra who seemed happy to discuss something innocuous.

"Do you agree?"

She took another bite of the beef. "I suppose I agree with the principle of ethnocentrism guiding modern scientific discovery, but I don't think it's that simple. Concerning your example of the coelacanth and applying folklore, I disagree. The fish wasn't a part of the local African folklore. It was just common knowledge that the big ugly fish that was a thousand years old would turn up in the fisherman's nets. They didn't tell stories of a grand, ancient fish from the depths of hell. Also, I don't believe in Sasquatch precisely because I'm not ethnocentric."

"What do you mean?" the young man asked.

"There are stories of a hairy bipedal ape creature across the world: the Yowie, Yerrin, Yeti, Oranganpak, Asaanbosam, Sasquatch, Skunk Ape. It's just the way people project their hairy past onto nature. The same way we need spirits to assure us that something happens after we die."

"Well I still believe," the young man said, nodding in agreement.

"Many people believe in spontaneous human combustion, but why do all the cases come from 1930-1958? It is because people smoked more regularly back then, so it was harder to tell when they fell asleep with a cigarette. Every room had an ashtray. Everything always smelled like smoke. I mean for God's sake, did you know the sturgeon is a prehistoric fish?" she asked.

"Who cares about fish?" Castro said, taking a gulp of wine.

Cassandra got home later that night. Exhausted from the conversations, she fell backwards onto her mattress and listened to the thunderstorm beyond her window. She watched streaks of lightening imprint themselves into the sky like blood vessels popping in and out of existence. She cracked open the window only to hear the rain pelting the roof and feel the cooling water splash against her cheek, again letting her hand catch a little rain water before she used the moisture to caress her clitoris. Masturbating during thunderstorms was a ritual she began in college. It allowed her to clear her mind. The older she got, however, the less it helped as she came closer to the realization that what she wanted was a partner. As she massaged her clitoral hood as the lightning struck, water jumping up from the sill through the opening of the window like a swarm of insects drenching her pillow and face, she thought about Erik. She thought about him in the strangest way. He reminded her of Tennessee and everything awful that went along with it, but recently she also longed for her first impressions of him and the night they shared together in the hotel room. Despite her apprehension toward having sex with a man so much younger than her—the same way she had spurned the advances of older men years before—everything felt so natural, so comforting, and so perfect during that night together with him. She continued to masturbate even after the storm abated, the corner of her pillow drenched as streaks of water ran down the side of the wall, pooling beneath her bed. It took her longer to finish as her arousal dropped while her mind wandered. She lay in bed, looking up at the textured ceiling. She thought about Omar Castro and Juan the shuttle driver, about marijuana and Erik. She thought about red wine and Coca-cola. She thought about her first couple months in the United States. Her ex-boyfriend was able to find her under-the-table work at a Mexican restaurant and bar where, according to him, most of the clientele were Mexican anyway so she wouldn't have to speak much English. On her first day, she stared at a sea of white faces in the dining room. Not one of them spoke a word of Spanish. On her lunch breaks, she took a plate of rice and beans, that had been untouched by a family of four, behind the decrepit building, and sat atop a rusting, abandoned washing machine to eat it. On her second day, she noticed an old man sitting in the corner. He had been sitting there the day before. He was the only one that looked Mexican. She went to his table and asked him in Spanish what he wanted to drink. He smiled. She asked him again. Then he explained that he couldn't speak Spanish and told her his name was Mills and that he was a Cherokee Indian. After a long embarrassing conversation with her new boss, Cassandra learned Mr. Mills was a prominent member of the community, known for his endowment to the first Baptist church and the 24-hour clinic. Days went by as she continued to work in the little Mexican restaurant, enduring the blank, pit-eyed stares of the Appalachian folk as she painfully learned English the hard way—table by table. At night her boyfriend beat her for flirting with every man in the restaurant and stole her tips. During the day, she worked at that hopeless Mexican restaurant because suddenly she had no other choice.

Years later, as she attended college, she wondered why the Americans that ate there hadn't minded a waitress with a split lip and a black eye. Some people were so crass that her poor English skills were more of an issue than her horrid appearance and broken demeanor. They would berate her for mispronouncing 'enchilada', 'adobda' and 'al pastor'. It had only been Mr. Mills, the Indian, who had noticed her unhappiness. Once, during her lunch break, Mr. Mills had approached her as she sat on the rusted washing machine. Without saying a word, he reached over to hold her chin between his finger and thumb, lifting her head up. Her long hair parted and he inspected the black eye.

She set her plate down and leaned forward to hide her face from him.

"Who did it?" he asked.

She shrugged.

"Mr. Rodriguez?"

"No."

"Well then who? Who?"

A few days later, when she was feeling brave, Cassandra told Mr. Mills who had been beating her. He found her another place to live: a small apartment complex northward on the mountain overlooking the county, not too far from the restaurant. It was there a young man who lived down the hall, and a girl, a very young girl from Eastern Europe, asked her to visit a house with them for what they promised to be a party.

Cassandra fell asleep in her bed thinking about Tennessee as another storm rolled in bombarding the city, rattling windows, blasting stray branches and bits of foliage into the streets, igniting the sky in flashes of blue and faded violet. She dreamt about driving down a secluded mountain road in the pouring rain. The rain was so intense that she couldn't see anything beyond the windshield. The car broke through the steel safety guard like ribbon and she was in free fall. Dire situations never seemed so dire in her dreams. The car fell as a huge rush of adrenaline built inside her. The car landed somewhere in a vacant field with no problems. The point-of-view in her dream split and she watched her seventeen-year-old self speak to Erik in the field as the rain clouds parted overhead.

2.

The joke began with a familiar scenario: men walking into a bar. In this joke, there were two of them, both Oxford professors of ubiquitous Anglo-Saxon Protestant stalk, who happened to be in rural Mississippi for a conference. For the sake of the joke, one had to suspend their disbelief, understanding that no English professors from any college, much less Oxford, would be in Mississippi for academic reasons. After these two English professors finished whatever made-up scholarly duties they had planned for the day, they weren't about to sit in their hotel rooms with nothing to do. They were English weren't they?

"No, I say dear old chap, let's find a pub or whatever passes as one in these rustic parts," one said to the other.

"Spot on old boy. My god, I hope these yanks have a passable stout."

"We'll find out won't we?"

The two Englishmen drove around the small town in search of a watering hole until they came to a tiny, weather-beaten shack tucked in the wood.

"Well, I think this is it.

"I suppose it's better than nothing."

The two Oxford professors walked into the redneck bar and found a tiny table a few feet from the bar. The bartenders had never seen leather elbow patches. Most of the patrons didn't even wear sleeves. The professors squinted through the half-light at the many mullets and scraggly mustaches. Three men interrupted their game of pool to stare at the limey boys, leaning heavily on their cues. As it turned out, the saloon didn't serve stout.

"Two whiskeys and two pints of lager to back them my good man!"

When the Englishmen were done with the whiskey and a few sips deep into their lagers, one of the mullet-sporting good ol' boys slammed his fist against their table.

"Now, I've just about had it with you two Nancy boys. This is a local bar, for local people only. Finish your drinks and get the fuck out."

The professors smiled at him.

"What? What are you smiling about?"

He demanded to know.

"We were planning on having a few more drinks. I see you were playing a game of billiards. Are you a gambling man?"

"Yeah," he said.

"Well, what say you to a wager?"

"What kind of a wager?"

"If we—I mean just me and my colleague here—can drink more than you and your seven friends back there, we can stay as long as we'd like and come back tomorrow night as well."

"You crazy limeys are gonna be in the hospital in an hour." He turned to his friends. "Let's get these deal-making liberals out of here."

Three hours later nearly everyone in the bar was unconscious, sprawled out across the floor in pools of vomit, except the two Oxford professors who sat at their same table discussing the version of Beowulf translated by Seamus Heaney.

"How about another round old boy?"

"Yes, I could go for another round."

They stared at the depraved mosaic of drunken hill folk.

"It's Australia all over again, chum."

Cassandra closed the book and giggled. Wilfredo García's *New Jokes from Around the World* had outsold *Encrucijada del sur* by 700 copies. It hurt to say it, but Benedict deserved it. It was a wonderful book.

She walked into the kitchenette, wearing a Motörhead t-shirt and her pink underwear. The sun was shining through the curtains. She tossed the book on the counter and opened the refrigerator. She pulled out the eggs and placed the skillet on the stove. She reached into the freezer, which she always turned to a low setting, bypassed a few beers and grabbed a Diet Coke. She liked to drink Coke in the mornings. The eggs were cooking and, like a true Mexican, she dabbed a little chili sauce inside the whites before they hardened. She looked at the clock. It was already 12:18 P.M. Where was the old Cassandra who got to work by 8 o'clock? She flipped the eggs over and turned off the stove. As she ate, she continued to look at the book sitting on the counter. The feeling of inadequacy rose over her like a tidal wave breaking onto her apartment building, blocking out the sun, shattering the window, killing everyone in sight. She thought about her bank account–though she had more money at the moment then the average Mexican could hope for–slowly diminishing everyday she that wasn't writing, every day that she was lost in the awe of other books that were more profitable. Who was she kidding? She was almost 50 and still living like a 20-year-old. She had gotten fat. She had sold out and sold herself short when she left the newspaper. She could have gone to prison and become a martyr for Latin American free speech. Now she was writing ghost books, sleazy, uninteresting ghost books, ghost books that people were less and less fond of; the literary equivalent of bottom-shelf tequila. She didn't want to write another one in Baja California del Sur. She didn't know what she wanted to do. Morning-time anxiety overwhelmed her. A voice within her said she shouldn't feel like this. Why was she worrying about something as petty as money and popularity? Why wasn't she re-inventing herself?

She finished her eggs and walked to the living room where she pulled a copy of an older *Encrucijada* book off the small wooden shelf. It was one of the few books she hadn't had to travel for. It was a thicker volume than the others. It was also more horrifying and only a few of the stories in it were paranormal, everything was real.

Chapter 4: Nazi's in Chile: Villa Baviera.

The moon over Northern Chile shined bright enough to il-luminate the fine details of a hand-written map, a pair of untied shoelaces, or a small child running across the distant chaparral. Pale light spread from the borders of Colonia Dignidad, past the crushing river, and onward through the landscape rigged with spiked pits and bear traps. With odds so obviously against any single human being, there were no watchmen to guard the outskirts of the religious compound. Couples, banned from sex-ual intercourse, escaped only within the confines of a splintered casket. They were buried away from the church without markers.

Klaus, a boy of thirteen years but with the features of an eight-year-old due to the compulsory injections of hormone-stunt-ing medication, jumped from his window twenty minutes after lights out. He ran toward a sea of the extraterrestrial crater for-mations and sharp, brittle thickets. His skin was already throb-bing from the fresh rope burns around his wrists, back, stomach, and thighs. He was finally leaving Villa Baviera: the colony of dignity, a small settlement of German expatriates in rural South America. The full name of the colony was Sociedad Bene-factora y Educacional Dignidad There, they had built a small residential complex, a working hospital free to the public, and a German kitchen for all Chileans to experience Kaiser rolls and marzipan. Many natives traveled for miles to seek hospice for their loved ones, and the Chilean government worked closely with Paul Schäfer: the former National Socialist Party member and leader of the sermons in their church. Schäfer had proposed they emigrate from their brutally impoverished homes to a new land of operation. Men worked day and night to construct the colony. Some gave their lives.

Klaus came to the precipice of the river and looked back only once, thinking of George, the man who, at times, treated him like a son. George helped run the orphanage, often beating misbehaving children and actively separating the whites from the natives. He had seen something worth fostering in Klaus, who accompanied him on his evening walks up the northwestern hills. He would sit on the top and watch the twilight emerge, stroking his beard and speak to Klaus in grandfatherly tones.

"You're a good boy, Klaus. You will remain a boy for some time, but when the time comes for you to be a man, you must never displease God. God doesn't forgive men. We think he does but we hang to closely in the balance to be assured of any lasting grace."

In exchange Klaus told George of Paul's unwanted kiss and the progressing abuses. George replied that neither men nor boys discuss such things.

When the screams of the tortured opponents of the Pinochet regime echoed through the basement of the orphanage, Klaus had hatched his plan to leave.

An older girl from the bakery had given him a map she had drawn on a scrap of butcher's paper. She had once, and only once, driven out of the colony in Schäfer's truck to purchase baking supplies from the nearest town. She crumbled the map in his palm and closed his fingers with both her hands.

"You have leave and tell others what's happening here, Klaus."

A single tear fell down his cheek as he stood at the edge of the river. His dying world behind would remain just as sick as he had left it. He dove into the water, hoping his feet would touch the bottom. Instead, the stream pulled him away from the bank. He couldn't get his footing. His only hope was to swim, but he didn't know how. Klaus stretched his arms out from above the icy liquid. Reaching toward the dark sky, he screamed at the false God he had been taught to believe in and kicked and grabbed at the stream as best he good, hoping he was moving forward until his body slammed against a sharp rock. It felt no worse than Schäfer's broken chair leg and electric cattle prod. It felt no more humiliating than being tied to a bed and fucked until his rectum bled for days. He would trade any tribulation of nature, any turn of bad luck, any sharp rock or animal attack for his life back at the colony. He would gladly walk across the desert forever in aimless wander.

The jagged, slick rock dug into his side. He leaned to the left to get a grip but the rock was too smooth. His hands slipped away at each grasp. The stream eventually pulled him further. He was in free fall, completely adrift. This pain was the price of his new freedom. He was happy to lie in the frigid stream and drown under the unearthly glare of the Chilean moon.

After four minutes his legs lodged under the side of a submerged rock giving his body momentary balance. He took advantage of the opportunity instantly, a skill he had learned while working with the men who built the church. He had learned to pounce on any nourishment possible in their situation. He used to kick the other children, white and brown, away from his biscuits when George or Señora Stickfort where kind enough to salvage scraps from their own meager rations. Klaus dove outward, fighting the stream. He exerted himself to the brink of submerging. When his arms where almost too cold to extend from his torso, he felt the soil of the opposite bank and pulled himself onto shore. He lay in agony and, exhausted, fell asleep.

At dawn, the clothes on his back had nearly dried from the early-morning heat, but his body was still frigid from the night. Shivering, he fought to stand and vomited the river water he had swallowed while crossing. The folded map had fused together in his pocket. He didn't dare risk tearing it open. Instead, he held the withered scrap to the sun and saw the path past the crudely drawn river. He stuffed the lifeline into his pocket and walked across the terrain where bushes rose above his hips. Here, the trees began and he could see the white tips of the mountains in the distance. He knew nothing of the outside world, nor which country he lived in or why German was spoken along with the Spanish. To his left he saw the graves where Luis, a young friend now deceased, had told him that Hugo and George had executed spies for a payment from the government. Worn mounds of dirt marked the graves. He imagined George and Hugo sharing a cigarette before shooting the two men. Luis had said that the gunshots echoed beyond the river.

Now was not the time to think. Klaus trekked through the dense trees and followed a dirt road for two hours. A small voice inside him kept saying further...go further...

Today, *Klaus Peikel lives with his wife in Ayutla, Guerrero where he runs a grocery store. He hasn't returned to Chile since escaping from the compound. In 1983, he became a Mexican citizen.*

"I never really thought about taking on the Mexican identity. It just seemed pragmatic at the time. It wasn't symbolic."

A tall German man, he's easy to notice in a town that's almost completely Mixtec. The locals cheekily refer to him as the ambassador. The name has caught on, so much so that he changed the name of his grocery El Embajada.

Paul Schäfer wasn't tried for his crimes until he was extradited from a safe house in Argentina that the Pinochet regime had sent him too. He was charged and convicted molesting 26 children of the colony. Twenty-two other members of Colonia Dignidad have been found guilty of aiding child molestation. An overwhelming majority of the survivors of Villa Baviera still live in Chile.

Cassandra stood in the living room, early afternoon light heating a third of the cool tile floor creating an almost perfect right triangle of shadow draped over the white couch. The open book in her hand grew heavy. She read the paragraph over again. The rhythm, the words, and the mood seemed alien to her. She was the author of seven books and countless articles. She had written in the morning at her bedside, salvaging lines of hypnagogic transcendence from the annals of her subconscious, on trains in midday where breakthroughs came to her as fast and unrelenting as the desert vistas and European mountains that washed across the gritty window, at her desk in the night as the thunder and rain of summer roared on the outskirts, and in the unexpected evenings out with her friends or sunny days by the poolside on vacation. She had always written. She had always persevered, but now, staring at her own words in the form of a proper book, it was as if she had written nothing. Her many identities, a student, a journalist, a hack travelogue writer, a victim, no longer existed—her words were meaningless to her.

The electric buzzer rang through the apartment, jolting her out of her thoughts with a painful immediacy. She ran to the intercom beside the door.

"Yes, I'm here," she said, noticing the stutter in her own voice.

"Is this Jimenez? Cassandra Jimenez?"

She didn't recognize the crackling voice.

"Who is this?"

"Claudio."

It was Omar's latest boyfriend. It was hard to keep up.

"You know, we had dinner last night?"

"Right, okay, let me buzz you in." She pressed the second button down for a few seconds then returned to her room and quickly put on a pair of jeans. She waited by the door, listening to the footfalls coming up the stairs. A strange panic came over her when Claudio stepped inside singing a loud and sorrowful ranchera. It could have been Chavela Vargas, but she wasn't sure. Claudio was dressed in drag so convincingly it took her a moment to recognize him. When he saw her he stopped singing and said, "Why is the world going south, my dear, spinning on its axis crooked like it's going to fall off the table of the galaxy?"

"What are you talking about?"

"I don't know. Maybe I watch the news too much." He paused to look at her. "Omar gave me your address last night after dinner. Don't freak out. I was just wondering if you wanted to go get a drink."

"You couldn't have just called?"

"Yeah, I could have, but it's better to actually show up. It makes it harder for people to come up with an excuse or, god forbid, they lie to me. People do that to me all the time. Could you imagine that?" He blew a few strands of hair off his face. "And don't even try to tell me you need to start writing Omar a book."

"I don't think I'm going to be doing any writing for a while."

"Perfect, come out with me. You'll get inspired."

"I better," she said.

3.

The rattlesnake was curled at the edge of the dog carrier, tightening itself into a coil, its forked tongue hovering like a sliced red typewriter ribbon. Erik looked at the distinct white markings on each side of its opaque, dark-matter eyes, and the writhing Mexican rug patterns inscribed on its feathery scales; each one transforming as the muscles beneath the skin tensed to mimic the rigid lines of tree branches.

"Mussolini's as dangerous as he is old," Fillmore said as he poked at the dog carrier with a stick to make his point. Mussolini was a five-foot long, adult male Eastern Diamondback rattlesnake. The long rattle at the tip of its tail rose above the coil, shaking with frenetic tension. The guest preacher, Elden Collins, placed his hand on the carrier and closed his eyes. Erik didn't like the new preacher. He was a stout man with black curly hair and spoke with the remnants of an Irish accent. Erik introduced himself as the church van driver and nothing more. The preacher gripped his arm.

"Eric huh? We know you've been working hard for those biceps. I'll tell you, when the old Rev told me he had a South African in his employ, I'as expectin' a real 7-foot bulge-lipped grinner, but you as white as an Aberdeen highlander, ain't cha, Eric?"

Whenever he thought of Erik's name, he spelled it with a hard C in his mind.

The Reverend had brought Elden Collins down from an obscure church just over the border in the coal country of eastern Kentucky. For legal purposes, he needed a separate preacher to preside over the snake handling ceremony. He offered Erik $300 to drive the second church van up and back down the winding roads to the mountain where the sermon was held annually.

"As long as I don't have to take part," Erik had told him.

"You can sit your ass in the van all night and eat a orange for all I care. I'm payin' you for discretion here," the Reverend had said, the odor of whiskey emanating from his lips. Discretion was the highest maxim when it came to snake handling. Only half the congregation took part each year, hiding the details from the police officers and community leaders who attended the church.

"Why even do a thing like this?" Erik had asked a year before.

The Reverend vehemently answered. "It's a part of our heritage that must be hidden. The times have slipped away from true scripture. An ancient practice between God and man, taking up serpents. It's part of our white heritage and we practice it out of reverence to the forefathers. You wouldn't deny an Injun the right to go on a vision quest or a nigger the right to walk across the hot coals would ya?"

Elden Collins was apparently one of the best handlers in the region, having studied with Pastor Fred Ward in La Foilette, Tennessee. The preacher pulled his hand away from the carrier and opened his eyes. "Ya'll ever used this one for a ceremony?"

"Mussolini's a seasoned veteran," Fillmore said.

"Is that right?" Elden turned to Erik. "You ever handle 'em, son?"

"I just drive the van," he said.

Elden smiled. "Well, we'll turn you into a Christian

yet."

Erik didn't respond.

Fillmore set the stick into the corner and draped the canvas tarp over the dog carrier. The three of them stepped out of the church basement.

"Now, I understand that you brought a couple timber rattlers along with you," Fillmore asked the Kentuckian.

"Yes," he said. "What's the problem?"

"If you handle 'em all together, Mussolini's gonna gobble 'em up like worms."

"Not if God's with us tonight."

Fillmore looked at Erik then back at Elden.

"We'll just pray then."

The three men walked outside to the overcast parking area lot separating the graveyard from the main church building and the smaller annexed buildings. The dark half of the sky loomed over the misty silhouette of the mountain, while the church steeple still scraped the light, cloudless half, but the thick, dismal grays and deep unreflective blues were moving quickly overhead, bringing with them a chilling wind and the stench of moist copper.

Elden stared at heaven and spoke to anyone who would listen.

"Some weather. This gonna put a cork in your plans?"

Fillmore set his hands in his pockets and kicked a piece of gravel across the tarmac.

"Might make the driving tougher for us, but the spot's got a sturdy roof."

"Well then, gentlemen, I think we shall reunite for the drive up. I need to catch up on some reading." He patted them each on the shoulder and walked back into the small annex where the church had afforded him a place to sleep.

The Appalachian preachers hewed a monkish existence compared to their uptown, suburban counterparts.

"8 o'clock sharp!" Fillmore called out after him.

Elden gave him a thumbs up and disappeared.

Erik lit a cigarette as soon as he was gone. "I hope this shit is worth $300."

"Who said we were getting paid?" Fillmore scoffed.

"The Reverend."

"Well Hell, Erik. Don't you think that's a little disrespectful?"

"No, I think it's money well spent and well earned, especially with a storm like this one coming in."

"The Reverend ain't payin' me."

Erik shrugged as the smoke from the cigarette, held in the crook of his long, bony fingers wafted between them. The tobacco smolder lingered in the humid air, unable to lift itself upward to the sky.

"I'm gonna get a bite to eat. Do you want anything?"

"No, I'm just going to walk for a little while," Erik said.

"Suit yourself."

Fillmore walked away and jumped into his pickup truck. The diesel engine rattled down the road, shooting and hissing like the cast-iron coal chamber of a grinding locomotive.

Erik sucked on the filter of his Maverick and blew another stagnant waft of white smoke. He looked back at the church then looked at the foliage beyond the two-lane road. The rhododendrons, the poplars, and Empress of China leaves conformed to the wind as the faces of monsters staring him down with expressions both lecherous and foreboding. Erik walked away from the church in the tall sweet grass parallel to the road where the snakes basked in the morning sun and woodchucks grazed like listless cattle after nightfall. In the woods to his right, he could see that a washing machine had been discarded in a red dirt gulch. The ounce eggshell-white metal finish had accrued a fecal-colored layer of rust, but the warning sticker remained. He imagined a possum crawling out the top. The gas-station up the road was now visible even through the kudzu and chain link veil. He put another cigarette between his lips and lit it with a sharp snap of the automatic lighter. A gust of wind blew through, displacing the humidity, sending the smoke to trail behind him. He set his hand on the top of the fence post near the gas-station's parking lot, leaning to one side, smoking quickly as if he needed to. The old station's gas pumps where severely worn and outdated. The rubber was falling off around the edges of the handles and credit card readers had been precariously attached to the tops of the dials where the paint was chipped and resembled flakes of rotten skin peeling off diseased muscles. The weeds were taking back the small patch of earth the asphalt had once suffocated them, rising up as tall flags of victory from the canyons and crevices harboring specks of green and brown beer bottle glass and stomped cigarette filters. A network of brown vines growing on the side of the aging structure worked its way into the cracks and depressions of the enameled brick. He stepped past the ice bin and through the glass door defaced and obscured by cigarette, beer, and energy drink logos. The metal frame of the door hit the bell tied to the ceiling. An older white woman moved behind the counter with a magazine in her hand. Her blonde hair was wrapped in a silk scarf. A stick of incense burned in the ceramic tray beside the onyx Buddha vigilantly guarding the cash register.

"You can't smoke in here," she said.

Erik had forgotten he was even smoking and clumsily walked back outside to stab out the butt in the communal ashtray atop the garbage bin. He went back in and apologized.

"You've got an accent," she said.

"What about it?"

"Are you fooling me?"

"No," he said.

"Are you from South Africa?"

"Yes."

"Afrikaans," she said. "You're an Afrikaner."

"I was," he said.

"You were?"

"I'm an American citizen now."

"Oh, no. You can't be. That's awful."

"A bit over dramatic, but I'll respect it."

"I don't need you're respect," she said.

"I'm just stating a fact." He moved to the opposite side of the gas-station. "Where's your coffeemaker?"

"It's over by the ATM."

He turned around and saw cups stacked next to the bubbling coffeepots. He poured a small cup and added one packet of cream. When he paid, he asked the woman behind the counter what kind of incense she was burning.

"It's called Vanilla Kalachakra," she said.

"That sounds special."

"It's 99 cents a stick over there next to the porn videos."

He turned around and looked at the colorful incense display.

"This place smells like ass if I don't burn it," she said.

"It certainly looks like ass," he said, before walking outside. Specks of rain pelted the dry road. He wandered under the leafy canopy as the rain began to fall. Thunder echoed in the distance. He was still dry enough to light another cigarette. There were seven left in the pack.

"The seven disciples of nicotine," he said to himself absentmindedly. When he made his way back to the church, the washing machine was gone. The gulch of red dirt just a few yards from the road was empty.

The faithful few, privileged to know of the snake handling that was planned for the evening, crowded under the aluminum roof of a small walkway connecting the several buildings of the church. Elden Collins stood in the crowd with his camouflage rain jacket on as if he were just another member of the flock. Erik and Fillmore walked out in the rain to load the snakes into the first church van. Mussolini remained in the dog carrier with the canvas tarp wrapped around it, while the timber rattlers were left to writhe at the bottom of a threadbare pillow case.

"Alright, we're good to go," Fillmore announced to the crowd.

They filed into the two vans, trotting with a sense of urgency as they passed quickly under the rain. Not one of the two dozen parishioners appeared crazed or in any way unusual to Erik. They talked about sports and politics, books they were reading and television shows that they followed. They talked about the lives of their daughters and their sons, their pets, and their mortgage woes. All of them were white. The men were well-dressed in white button-ups and black pants while others wore blue collars with retail or factory emblems stitched to their breasts. The women wore practical clothes and tennis-shoes. Many of the women had their husband's coats around their shoulders like capes. They sat close to one another cozily in the dark inside the van.

"I'll ride shotgun with Eric," Elden said as he raced around the front of the van and jumped in.

Erik did his best to smile.

"All aboard!" the preacher yelled, hoping to create the facade of a good humor.

The vans sat in the church parking lot for a moment. Fillmore, who drove the front van, was stalling for some reason. Erik drummed his finger on the steering wheel.

"What's taking them so long?" he asked the preacher.

"I don't know," Elden said.

"Do you want some music?" Erik gestured toward the radio.

"It's better not to dilute your witness on a journey like this."

"I don't understand."

"You should use the drive up to prepare yourself spiritually. It's best not to get distracted by television or radio or anything like that from the secularist media," Elden said. "Come to think of it, let's take this opportunity to start in prayer."

Everyone in the van joined hands as if on cue. Elden set his hand on Erik's shoulder and commenced the prayer: "Lord we ask you not only to watch over us tonight, but to also move through us if we may be so bold, and to protect us as we exalt you in our own way. Lord we ask you to keep our drive safe to the mount this night and to move through our driver Eric's hands and to be his quick judgment. Lord, we thank you for bringing our boys Eric and Fillmore back from the war and we humbly ask you to help them see your glory tonight. Please help Mabel and Jerry with their strife and struggles by offering them protection and cleanse them in your burning word. In your name we praise, Amen."

An endless stream of Amens followed. Fillmore had already moved out on the road. Erik put the van into drive and stomped on the gas pedal to follow.

"So," Elden said, staring out the windshield. "I can pretty much bet that you're not a believer."

Erik chose not to respond. The preacher remained silent, accepting Erik's choice not to answer. The two vans drove through the rainstorm in a single file like a police convoy. The highway melded into two-lane country roads, which gave way to a dismal back road where the wind-blown tree branches hung overhead, living, breathing, like a shifting membrane of dark green algae floating above the high beams. Erik had the windshield wipers on the highest setting and still he was forced to hunch over the steering wheel squinting his eyes to see through the torrents. As the road dissipated into mud, the wind accelerated, picking up waves of ghostly mist that jetted and broke across the black asphalt canals. Stray twigs and branches fell from the canopy in front of the van, jolting the already strained suspension causing the van to bounce up and down as the tires crushed over them. Erik barely could see his passengers' faces in the rear view mirror. They were neither excited nor terrified. Written on their faces was the violent expression of pure belief, a look he had only seen in his father and, in brief flashes, in the old

Reverend. At any point during the storm the congregation members would be happy to ride the van down the side of the mountain to their deaths. Looking at Elden, Erik saw that he sported a different expression: one of a show-man, an entertainer. It was the expression of a magician, a dictator, a master manipulator. It was the expression of a man who needed the crowd and, above all else, needed the control.

Three mallards scuttled across the road in the glare of the headlights.

"Did you see that?" Elden asked.

"Yes I did," Erik said, maneuvering around a corner.

"How the Hell are their ducks up at the damn—I'm sorry—the dern mountain?"

Erik managed to force a smile. "There's a lagoon not far from here."

"You know these mountains well?" Elden asked.

"I hike here," he said.

"I'm impressed a heavy smoker like you can handle it."

"How did you know I smoke?"

Elden chuckled coyly. "Are you kidding me? I can smell the tobacco on you from the other side of the moun-tain."

A man sitting in the very back of the van raised his head attempting to pry Erik's attention away from Elden Collins. Erik immediately caught the gesture and gave him the floor.

"Yes, sir," Erik asked.

The man spoke. "I quit smoking three years ago."

"Yeah?"

"One of the hardest things I've ever done in my life,"

he said.

"I can imagine."

The first cigarette he had ever tried was a long, thick twist of tobacco lifted from his father's work desk. Erik and two other boys had smoked it under a Wonderboom fig shading a mossy outcrop in the blazing heat. Their faces went pale from nicotine sickness and, after a few minutes of stumbling through the forest, Erik had vomited into a creek. Years later, he smoked with the street children of Sierra Leone, puffing dirty hand-rolled bunches of cheap tobacco stem matter. On rare occasions someone might have had bootlegged Marlboros or, even more seldom, an actual pack of Spanish or French cigarettes. When he first came to Europe, he always carried a pack of Lucky Strikes in his coat, smoking them on the street corners, at cafes, and while loitering near Gothic fountains. Erik had always smoked. At times, it seemed more important than eating, especially in the war when offering someone a cigarette was saying a prayer for them. It was a way of extending their life a few minutes longer, just long enough to burn one down to the filter. He never had to worry about losing lung capacity, or black chunks growing inside him. He didn't even have to worry about his teeth.

The same man raised his voice again. "It was the best thing I could have done for myself even though it was hard. I just wish I hadn't smoked for so long. You really should think about quittin', son." Why was everyone calling him son? The man's wife nodded, closing her eyes to emphasize the hardship. The rest of them nodded silently, just enough to agrée with the sentiment but without a concrete expression of judgment. Erik's passengers began to seem more zombie-like to him. He was learning to anticipate the eerily prescribed nuances of Southern Baptists. He looked at Elden with disgust and thought about the oranges he would eat during the sermon and the cigarettes he would smoke.

A woman spoke up on the issue: "A friend of mine always gets terrible headaches when storms like this come in since her ma smoked when she was pregnant. She's got smaller capillaries in her brain now."

The parishioners nodded again.

Elden looked out the narrow corridor of foliage on either side of the vehicle. Fillmore's van steered into the sea of green ahead of them.

"Alright," Erik said to the group. "It's about to get a little bumpier."

He turned the van to the left and swung it back around into the slight opening of the bramble patch. The tires sunk deep into the mud, rolling atop the imbedded rocks to move forward. Both vans moved from side to side, hauling their immense weight up a shallow, inclined creek. He did his best not to floor the gas pedal while maintaining the necessary momentum to keep them going. Fillmore was lagging. He was paving the way by parting the mud for Erik, but his own vehicle was teetering back and forth unable to move. Time slowed as Fillmore revved the engine to no avail.

"We didn't factor in the bloody water!" Erik said in fear. "We're not gonna make it up the road!"

"Park it on the side!" Elden said.

"Where! In the trees? There's no space. It's either forward or backwards. That's it."

Elden began to pray silently.

"Come on Fillmore," Erik mumbled.

A loud crack sounded through the wood. A deadly omen. Fillmore's van, caked in long streaks of mud like dried wounds, had slid a few feet back before anyone braced themselves. The two vehicles collided and the air-bag burst through the steering wheel, wiping Erik's line of vision clean, shielding his face from the glass. All he could hear was screaming. He pressed his foot on the gas pedal trying to slow their descent, but the engine wasn't strong enough to pull the weight of just one van and their spinning tires launched them down the creek even faster than before.

"It's not doing it," Elden yelled. He kept his left eye closed to prevent anymore glass from getting inside. Black blood poured from a gash in his forehead, down the middle of his face, along his nose, dribbling off his chin.

Erik saw himself in an armored Humvee lumbering down a dry beige rocky mountain range and, in a thought-less moment of pure action, hit the break petal at the moment he cranked back on the emergency break. The van spun to a halt, fell onto its side, skidded down the creek, and slammed into a black oak. Fillmore's vehicle contin-ued down the incline past them before crashing loudly into a rock below. Dazed, Erik discovered that he was still in his seat pinned to the ground. His legs didn't feel broken. He wiggled his toes beneath the airbag and touched his knees. They definitely weren't broken. The trouble with healing too fast was healing badly. If he had broken his leg, he'd have to keep breaking his legs again and again until the bones lined up. He lingered for a moment. Cool droplets of rain pelted his face from the shattered window above him along with hot specks of blood dripping from Elden's dangling body. Elden's seat belt had worked in holding him in place. Erik reached up and nudged Elden's shoulder. His head slumped forwards as if his neck was boneless, and more blood dripped onto Erik's face.

"Nevermind then," he wheezed under his breath, squinting in the falling rain. He looked back to the parishioners. A few were missing having been tossed through the windows and two appeared dead or at least unconscious in their seats. He pulled his legs out from under the wheel and unbuckled the seat belt.

"Don't worry. I'm fine and I'm going to get help. Don't move and don't fall asleep if you can help it," he said out loud.

A few people granted him a nod of approval without saying a word.

He crawled up through the passenger door across Elden's body. The passenger side glass fell inside the vehicle from the destroyed window. He jumped down into the shallow water and navigated his way through the rocks and mud. A few bodies were strewn out along the forest floor and the babbling creek.

A woman lying in the distance raised her hand up. He could barely see her in the twilight. He jumped across the creek, stepping along the slick amber clay filled with exposed roots like exposed arteries. She was lying in a patch of leaves and pine needles.

"Help!"

"I'm right here," he said.

"I can't feel my legs."

He looked down and saw the white shard of bone piercing her jeans. The other appeared crooked, bending sideways at the kneecap.

"Your legs are broken," he said, glancing down into

the darkness to see a glowing mist rising from behind a boulder.

"Just wait here. Lie down. Don't move," he told her.

"Call for help!" she pleaded.

He trekked down the muddy bank and saw Fillmore's van smashed up against a rock the size of a small car and wedged between two mossy tree trunks. The impact had warped the side door like a piece of wrinkled aluminum and split open the base of the trees, exposing the splintered fresh wood inside the blackened outer layer covered in hairy, rotten-looking moss and speckled white lichens. The van's headlights were still on. The mist he had seen was smoke rising from the engine. The windshield was cracked but not completely shattered with glass fragmented in the shape of a mandala, a tiny hole dead center. Erik opened the driver door to find one of the parishioners slumped over the steering wheel. There was a bullet wound in the back of his head. He lifted him upright in his seat. An enormous section of skull was missing from his forehead, suggesting an exit wound. He let the body fall to the ground after ripping off the seat belt and crawled halfway into the van to look inside. Fillmore was crouched behind the driver's seat, letting the blood from his broken nose pour into his cupped hand.

"What the hell, Fillmore? I thought you were driving?"

"No."

"Why the fok not? What's going on?" Erik yelled.

"This whole thing isn't what you think it is."

A tall man in a bloody shirt and beige pants jumped over the seat and grabbed Fillmore from behind. They struggled for less than a second before Fillmore managed to press a Ruger to the man's chest and shot him.

"What the hell did you just do?"

Fillmore winced and raised the pistol. "You should play dead for a while. That'll keep you safe." He shot Erik three times. Once in the chest. Once in the head. Once in the throat. He fell backwards into the creek.

Fillmore stepped out of van behind him locking the remainder of screaming passengers inside. Their hands pounded against the door knobs and the tinted glass. They cracked the windows where they could but weren't able to smash them. The vans were transformed into cages.

Erik lay in the mud sucking air. Fillmore sat down beside him and spoke: "You see the driver usually gets hit first in these pickups and since I'm just a man, unlike you, I couldn't afford to be front and center."

Erik blinked erratically as blood bubbled up from his throat.

"Man did it get messy. We're supposed to be up top over yonder, but shit got all fucked up and I had to shoot that guy anyway. Didn't really do me any good after all. Well, such is life."

He pointed to the dead driver lying next to the muddy tires with his Ruger.

"Look at the inside of his head. It's empty. I didn't see anything like that even when we were deployed. You did though. Oh yeah, you did! You saw it when the fuckin' sarge died. Cause you're the one that'd done it, right? The guy had him in a head lock with a knife to his throat or something?"

Erik's skull and brain matter started to reconnect. The hole in the back of his head was still big enough to accommodate a tennis ball.

"Kukri knife," he managed to say.

"That's right. He got his throat slashed wide open and you shot on through him to blast that towelhead. Now I recall. That was a hell of a decision you had to make then, son. But those are the decisions we have to make, cause sometimes we have to do a shit job. Sometimes you gotta just do a goddamn, motherfuckin' shitty-ass job. You gotta work at Applebee's to keep yourself in good beer and good weed. You gotta go to Afghaniland to kill a bunch of brown people. And sometimes you gotta do shit like this to keep things even. Evil? Sure it's fuckin' evil, but you've had to do crap like this, so you can't lie there and begrudge me any of this."

"What?' Erik croaked.

"My god, look at you. Your neck is healing before my eyes. It's sickening. Not to watch, just the idea." He watched parts of Erik's neck reattach themselves with every heaving breath. "The idea that I can't do that. I can get torn apart by wolves, destroyed by IEDs, stabbed to death in my sleep, and die from the flu if it gets infected. You just walk on through life like nothing matters. That's God's inequity and I can't stand it."

Erik lifted his head slightly, preparing to sit up. Fillmore shot him twice more through the throat and chest.

"Naw, I think you'll stay down for a while longer. I like you better that way, Erik. Now I actually get a chance to talk."

A man pounded his fists from inside the pulverized van. "Let us out! We've been bitten!" A woman's frantic screams echoed through the forest.

Fillmore pressed his index finger to his lips and fired a round through the metal door. "Time to be quiet now."

Erik attempted to speak but only spit blood.

"Uh oh, looks like we got a leak," Fillmore said, wiping even more blood across Erik's face. "They'll be here any minute you realize. Then I've got to put myself on the line and hand over all these nice people. Now that's dirty work. That's a fuckin' shit job. But I do it gladly. I do it gladly or I don't do it at all. We have to give these people over or else they come trolling through the town. So we keep the peace. We make the tough decisions."

He paused.

"But shit man. It's not like I feel any better about it," he said. "You know we got one for ourselves. Found her in the woods one night up in Jackdaw. We're trying to understand' em better. Got her in the basement of the old Llewellyn Ranch. Can you believe that shit? We got us a vampire."

Erik's body twitched.

"Remember that last batch a shine we pulled? Man, that shit had body. You could smell the creek water and the rocks and the pines, and the fresh air. It was like going hiking in a bottle of licker. We were smoking cigs by the cooling tank and the Rev was all 'Get your ass away from there. You gonna blow us to hell.' Shit, that moonshine smelled like it does out here." He inhaled the air loudly. "The cool mountain air, flowing through your lungs. God damn it, it's nice!"

Fillmore watched as Erik eyed the massive pistol in his hand.

"You gonna live through this one buddy. You gonna live through this one."

More screams emanated from the van.

"There's still some alive by you right?" he said as he pointed above the incline were the upturned van still sat.

Erik didn't answer, keeping his eye on the pistol, struggling to pull in a dry breath. His healing lungs ejected the pooling blood out his mouth. To Fillmore, it appeared as if Erik was vomiting pure blood.

"Oh come on now, you've shaken off worse than that and torched up a cigarette after."

He paused.

"Actually, now that I have a chance...Think I might trouble you for a smoke?"

He rifled through Erik's pockets, finding the Maverick pack and pulling one out along with Erik's lighter.

"Wow, they're still dry."

Erik's eye remained on the gun. He watched Fillmore trying to spark up the clear butane lighter with one hand. It wasn't working and for an instant he put the gun on his lap to shield the flame from the wind with his other hand. Erik took his chance and reached out for the pistol, but his hand moved slowly as if he'd had a stroke. His body was going into shock and he could barely control his extremities. Fillmore promptly snatched the gun from his lap. He was right, Erik had endured worse, but the times were changing and he could no longer subject his body to the tortures of war, the tortures of Africa.

"I don't think so," he said as he puffed opalescent smoke from his lips, and shot Erik in the stomach.

The flame from the barrel briefly illuminated the clearing before the darkness returned where all Erik could see was Fillmore's silhouette and the glowing ember hovering a few inches from his face. He took a few more short drags on the cigarette and leaned toward Erik.

"Do you remember that story you told me and Jeremy a...well let's see...hell, that was a long time ago now. You know the one about the African tribe that ate little girls? Remember that one? I remember that one very well. It haunts me, Erik. It haunts me because it's an unnecessary sacrifice. That girl didn't need ta die. But these people. These ones ain't got much kin. These one's lived a good life. I'm willing to accept the wrongs but the world's gonna have to understand the reasons. They got to go. In many ways...I guess in most ways really...I'm no better than that tribe a niggers, but there's one giant, giant difference. If we didn't give these people over to them, they'd stalk through the neighborhoods picking off anyone. Picking off someone's child for God's sake, so we'll do what we can to sequester them to the mountains."

Erik thought could see the little girl standing on the sacrificial mound. Her stomach bulged with a mixture of goat and, unbeknownst to her and perhaps even the village cook who prepared it, human buttock meat. Her whiteness marked her death. She was standing just a few feet from the van, staring at Erik, lust in her expression. Her eyes where white and steady but the rest of her body twitched with the momentum of a crazed person held back by an invisible force. She appeared to be seizing while standing up. Erik attempted to interact with it, shooing it away with trembling hand motions. She had to leave. Couldn't she see this place wasn't safe? The tribe was about to sacrifice her and eat her heart.

"Get out of here," he croaked as loudly as he could.

Fillmore jerked his head to the left and saw a pale, naked girl in the distance. The cigarette dropped from his lips and he stood up quickly, raising his hands, taking the precautions of a man confronted by wild animals. He fired a shot in her direction and she paused, then scurried back into the woods.

"Looks like they're here," he said. "Better getty up."

He rolled up his pant leg and pulled a long baton-like cylinder from his sock and set it in his teeth while he ejected the spent clip from the Ruger. It was hot and sizzled in the mud where it fell. He grabbed a fresh clip from his back pocket and inserted it into the handle then pulled back the slide to chamber a round. The grinding noise of metal, the quick jerk of a handgun or the pump of the shotgun had excited Erik as a younger man. Now, it made him feel sick. It was almost worse than screaming. To hear that noise in the distance or close by meant nothing but suffering was to come of it. Fillmore took the cylinder from his mouth and ripped off the top, which immediately burst into a white, magnesium flame. He waved the Orion emergency flare back and forth, creating more smoke than light.

"I may not be a learned man," he said without looking at Erik. "But I know a symphony when I hear it."

Erik listened to the quiet hissing of the flare, a shuffling noise like the patter of the rain as it dropped through the leafy canopy and again as he fixated on Fillmore's pistol. It shook with a light percussive quality as Fillmore's hand fidgeted on the grip. His finger touched the trigger and curled back to the side, sliding along the fitted grip. These were the noises that lingered when all else washed away. Erik listened to the sounds around him just as attentively as Fillmore had and, for the first time amid the torture and the screaming, understood exactly what his old friend was talking about. The symphony continued as seconds passed by like coal sludge dripping down a tainted river basin. Nearly silent footfalls surrounded them accompanied by the deep splatters of those strong enough to

pull themselves through mud. Agonized screams perme-
ated the darkness. The metal doors of the van screeched
as they were pulled off. The suspension strained as the
vans were invaded. Glass shattered. Another scream
sounded closer to them. It was a woman with broken legs.
Her attacker ended her screams with a muffled crack. Had
it been her neck? Her back? Her skull collapsing between
two inhuman palms?

Erik could feel his wound healing and through the
delirium stood up. Fillmore pressed the barrel of the gun
under his shoulder.

"Don't do anything fancy, and don't make any quick
movements. Just play dead," he said.

A crescendo of violence swept over the forest. The
abrupt and wet sounds of limbs being torn from bodies
floated down the incline. The smell of blood was thick and
putrid. It was a frenzy, an orgy. Not since his days on The
Liberian border had Erik been in the presence of so many
mud bathers, corpse burrowers, shroud eaters, night
breathers, bloodless children with vacant eyes. He turned
to Fillmore and explained that he had to run now. If they
smelled his mixed blood they'd tear him apart. Fillmore
pushed him away with the barrel of the gun.

"Run then, but you can't go back. The Rev wanted you
dead too. You were nothing but a driver now."

Erik wasted no time contemplating and ran into the
woods past the brambles and wild patches of blackberries,
twice falling over decaying stumps.

Fillmore called after him, saying "I grant you exile!
It's my gift, old friend. My debt is paid."

Erik ran into the wooded no man's land until he could
no longer hear the carnage. He found the river by sheer

luck and spent the night healing on a boulder. His dreams were filled only with the chatter of cicadas, rushing water, and the texture of the stone against his face.

4.

Claudio didn't take Cassandra to an upscale restaurant or another open-air cafe, but to a dark smoky bar deep within a completely unremarkable barrio where the streets were dusted in soot and the business signs appeared stark and pragmatic rather than flashy and sleazy or decadent and inspired. The boulevards let out into narrow streets that were uncrowded and almost completely silent were it not for the rumble of the garbage trucks and the occasional hum of buses cruising past the shop windows and apartment buildings like small oil tankers bellowing diesel fumes from their rusted exhaust pipes. For the first time in a few days, the sky was clear and the air was plagued by a northerly dry heat. Claudio walked with a pep in his step, talking very quickly about numerous unrelated topics.

"Your hips are magnificent," he told her. "I'm stuck with this swimmer's body but I can't swim. I've always wanted to have a voluptuous woman's body."

"Does Castro know?"

"Know? About my dress? Omar Castro is the most avid transvestite I've ever met. He even goes to bed in a wig sometimes. He knows just about everything about me. Some mystery is important. Don't you agree? I think it's just easier for him to stick with what he knows and to do business in the gender he went to school as. I mean, it doesn't have to be bad that he doesn't dress like a woman all the time. There's a higher freedom to getting what you want when you want it if you play by the rules."

Cassandra thought of all the transgender people who didn't eat at expensive restaurants and didn't have the luxury to slip in and out of their own lives shamelessly, the ones who were heterosexual, the ones who had abandoned the Self.

The bar was in a basement below a faceless building used either for archiving clinical records or the financial records of Cartel members, something shapeless, abstract, and questionable. Claudio led her down the concrete steps into the dim lights. It took a moment for her eyes to adjust to the near total darkness of the barroom. When she got a good look, she felt nervous for Claudio in what was obviously a working class hangout.

"They have Agavero here. Have you ever had it?" he asked.

She shook her head. "What's that?"

"It's a tequila liqueur. It's full of sugar so it's softer on the pallet than the normal stuff."

"Oh no, tequila fucks me up quick. And I can't have anything with extra sugar, I'll be vomiting all night," she said.

"Ah hah! I didn't figure you for a proper drinker last night, since you had Perrier with dinner, but it sounds like you got the stomach of a whiskey man. Do you?"

"I prefer bourbon," she said.

"Then I'll get me an Agavero and you a half-glass of Jim Beam."

"I think I'll just stick with beer."

"Let me guess, Guinness?"

"How about just a Corona."

"Ah, you're too worried your lips will get loose. Let's settle for a proper beer for you. How about a tall Dos Equis

Dark?"

She smiled coyly and said, "Okay, I'll make that concession."

"Perfect."

He raced up to the bartender to order.

Cassandra looked around at the wood-paneling and the dim, vermillion bulbs hanging from the black power cords. Some were covered in blown glass carafes with bubbles of imperfection, others just dangled naked, haphazardly. A man in a postal uniform sat in the corner, drinking an espresso and smoking a cigarette. The smell made her crave one and she lit her first cigarette of the day. She took her cigarette pack everywhere as if it were permanently affixed to her wallet. When Claudio returned he acted surprised to see her smoking.

"You smoke?"

"Only recently," she said. "You know, since I was 19."

He laughed. "Did your parents smoke?"

"No." She took a sip of beer.

Claudio stretched his arms and bent his neck from side to side before saying, "So what are you worrying about these days?"

"What am I worrying about these days?"

"What insidious thoughts are wriggling their way into that mind of yours?"

"Why do you ask?"

"Because you were in a panic when I dropped in on you."

"Was I?"

"Don't play dumb with me, something is eating at you. I can see it in your demeanor. All your conversations last night were perfunctory and you looked at Omar sometimes like he's done you an unforgivable disservice. And your Bigfoot explanation...hmm...let's face it Honey that was goddamn nihilistic."

"I have writer's block," she said. "I have writer's block and I don't want to go to Baja California del Sur to do another fucking ghost book and I'm tired and I'm afraid to do something else and I'm stressed out about money and I'm too fucking old! I'm going to be 50. I just...I just don't know."

She slumped to the side of the booth and took an immense drag on her cigarette.

Claudio paused for a moment then lifted his chin as he spoke. "You spill the beans pretty quick. I thought you were going to evade me all evening."

"Maybe, I should have," she said.

"No, no. You've done the right thing, and you're talking to the right person. I can convince Omar of a lot of things. If you don't want to go to Baja California, you don't have to."

"No, don't do that. Don't tell him I said that."

"I'm not going to. I can be a lot more strategic about it. You might not know this but Omar is very fond of you, and if I convince him that you're tortured about the new project and too afraid to tell him, he'll be overcome with tremendous guilt and let you off the hook. How does that sound?"

"Can I trust you?" she asked.

He took a sip of his sugary tequila and said, "I'd like you to, but that's your judgment to make."

Cassandra sucked on her cigarette and blew the smoke back out. "God, I'd like that a lot," she said, then quickly scaled back her enthusiasm. "I'd appreciate it if you'd do that for me."

"Think nothing of it. Now that that's taken care of, what else can I do for you?"

She drank more of her beer. "You bought me a drink and put my mind at ease. I don't know if there's much else."

"Isn't that the nicest thing anyone's ever done for you?"

She smiled and said, "No, but just about."

"What was the nicest thing?" Claudio asked.

"A young man from South Africa killed a couple people for me once. It's okay though, they were trying to rape me."

Claudio laughed. "I like your sense of humor. It's intense and personal and filled with non-sequitors, just like life. I think you and I are going to be friends, even after my relationship with Omar is over. But, of course don't tell him that, it'll last long enough for me to get you a different book assignment. No worries there," he assured her.

"You don't think it'll last between you and Castro?"

"Nothing lasts. Everything changes," Claudio said flatly.

"So are you one of those typical gay guys that jump from relationship to relationship?"

"I am what I am, and that's just about all I am," he said.

Cassandra stubbed out the cigarette in the tin-foil ashtray, the brief image of a bird flashed through her mind.

"Have you ever had sex with woman?" Claudio asked.

"I might have," she said without hesitating.

"What the fuck? You might have? Did some chick fingerbang you at college and you're too straight and stuck up to admit that no man could ever satisfy you like that?"

She gave him a sardonic expression.

"I mean, I might have had sex with a woman in college, but I was so focused on forgetting my trauma from the past and studying like a maniac."

She paused.

"Did you ever notice how 'sexually liberated' people who don't really care about sexuality, or maybe I should say, regard sexuality with a kind of agnostic detachment, are completely willing to fuck either genders but usually don't and just stay heterosexual or homosexual, usually monogamous?"

He could have said anything. He could have told her it was a broad statement she was making, and that plenty of liberal-minded college students bumped cunts and sucked dick. Instead, he immediately agreed with her.

"Yes," he said. "I used to live in a rooming house in Durango with a big group of straight boys. All of them had girlfriends and all of them were Catholic. One by one, I fucked them all. None of them knew the others had been doing it too. I became the problem! I was the deviant. I became their great secret. It was fantastic, mesmerizing even."

"Amen," she said and raised her glass to touch Claudio's.

They talked for another hour. Mostly about sex and homosexuality which inevitably lead to the topic of art and culture. Claudio brought up Andy Warhol, and the idea of American disenchantment, linking it vaguely to Mexican communists like Diego Rivera and Pablo O' Higgins. Cassandra found it interesting that Andy Warhol was such an inveterate believer in capitalism and much worse things like materialism and consumerism.

"The man painted Brillo pad logos and soup cans and

traced over pictures of Mao Zedong as if to mock communism, turning it into something copied and shoddy unlike his lustrous and brilliant Coca-cola bottles. The man was capitalism incarnate, nonsensical, and lazy. He was a complete fake. He used to say that he wanted to be an assembly-line. For God's sake, he called his studio The Factory! But that was his career. In his personal life he was such a timid little queer who only wanted his scrap of the pie, and he genuinely cared for people. He loved his boyfriend. He loved his friends. He loved his mother immensely. She was Slovakian. I think there's something to be said about Americans who've been raised by foreigners."

"What would that something be?"

"I can't seem to think of it. What was I talking about?" she asked.

"Andy Warhol. He was a petty capitalist and a good person too, ironically."

"That's about all there is to Warhol. As for Rivera, Rivera was disgusting. He ate whatever he wanted. He fucked whomever he wanted driving his wife to insanity. And he was the one who painted 'the people's walls' and believed in the equality of mankind."

Claudio finished his Agavero and looked at the bar's entrance then back at the postal service worker who had just gotten up leave.

"How is it that you've come to this bar?" Cassandra asked.

"What do you mean?"

"This isn't a transvestite club. It's a bar for factory workers. Aren't you afraid someone's going to attack you in here?"

"No, I live life fearlessly."

Cassandra appeared shocked by what she heard as if she were staring into a floating ball of white light. Claudio put a smooth piece of ice in his mouth and crushed it with his molars. "You look confused," he said.

"Perhaps I'm a bit impressed," she admitted.

Claudio leaned in and spoke softer. "You're a skeptic right?"

"When it comes to certain things."

He stroked his chin, an unusually masculine gesture. "My friends keep telling me about this fortune teller."

"I knew this was going somewhere I didn't want it too," she said.

"No, no...Don't ignore me. Listen, there's this black woman who gives free advice from her apartment. It's free. She doesn't charge money. Almost all of my friends have seen her, and they say it's pretty uncanny and sometimes scary what she has to say."

"Is she Mexican?"

"No, she's from...uh...Africa...South Africa! That's it! She's from Port Elizabeth, South Africa. Speaks beautiful Spanish though."

"Yeah?"

"Look," Claudio said. "I liked what you said last night. You don't let your will to believe get in the way. You are the perfect skeptic. Plus you've seen hundreds of reported paranormal incidents. What's one more? I just need another someone to talk to her. Someone not so easily tricked like me and my friends."

Cassandra drank the last dregs of her beer. "When do you think we would go?"

He smiled at her, walking his fingers up and down the table in nervous anticipation.

"We could go now," he said.

"Now?"

He nodded.

"She lives across the street."

Cassandra lowered her hand and pulled out her cigarettes before sighing. She knew everything now.

"You son of a bitch. You set me up bringing me here."

"Only with good intentions," he said.

"So that's why you picked this bar. I thought you lived life fearlessly."

"I don't want you to come with me because I'm afraid of her; I need you for your scientific detachment. You might see something I miss."

"Okay, I'll go. But I'm not getting my fortune read," she said, placing a cigarette between her lips, lighting it with one hand.

"Oh come on, that defeats the purpose. She's already read mine. I just need to know if it's true of if it's a trick."

"Alright, fine." She blew smoke from the side of her mouth. "So the whole thing about talking to Castro was bullshit, right?"

"No, I'm actually going to get you out of that assignment. You'll see."

She believed him, knowing for sure that he was a skilled manipulator.

"And you're sure she's South African."

"Yes, I'm almost positive."

"Interesting."

5.

Cassandra watched Claudio cross the street in the path of an on-coming bus as it kicked up the beige dust of the street: Mexico's equivalent to London fog. Waiting for the bus to pass, looking both ways first, she followed him across the street and stared up at the building opposite the bar. It was covered in the same blackened grit that grew like mold on all the old buildings in the federal district. Claudio motioned for her to move faster but she tuned out his unnecessary frantic gestures and moved at her own pace. Finally, after Claudio had already gone inside the green door, she scaled the stoop and pushed open. Cool air caressed the sweat on her brow. She could smell vegetables stewing. The white hallway was also covered in black soot and grit like the faded crosshatching on a vellum sketch. Claudio was standing by the wrought-iron mechanical elevator.

"Do you think we should take the stairs instead?" he asked.

The beer had slowed her senses. She could barely think, processing everything she saw languidly with a sense of unhappiness shaping the experience.

"No, let's not take the stairs," she said. "Let's take our chances with this cage of death."

He pulled back the retractable guard and stepped into the elevator. Cassandra followed, trying to look complacent and unamused.

As the elevator lifted, the scent of chicken broth and vegetables was replaced by the stench of ammonia. The metal gears ground against each other. The car jolted to a stop as they reached the third floor. Cassandra grabbed Claudio's shoulder and didn't let go until they had both walked out. The hallway had been defaced with thousands of swastikas carved into the plaster.

"Nazis," Claudio said.

"Or Hindus." Cassandra then saw the hermetic German graffiti on the walls just above the empty fire extinguisher case. "Okay, Nazis."

Claudio led her to room 303.

"This is the one," he said.

The door had six locks. It was also the only door void of swastikas. As the boards creaked underfoot, the beam of light behind the keyhole disappeared. Someone was looking at them.

"Oh, shit," Claudio whispered.

Unfazed, Cassandra knocked on the door. The voice from the other side said, in Spanish, that they would have to wait a moment. Light returned to the opening in the keyhole, followed by the tedious clatter of the locks opening as if a mouse were climbing through the obstacle course of an old-fashioned grandfather clock. The door opened and they were met with a short black woman wearing a man's button-up white shirt and black dress pants. She wasn't as old a woman as Claudio had explained. Cassandra wondered if the woman standing in front of them was even the fortune-teller.

"We're looking for the psychic," she said, unable to shed the abrasive of aura of flippancy from her voice.

Claudio looked at her, widening his eyes as if to tell her not to screw anything up for him. He turned back to their reluctant host and said: "Excuse us. She's just nervous. We're hoping to ask for a basic reading, if it's not too much trouble."

"A reading?" the woman asked. "You want to know?"

"Yes," Claudio responded. "More than anything."

The woman sighed, then moved out of the way, ushering them into the small apartment.

"Please, wait in the kitchen."

"Of, course." Claudio said as he pulled Cassandra down the hall after him. As she was dragged into the kitchen, she caught a glimpse of an adjacent room where the radio was playing on an eerily low volume. She recognized the song. It was Atahualpa Yupanqui's *Tierra querida*. An old man wearing a fez sat in a rocking chair beside the window wrapped in a knitted blanket. He looked directly into Cassandra's eyes and remained still, indifferent to strangers walking through his house. He must have seen hundreds of visitors come and go, searching for the truth and the future.

Together they entered the antiquated blue-tile kitchen and sat down at the table: an ordinary wooden spool for electrical lines that had been upturned and shellacked on the surface by hand. The music from the radio stopped and the ancient crackle of a record player filled void. The old man might have been a haunted manikin moving only in the absence of close observation. More music started to play. The nasal bray of a donkey started off the song followed by the staccato plucking of a semi-tuned guitar. The singer belted out words in a language unfamiliar to Cassandra, not quite German but of the same ilk. Naturally, the singer was singing about a wonderful donkey.

Claudio looked around the room. The cabinets were painted red. The refrigerator was an antique with a loose handle lock. Two coffee mugs lay in the otherwise pristine sink beneath the leaky faucet. Cassandra thought it was strange that the kitchen had no scent. There were two mugs in the sink and a pot on the stove, but where was the lingering musk of the morning's brew?

The black woman entered the kitchen with a dusty,

corked bottle of white rum. The label was fraying at the edges.

"Forgive this," she said. "But it must be done."

Neither of them spoke as she swigged a bulging mouthful of rum and spewed it into the four corners of the room. She re-corked the bottle and set it loudly atop the refrigerator from where she pulled a deck of cards. She sat back own and lay them flat on the glossy surface before them.

"Tarot cards?" Cassandra asked.

"Bicycle," the woman said in English.

Cassandra presumptuously inspected the top card. It was a joker. She thumbed through the rest of the deck. Every card was a joker.

"What is this about?" she asked.

The woman sat down at the table and picked up the cards expertly fanning them out with one hand to reveal each card was now unique, making up a full deck of four suits complete with two jokers and an instructions card. She set the deck back on the table, placed her hand over it and closed her eyes.

"Which of you want a divination," she asked, her eyes still shut.

Claudio pointed to Cassandra as if the women could still see and said: "Give it to her. She wants a reading."

Before Cassandra could react the woman had reached across the table and grabbed her hand and began lightly touching her palm with her thumbs.

"Try to stop thinking," she told her. "Just feel my hands and let all your doubt about this go. Stop thinking about my father in the next room. Stop thinking about the coffee. Stop wondering why I'm dressed like this. Stop thinking about your friend sitting next to you."

Cassandra closed her eyes in a meditative trance.

"No no no, keep them open," she said. "Let me be the one with closed eyes."

"How long have you been in Mexico? You're Spanish is wonderful."

"Do you want a divination or not?"

Cassandra stopped talking.

The woman started again.

"Stop thinking. Just feel my hands and let all your doubt about this go. Stop thinking about the beer you drank. Stop thinking about the cigarettes in your pocket. Stop thinking about vampires. Stop thinking about how I know this or how I might have figured this out. Stop. Stop everything. Take a deep breath."

She took a deep breath as instructed, still wondering why she had to keep her eyes open.

The woman kept massaging her palm. It tickled but it also let Cassandra lower her guard. The kitchen didn't look any different but the colors and the cracks stood out conforming to a single mass as if she had been living in that room alone for years. She was still afraid or, at least, vigilant that something might go wrong. It could have all been a perfect con in which Claudio was the recruiter. She didn't really know that much about him. Omar Castro had only been dating him for a few months. She could see the entire scenario in her mind. As soon as she relaxed, Claudio would sucker punch her, or drug her, or choke her until she passed out. She'd wake up on the outskirts of the city without money, her cell phone, or most of her clothes, having to hitch-hike back to Coyoácan. By the time Omar knew, Claudio, if that was his real name, would have dropped out of his life for good. It could turn out that he was dressed like a woman so no one could recall seeing him lead her into the building. Then again, it all did seem a little strange that he'd go through this much pageantry and deception to do little more than rob an unknown writer, whose tiny sliver of popularity had been waning for some time.

The South African woman turned Cassandra's hand up, facing the ceiling, and took an enormous breath, the kind of inhalation that Cassandra identified with anxiety and extreme boredom. She lay the hand down flat on the table and tapped her middle finger on the deck of cards, then took her left index finger and slowly moved up from Cassandra's palm down her wrist as if she were sliding up a button on a control pad. Immediately, the woman started to convulse and began trembling. She strained her eyelids shut. Heavy beads of sweat ran down her forehead. Her neck strained, making the jugular vein visible. She got halfway up her forearm before Cassandra pulled her hand away and stood up from the table. The cards scattered across the room like magnolia petals. The cards that lay face up had gone completely blank.

Claudio tried to catch his breath. There were tears in his eyes.

The soothsayer pushed her chair back from the table and stared up at Cassandra with an expression of unmistakable indignation.

"You did not need to let me see all that," she said as her lower jaw began to tremble and her eyes welled up with tears.

Cassandra said nothing. Her body was poised as if to leave but she remained still.

"It's disgusting what's happened to you," the woman said. "The baby. The boys you watched die. The man you shot."

Cassandra swallowed loudly and raced to the door.

"You shot a man," she said again.

"He got back up," Cassandra said as she hurried through the hallway, abandoning Claudio who sat in awe of everything he had heard. The old man wearing the fez appeared beside her and grabbed her shoulder tightly, keeping her from leaving. His strength was unprecedented for a man his age. The white of his eyes were all that shown. She tried to fight him off but couldn't. He grabbed her other shoulder and pulled her closer and spoke: "Ek gevind hulle wat jou baba gesteel het. Jy het om hier te kom, maar wees versigtig. Dit is die kerk. Hulle is verbind tot die kerk. My probeer ombring. Ek het ook gevind iemand ons kan help. Jy weet hierdie persoon."

She found the strength to break free and ran out the door as fast as she could, racing down the hallway. She took the winding stairs rather than take the elevator back to the first floor.

For the remainder of the day, she wandered the streets of the barrio, asking strangers for the nearest bus stop. No one cared, pointing vaguely in the distance where she encountered no bus stops. The sidewalk led her to the edge of an industrial park where the whine of trucks and the grinding of machinery drowned out the rumble of the city and, quite possibly, the pleas of kidnapped businessmen. But none of this truly mattered to her. She recognized the language the old man had spoken as Afrikaans not because the words themselves meant anything to her, and not because the sound was easy to recognize, but because the cadence in which he had spoken was not his own. It was Erik who had been talking.

6.

Erik was lying on his side, half-asleep and gulping unconsciously, when the first beam of morning sunlight broke through the canopy to shine on a patch of sumac beside the rushing creek. He opened his eyes and slowly sat up, expecting his back to hurt from lying on the rocks but, miraculously, the boulder he had slept on had been smooth enough to reinforce his spine comfortably through the night. Moving around he noticed that his right leg felt unusual. It felt as if the muscles were tight and strained, keeping his leg stiff. He looked past the mist floating over the creek water and focused his eyes on the deep fuchsia buds of the sumac, a plant he didn't know the name of but always recognized, believing it to grow only near the highway and just outside the fences of goat farms. Yet here it was, blooming in the middle of woods, imitating Prairie-Fire from the West. The creak side was covered with greens, bright grays, and red soil which appeared beige from a distance, but there, in the only beam of light like a religious sign, grew a plant yielding giant cobs of deep purple fiber. In spite of everything, he found the sumac beautiful.

It was still early enough, with the sun cresting over the mountains, to still hear the night noises: cicada chirps syncopating with the whines of crickets and the croaks of all other creatures unseen, the endless babbling of creek water too great to be a trickle and too mild to be a roar, the hushed bellow of the wind pushing the leaves sideways and passing, almost inaudibly, by dull ears.

Erik's first impulse was to stretch his neck from side to side, then to pat down his pockets until he found his cigarettes, which he in fact still had. He smiled to himself. After setting one in his lips, he searched for the lighter. This, he did not have, nor did he have his wallet or his cell phone. He lay back down on the smoothed rock and pretended to smoke the cigarette, then angrily threw all of them in the creek. He sat back up and glanced once more at the sumac. Part of him wanted to pull it off the stalk for closer inspection, but the idea revealed itself to be unnecessary. He moved to the edge of the rock, allowing his legs to dangle freely on the side, and then smiled when he thought about taking off his boots and toeing the water. His were sore. He planned on drying them in the grass. He chuckled to himself once more and began rolling up his tattered pants which were heavy with mud and rain water. He noticed the steel cable protruding from around his boots, just above his sock to disappear up into the canopy on the opposite end of the bank. He dug into the wet fibers of his sock and found a thin rubber-padded shackle device clamped around his ankle. Before he had time to do so much as touch the bizarre attachment, the cable went taut and he was lifted into the air and swung across the creek over clearing. The blood rushed to his head, straining his temples, reddening his ears. He managed to lift his head and see the cable from which he was now hanging wrapped along a thick oak branch. He curled his back and lifted his neck to see beneath him. There were no visible rocks on the forest floor just rhododendrons and, a few feet away from the base of the oak tree, he could see the grill of a muddy jeep with an enormous steel winch controlling the silver coil that had pulled him off the rock.

"Bastards!" he yelled.

A single voice called to him from below.

"Terribly sorry for the shock, old boy, but I thought it better to wait until you were up. Nobody likes to wake in mid-suspension." The accent was unmistakable. A nearly perfect British English with a South African curve around each of the vowels.

"Get me down from here!" Erik bellowed.

"In due time," the male voice said. "First, I must run the faithful test to see if you were bitten. People often lie, you know."

Erik struggled with the shackle as it cut into his ankle.

"I wouldn't do that. It'll just get nastier much like a wolf chewing its paw out of a snare."

"Shut the fok up!"

In the purple darkness of dawn, a violet spotlight, emanating from the top of the jeep, shined on Erik's body. He still couldn't make out the figure from behind the light. The man allowed him to dangle a little while longer before shutting off the ultra-violet lamp.

"Perfect then," the man said. "You're not exhibiting any signs of irritation, of the skin at least, so I'll bring you down."

"Do I have to behave?"

"Do as you please. I am heavily armed."

The winch's motor sounded and Erik was lowered into a patch of rhododendrons besides the clearing. For the first time, he saw who had been speaking. It was a tall Punjabi man with a long graying beard, dark skin, and a green Pagh wrapped tightly around his head, his broad frame filling the khaki shirt with a slight gut hanging over military-issue pants. Erik instantly recognized the rifle in the man's hands as a Bushmaster. A black angular Glock hung from his hip.

"I apologize," he said to Erik. "Come now, give us the leg."

Erik lifted up the foot still connected to the cable.

The man rested the rifle barrel on his forearm, keeping it pointed at Erik, and pulled out a metallic key from his pocket.

"What the hell is that?" Erik asked.

"It's a magnetic key for the leg band."

With one turn of the key, the clamp sprung open. It left a throbbing red mark above his ankle.

"Locks are dangerous. Things tend to bite when you're fiddling with a key."

"Why did you tie me up?"

"Because I plan to hunt you for sport. Off you go then. Two hours head start."

Erik didn't laugh.

"I'm kidding. You know why. Just off the road back there was another church feeding frenzy. People get bit. People change, slowly mind you, those that escape. Shine them with the UV cannon and it's over. It's like being trapped in a microwave. But no worries, you check out."

He rested the Bushmaster on his shoulder and offered Erik a hand. "Can you walk? I hope I didn't dislocate your leg."

He grabbed his hand and pulled himself up muttering, "I think I'm okay."

"Good. If you can imagine what it's like jamming an arm back into the socket, a leg is just needless cruelty. One might as well just saw it off."

"You're a South African," Erik said.

"And you're a Boer," the man said flatly.

Erik had forgotten what it was to be an Afrikaner among Africans, which was nothing like being a foreigner among Americans.

"Yeah, I'm a Boer," he said. "But I'm not like..." He hesitated. "My name's Erik van de Roer." He offered his hand.

"Gurveer Singh," the man said, shaking Erik's hand firmly.

Even though he had never met him before, Erik knew who he was. Adrenaline coursed through his veins like ice water to the heart. He attempted to speak, thinking of the old rhyme.

"My...my name is Gurveer Singh," Erik said.

Gurveer smiled and said, "And I sing all day long."

"I never shear my hair."

"For the lord says it is wrong."

"My homeland is India."

"Where my heart clings so tight."

"And I work for all that is good."

"And I keep up the fight."

"You're supposed to be dead," Erik said.

"Dead?"

"People think that you died out here."

Gurveer frowned and scratched his beard, silent for a moment.

"I joined the military because of you," Erik said.

"The goons in Pretoria?"

"No, the U.S. Marine Corps," he hesitated and then said, "I fought in Afghanistan."

"So that's what you're doing here."

"I am American citizen now," Erik said.

"Ah, well that's different then. Thought you were just another snot-nosed emigrant fleeing BEE."

"No, it's nothing like that. I came here for a different life entirely."

"How's that going?" he said as he pointed to Erik's muddy, ripped clothes with the barrel of the rifle.

"I should ask you the same."

"Fair enough, old boy. Fair enough."

Erik looked up at the sunny canopy. "Do you have anything to eat? I'm starving."

"Come along then. Get in the jeep. I'll drive."

"Really? A drive with Gurveer Singh," Erik said with the enthusiasm of a child.

"We'll have to get you some new clothes. Come on, I won't ask again," Gurveer said.

Like Erik, Gurveer Singh slept on a bed elevated by bricks and sectioned off by brick dust. His makeshift home was the maintenance building for a mining operation now long gone. Before that it had been a checkpoint for the Civilian Conservation Corps. And before that the building was erected as a blind tiger where moonshiners sold their wares. The derelict building had been extended several times through the years, shifting from a wooden homestead built on the mountain to a structure built inside the mountain, faintly resembling a munitions battery. Gurveer lived deep within the bunker, using the outer husk of a building as a decoy.

"If anyone were to shine a light in there," he said pointing toward the forward facing rooms, "all they'd find where two opossum eyes staring back."

He hid his jeep in the mine, driving it deep within the darkness and musty air, parking it at an intersection of down shaft before draping a dark green tarpaulin over everything but the tires. Erik looked up at the wooden pillars supporting the mud roof. Roots were growing down and twisting around them likes veins. He couldn't tell if the pillars where holding up the roots, or if the roots were holding up the pillars.

"How long has this been here?"

Gurveer smiled and said, "Perhaps it's best not to ask about that."

Gurveer could access the maintenance building from within the mine, coming up a small tunnel on a steel ladder through a submarine-like hatch, never having to pass through the decoy shack. The shelter was not comfortable. There were a few pieces of furniture that had been lifted from the roadside; everything else was rough, dumb and solid, or sharp, sleek, and dangerous. Gurveer had a hotplate where he cooked and a miniature refrigerator filled with plastic bags of venison. He had a generator down in the mine for the occasional luxury of electricity when he needed it, but the candles were his primary light-source. Dozens of them were oozing onto the bare concrete, forming a single mass of red wax.

"Do you like it here," Erik asked.

"I've said to myself it's more like a wartime occupation. But it's best to think of it differently. I'm not living here. I'm just camping out."

"How long has it been?"

"Six years."

"A long camping trip."

Erik took in the bizarre interior and saw the bed stilted atop red bricks, encircled in white chalk.

"Do you believe in the Tokoloshe?" Gurveer asked Erik.

"Of course, I do."

"Then you're more African than you are white."

"And you're more African than you are Indian."

"Besides the point that I've been a British subject since I was thirty."

"Do you have anything to eat?" Erik asked, feeling a bout of nausea coming on.

"Pardon me for forgetting." he said as he walked to the refrigerator and pulled out a short length of deer jerky and an apple, tossing them both to Erik.

"Thanks." he said as he started eating and immediately sat down in a folding chair.

Gurveer sat across from him in a shabby yellow armchair with stringy, fraying edges from the cat that had clawed at the family heirloom before it got chucked into a ravine where it was found. They sat in silence as Erik ate the apple in four bites and tore the meat away from his teeth with violent jerks of his wrist. He stared at the candles and realized they did more for the smell of the place than just provide Gurveer with light.

"You wouldn't happen to have a smoke on you?" Erik asked, breaking the silence.

"No, I don't."

Erik nodded and ate another bite.

"Let me ask you what your involvement with the church is, Erik. What were you doing up here last night?"

Erik swallowed and said, "What have you been doing here for the past six years?"

"Answer the question," Gurveer ordered.

Erik remembered that the man across from him still had a gun on his hip and had gone years alone in the mountains. He'd probably kill him for being a dhampir, but now that he was connected with the church, and not dead, it must have looked even worse. The best course of action, he thought, was to tread softly.

"Give me some time to explain myself," he said. "It's a really terrifying coincidence why I ended up here."

"Time? All I have is time," Gurveer said.

Erik explained his nomadic life to Gurveer. He talked about his days in West Africa and later in Holland, about how he moved to Knoxville but ended up homeless for a time before deciding to join the military. He told him about meeting Fillmore in Afghanistan and their common connection to Tennessee. He talked about working as a cook and moon shining with his friend and the church members on the side to supplement his income. He told him everything about the night before in perfect detail.

"So after last night, you're basically in exile now," he said.

"Probably so."

Gurveer leaned back in his chair, stroked his beard, and thought silently.

"This may be an opportunity for the both of us then. Perhaps, as I've always suspected, I can't go it alone."

He paused for a moment then quickly looked back at Erik and said, "I could use you!"

"Use me?"

"You've got knowledge of that church that I couldn't get even if I tried. I've been an outsider looking in. But with you, things are different."

He stood up and began pacing.

"There's an old fire tower not even half a mile up. I've left a cot and some provisions there for safe keeping. You should stay there until we plan a course of action," he concluded.

"Plan? Are we a militia or something now?" Erik asked, confused.

"A militia? Don't be ridiculous. We're both professional soldiers. This is an army. Prove your worth and I'll let you skip rank to lieutenant."

"What are we fighting?"

"A little girl," Gurveer said.

8.

Gurveer sent Erik up the mountain with a full rucksack of food and military clothing. Nothing felt uncomfortable. Even the boots went on easy. They were a snug fit, but they fit nonetheless. He had also given him a loaded Winchester and a black Beretta M9 to keep in a holster at his hip.

The hike was arduous: a long trek straight up through the underbrush, poplar, blackberry thorns, stumps, and fallen oaks with no trail. When the inclines were steep, he used the butt of the rifle to keep his balance. He stopped only twice. Once to look at the wall of stone overlooking a peculiar dip in the valley. There was no waterfall, but moisture trickled down from the white rock and a thin layer of exposed sediment formed where the tree line ended as if the terrain had been sliced in half by an unseen monolith. He walked up the gash in the mountain and placed his hand flat on the granite-like surface. A slight film of water flowed across the creases in his knuckles and matted the hair on his arm. The second time he stopped was to hide from of a black bear. He had seen something in distance and quickly mistook it for a something ancient and malevolent. Slowly he realized that he was spying on a bear instead. The adolescent had been opening a rotten log for the grubs. Erik gripped the stock of the rifle. He'd fire it in air if the animal came to close. The bear meandered around the incline, digging it's dog-like snout through the dead leaves and porous, soft wood with the listlessness of cattle then shuffled on further until all Erik could see was his tiny black rump bobbing up and down in a wild cherry bush. From there, Erik moved up to higher ground, pulling himself up on the thin maple trunks.

The fire lookout had once stood above the tree line but now there were at least six oaks and an ash tree blocking its western view. Their branches curled over the roof already blemished with stray leaf matter and twigs. A red cedar was growing at the foot of the metal stairwell. He climbed up without worrying about the aging stairs. He was more afraid of finding an animal's net, or a vagrant living in the cabin lookout. By the time he had gotten to the fire lookout, the sky began to dim with dusk quickly approaching. Rain clouds came sweeping across the Appalachian mountains from the east. Halfway up the reverberating metal stairs, he set his gun and rucksack down to look out over the mountain vista. There was something distant about the sky in North America. In Europe and southern Africa, the clouds and sunshine appeared low enough on the horizon that a man could reach out and touch them or find the point at the edge of the wheat field where the moon and clouds sank into the earth. But here, one could sit in the valley or stand atop a mountain and, always faithful to its arbitrary nature, the firmament remained unreachable. He looked back to the rusted stairs and continued the monotonous trek to the fire lookout, dragging the rucksack behind, a firm grip his gun.

Crouching down to avoid the nails in the floor boards, he slid beneath the lookout cabin and used the barrel of the rifle to open the trapdoor. The inside was not what he expected. He thought he'd see dead birds and piles of feathers strewn across a splintered rain-damaged floor. Instead, the cabin was well sealed from the outside world with clean windows and a ceiling unsullied by paper wasp combs and spider webs. He jumped up through the trapdoor and pulled up the rucksack. The lookout was filled with boxes in one corner. There was a short green file cabinet next to the boxes. He didn't look inside them. There was a thin cot across from the boxes with an itchy-looking blanket and a lumpy feather pillow. The military lifestyle was unavoidable. His father used to tell him that being a warrior was in the blood then point to Erik's jugular vein as if to say that it was only in his blood, his bastardized, mixed blood. Lying on the cot, covered in the old wool blanket, he thought about his roommates, Andrew and Linda back in town. Then he thought about Fillmore and the Reverend. He was going to kill them.

It was raining when he fell asleep.

9.

In the morning, Erik awoke as the trapdoor violently slammed open. Gurveer popped his turbaned head up, screaming in a convincing Robin Williams' impression, "Good morning, Vietnam!"

"Jesus fokken Christ!"

"Ahhhhhhh!" Gurveer bellowed as his head bobbed from side to side, screaming at the ceiling. With only his head above the threshold, to Erik he looked like a bizarre and intricate puppet.

"What are you doing?" he asked.

"I'm greeting the day with tenacity! Ahhhh! I'm the fearless one! I am one with the sun!"

"Shut the fok up!"

"Don't be afraid of it, Leonard!"

"Leonard?"

"Is that not your name?" Gurveer asked, assuming a normal tone.

"My name's Erik."

"Sorry, good with faces bad with names," he said. "Meet me below Erik I've got some coffee in a thermos and two bowls of oatmeal." He disappeared, leaving the trapdoor open.

Erik took his time putting his pants and shoes on then crawled under the lookout to meet Gurveer on the rusted metal stairs, watching the sunrise over the valley. Gurveer was eating oatmeal from a wooden bowl with a plastic spoon. Bits were getting stuck in his beard. Erik sat beside him and picked up his bowl, sifting the spoon through the oats as if he were searching for a stray thumbtack.

"It's not poisoned, I assure you," Gurveer said.

"Did you add anything to it?"

"What do you mean?"

"I don't know like vanilla or brown sugar."

"Oh, the man wants sugar. This is the military, Erik."

"We had amazing chow in the Marines."

"Well, this is more like a militia."

"I thought you said this was an army yesterday?" Erik gave him a dead stare.

Gurveer leaned his head back in deep thought.

"No," he said. "I think I said this was more like a resistance movement, therefore you and I are a militia." He unscrewed the top of the thermos and poured Erik a shallow cup of coffee.

"Thanks," he said, taking a swift gulp of the weak brew.

"How is it?"

"Palatable."

Gurveer studied Erik as he shook the oatmeal from his beard.

"You're worried that I'm crazy aren't you?"

Erik shrugged.

"Don't avoid your own feelings. Do you think I'm crazy?"

"Yes, I think you're crazy."

"Why? Come now, what else? What makes you think I'm crazy?"

"You're a famous tracker and mercenary. Now, you're here."

"What's wrong with this place?" Gurveer asked.

Erik shoveled two enormous spoonfuls of oatmeal into his mouth.

10.

Three lanky young men pedaled their bicycles, in unison, whizzing past the tall grasses onto the lonesome back road. Ties flapping behind their shoulders, helmet visors bent low casting shadow over their eyes; they rode along the shambled asphalt as rivulets of sweat streamed down their cheeks. Their armpits were soiled as well as the backs of their white dress shirts. Each young man had a small black name tag on his left pocket and carried identical saddle bags on either side of their back tires. They had been sent by God to carry out a mission, a mission of long bicycle rides on unforgiving roads, some too poor to accommodate the suspension of the most trusted Fords and Chevrolets, and a million slammed doors between Knoxville and Nashville.

One of them asked the leading Elder for a water break. They could stop after the next mile marker.

Six months earlier, in Utah, the question of temperature had come up.

"Expect the worst, son," a relative had said. "Expect nothing but the worst!"

It was ninety-seven degrees Fahrenheit outside.

They kept pedaling. An engine sputtered up from behind them. They moved slightly to the right to give way. A dilapidated van covered in mud crawled down the isolated road, covering the cyclists in a fog of carbon monoxide and burned oil. The van sped past them, then pulled onto the grassy shoulder under the shade of an oak and stopped.

"Whatever he wants to throw at us or say, just ignore him. We can pray for him later," the leading Elder said.

The others nodded.

The driver of the van waited until the young men were pedaling on the opposite side of the road to step out. He was tall and dark. His hair was damp with sweat and his clothes were covered in engine grease.

"Y'all need a ride?" he asked.

"No, but thanks anyway." He spoke for the three of them.

"Alright, suit yourselves." He turned back to the door

then promptly swung around on the heal of his boot, finger pointed in the air like a gun, as if to impersonate Elvis. "Well, let me ask you this. Where y'all headed?"

"Bishop's Pasture."

"Oh, no. Not the Pasture! You guys ride that way every day?"

"This is our first time," the cyclist in the back said.

"Y'all ain't gonna make it on them bikes, not in this hundred-degree weather."

The two Elders looked toward their leader who frowned. He might have been wrong about something.

"How far is it from here?" he asked.

"Six miles."

"Oh, man."

"Yeah," the driver said flatly. "It's a ways."

The young men brought their bikes to a stop and stood idly unable to make the next decision.

The driver smiled. "Look here, I know y'all are Mormons. I'm a Baptist myself. But we're children of the same God here. I'm getting my church's van fixed. It wouldn't be a burden if you hitched a ride to town. I'm going there anyway."

The three of them looked at one another.

"Yeah, if you don't mind," the Elder said.

The driver smiled. "It's no trouble at all. Heat stroke is serious business, son."

The Mormon youth crossed the street and shook the driver's hand, one after the other.

"I'm Elder Cochran."

"Elder? You look pretty young to me."

"And I'm Elder Jenkins."

"Jenkins, alright."

"Pratt," the last one said.

"You're not an Elder?"

"No, I am."

"Alright then. Good deal, good deal. Here, come 'round back there's tons of space for your bikes."

They followed him to the double doors in the back of the van.

"What's your name?"

"Oh, sorry. I'm Fillmore."

"Velmer?"

"Nope, Fillmore."

"Fillmore."

"There you go."

He opened the doors and jumped inside to help them hoist up the bicycles. There was enough space to let them stand lengthwise against the back window.

"Sturdy enough you think?" Fillmore wiggled them.

"Yeah, I think it'll hold."

"Perfect."

He slammed the doors shut then took them around to jerk open the horribly dented side door. It roared along the warped track like he was opening the threshold to a train car or a warehouse.

"One of y'all wanna ride shotgun?"

They fell into silence until Jenkins spoke up.

"I'll go."

"No problem," Fillmore said.

They stepped inside the van apprehensively, still wearing their helmets. The seats where all covered in white canvas and, on top of that, plastic sheets. It felt as if they were sitting two feet higher than usual. Jenkins sat in front with grin of satisfaction he simply could not shed.

Fillmore had to rev the engine before he was able to pull the van off the grass and head down the road.

"So what happened to the van," Cochran asked, leaning forward to take a place at the front.

"Well, it basically fell off a mountain."

"Really?"

"Yeah. Now that's what I call tried-and-true, huh?"

He laughed nudged Jenkins in the shoulder.

"Why did it fall off a mountain?"

"That's a long story, son. A long story."

Jenkins turned to face Fillmore, resting his arm on the seat.

"You knew we were Mormon. A lot of folks think we're Jehovah's Witnesses, but we're not. Do you know much about The Church of Latter-Day Saints?"

"Are you all missionaries?"

"We are. We all have to do it for two years as part of our spiritual path."

"It's mandatory service then?"

"Something like that."

"Were any of you in the military?" Fillmore asked.

Dead silence.

"I'll take that as a no."

"Were you?"

"Marines. I served in Afghanistan."

"Wow."

Fillmore scratched his nose. "Yeah, it's rough living back here. But you do what you gotta do."

"What church did you say you were a part of?" Cochran asked, leaning in even closer.

"Bishop's Pasture First Baptist. Yes, sir. But, I'm open to other ideas."

"Have you ever talked to anybody at the center?"

"Center?"

"There's a Mormon center just outside of Knoxville. It's just an hour away?"

"Well I'll be damned. I didn't know that. Mind you, an hour away in Tennessee is an entire universe away to some."

He laughed to himself.

"You're in a whole 'nother world there."

He jerked the steering wheel to the right taking the van off the road and drove down a path along the edge of an old cherry orchard.

"Where are we going?" Cochran asked startled.

Fillmore sighed.

"You're not the dumb one, are you Cogburn?"

Cochran said nothing.

Fillmore noted his silence and said, "That's a good answer, kid."

He sighed.

"Look, I could tell you this is a shortcut or a fast-track, but you'd all know what the fuck was going on here. I'm driving you out into the middle of woods when I said I was taking you along the road to town. Any idiot'd know that ain't right. So let's cut the shit."

Jenkins pulled way, his face turning beet red.

"What do you want?" Pratt asked.

Fillmore stared into his face through the rear view mirror. "What do I want?" He switched his gaze to Jenkins. "I want you to pull me a bottle of water out of that glove box there, Slick."

Jenkins complied and quickly opened the compartment. Something brown immediately struck his hand. He yelped and writhed in his seat, screaming as tears ran down his face. His hand was bleeding profusely. Fillmore chuckled mildly as Mussolini slithered from the glove box to the dashboard.

"What did you just do to him?

"I didn't do shit. He's snake bit. Can't you see that?"

Cochran jumped up from the seat, wrapping his arms around the back of the driver's seat, feebly gripping Fillmore's throat. He was too afraid to put any force or momentum behind it. His adrenaline betrayed him.

Fillmore flipped open the center console reaching for the Ruger and fired a round into the missionary's kneecap. His leg split, exposing the white of his bone as he fell to the floor of the van. Fillmore pointed the gun at Pratt.

"Don't shoot!"

"Just keep your mouth shut."

Jenkins screamed, clutching his knee.

"I can't feel anything!"

"Shut up!"

Fillmore bashed him in the head with the butt of the handgun as his body began to tremor.

Mussolini was coiled the far side of the dashboard, his rattle rising up from his body like a smokestack.

"Why are you doing this?"

"Joseph Fuckin' Smith, you can't shut up!"

He looked at the radio.

"There's what we need. Tunes."

He turned on the radio and cranked the dial past the organs and sermons before turning the volume all the way up when he found a Tom Petty song. He glanced at Cochran bleeding on the floor.

"You gotta love Petty!" he yelled over the music.

"Oh my my! Oh hell yes! Honey put on that party dress."

The van puttered along the dirt path, straining the suspension, leaving a trail of smoke. Fillmore floored the gas pedal and made a sharp turn across a vacant field toward a distant cluster of trees, then over a creek on a gravel embankment. Finally, he parked under a willow on the edge of an abandoned ranch.

"Where are we?"

"Disneyland, ever been?" he said, before getting out and slamming the door shut.

Pratt looked at Cochran rolled into a ball on the floor.

"We're gonna get out of here, okay?"

He tried to open the sliding door behind him.

"Come on, really jam on it," Cochran managed to say.

"I'm trying."

The door wouldn't budge. Pratt sat down to cry into his open hands.

"Stop it! Stop it you imbecile. You can't give up. You have to keep going!"

The door roared open. Fillmore and another man with a gray beard grabbed Cochran by his mangled leg and pulled him from the truck. His screams were alien to his fellow missionary. It was so desperate and so agonizing it didn't even sound like his voice. He stared back at Pratt in the van as he lay in the dust.

Fillmore stepped over him and pointed the gun Pratt, motioning for him to get out of the van. He stepped out with his hands raised, snot bubbling out of his nostrils as he wept.

"Come on, Tiger. Pick up your friend," Fillmore said.

"Please, sir. Don't do this. Please, don't hurt us. We'll

do anything. My parents are loaded. They'll pay anything. I'll suck your dick. I'll let you fuck me. Just don't kill me..." he said as his face disintegrated into blubbering snot.

"Ain't nothing you can do and ain't nothing you can say to stop this. Now pick up your friend!" Fillmore lowered the gun and shot Cochran's healthy knee.

Cochran whimpered like a dog and passed out from the pain.

"Now pick'im up!"

Pratt struggled to lift his friend off the ground. After dropping him several times, he was managed to lift him across his back.

"There you go. Now, he's your cross to bear." Fillmore turned to the bearded man. "Come on the last one of'em is snake bit in the car."

They made Pratt lead them to the steps of the old Llewellyn estate while they carried Jenkins catatonic body like a rug.

"Get your ass in there, boy," the bearded man yelled.

"Don't crack an ankle on the fuckin' steps," Fillmore addcd.

Pratt mustered all his strength to lift his friend up the creaking steps and into the darkness of the dilapidated mansion. Fillmore and his cohort were right behind him. He stopped to let his eyes adjust.

"Nobody told you to stop. Keep going straight!"

They passed through a musty hallway into a kitchen where an old man sat at a wooden table pouring George Dickel into an iron cup. Thin bands of light shined through the gaps in the boarded window over the sink. The old man slammed the bottle down and slurped from the cup.

"One of'em is snake bit, Rev," Fillmore said.

The old man stared at Pratt with jaundiced eyes then slowly turned to Fillmore.

"You makin' this kid carry his dead friend?"

"He's not dead. Just in shock. I shot out both his knee-caps."

"What the Hell for?"

"He was gonna get away."

The old man averted his eyes the missionary's pleading gaze and told Fillmore to get on with it.

Fillmore pushed Pratt onward. They moved passed the kitchen down another dark hallway that ended in a lone door reinforced with what appeared to be medieval technology. He didn't tell him to open it. Pratt knew that already. There was a single candle burning at the bottom of the steps in an empty cellar. Just as Pratt put his foot on the first step down, Jenkins body collided into his back and the three of them fell to cool ground. The door slammed shut and locked behind them. Everything appeared orange in the candle light. Pratt pulled himself up and felt the gash in his forehead. He had bitten the tip of his tongue off in the fall and spit a mouthful of blood. Cochran's legs looked barely attached to his body. Jenkins was drenched in sweat and his trembling hand was turning blue. Either blue or purple, he couldn't really tell in the orange light. The skin was peeling back around his fingers and black welts were forming around his arm.

His world was overcome by silence.

While on mission, Elders and Sisters were given just two days a year to call their family and friends: Christmas and Mother's Day. But the center would know when something was wrong, Pratt thought. Someone would surely know that he was missing by this evening. All he had to do was survive. This was a test. The greatest test of all. He crawled to a corner of the cellar. Something moved past the corner of his eye. He winced. His eyes adjusted but he still could barely a make out the silhouette before him. It was a girl, a naked teenage girl.

"Hey," he whispered. "Did they get you too?"

She hobbled closer to him like a primate, her head hung low.

"Is there any way out of here?" His voice was slurred from the bite in his tongue.

She didn't respond.

"How long have you been here?"

She came closer.

"Can you not talk?"

He wondered if they had cut out her tongue.

She said nothing and smelled him like a dog.

"What are you doing?" he whispered.

She stuck out her tongue and licked the streak of blood running down his face from the gash in his forehead.

11.

Erik had placed seven tin cans filled to the brim with water on a stone embankment fifty yards downstream from where he lay with Gurveer. The barrels of their guns rested in the notches of the fallen poplar trunk. Water damaged logs lined the edges of the river. Twigs and stray branches floated in the deadened current and were swept up onto the sandbars as shelter for moccasins and copperheads. The sky was overcast again in spite of the bright morning, and the temperature had dropped so much that the mist rising off the river looked like smoke.

"Do you consider yourself a marksman?" Gurveer

asked.

"Depends on what I'm shooting at."

"Or shooting with. Have you ever fired a Winchester?"

"Nope. Can it hit more than forty yards?"

Gurveer laughed. "I've shot a target at 540 meters. That's about 600 yards."

Erik closed one eye and focused on the target. He pulled the lever in to enable the trigger and, after adjusting his shoulder, he fired a round. The shot sounded through the valley like a blast of dynamite. The can remained.

"Fuck that's loud," he said, pushing the lever forward to eject the brass shell.

"You missed," Gurveer said.

"I haven't shot anything at long range in years."

"This isn't long range. This is …"

Gurveer grabbed Erik's shoulder, staring keenly into the distance.

"What? What do you see?" Erik asked.

"Look above the pines there. Do you see it?"

"No."

"Keeping looking. Up in the trees. One o'clock."

"The crow?"

"Yeah, right there, perched on top. See if you can shoot it down. We'll roast it up tonight."

Erik aimed and slowed his breathing again. The bird was at least 300 yards off. He pressed the leaver to loosen the trigger and squinted to keep the bird in focus.

"I want to see what you can do with the gun, Erik," Gurveer said.

Erik moved his support hand up the barrel.

"It's going to fly away."

"I've got it."

"Well then..."

Erik squeezed the trigger. Another explosion resonated through the valley. The crow flapped its wings and leaped up from the branch unscathed.

"About a foot and a half too low," Gurveer said squinting. "But that was a tough shot and this is your first time with a rifle like that."

"It's not my first time, and how can you tell from that far away?"

"I can't. It doesn't matter how close you came though, you missed it."

"Maybe if you hadn't been breathing down my neck," Erik said, ejecting the shell.

"Or maybe you should try it with the scope." He pulled the scope off his Bushmaster and affixed it to the Winchester. "Now try to shoot that same place where the crow was perched."

Erik aimed again, loosened the trigger, slowed his breathing, and fired. A heavy plume of smoke rose from the barrel this time and the blast sounded like a bolt of lightning cracking just above the waterline.

"I hit it."

"Of course you did," Gurveer said. "Only thing better than a scope is a laser pointer. A perfectly calibrated laser pointer."

Erik started laughing to himself.

"What's so funny?"

"It's nothing," he said.

"Obviously, it isn't. Come on then."

"Were you serious about eating that crow?"

"You've never tasted the meat of a crow? I used to make stew from the white-necked raven when I lived on the Cape. They had a truly brilliant flavor."

Erik flared his nostrils in disgust.

"I haven't had crow, but I've had coot. A bastard from the church made it ounce. Said it was a delicacy. Taste like shit to me. Even the bible advises against eating crow, since they were known to eat the dead on the battle field."

"You have to find a bird with good meat on it, or a marsupial if you're opposed to eating a snake."

"They can't cook down here."

"Yes," Gurveer agreed. "The Southerners are plagued by one of the worst cultural afflictions of all, they *think* they can cook. I suspect they inherited it from the English."

"You'd think they'd know how to barbecue. I thought they'd invented it."

Erik aimed for another tin can, fired, and missed.

"I thought you were military."

"I wasn't concentrating. I was talking," Erik said.

"Then shut up and hit something."

Erik aimed the Winchester again and fired. He hit nothing.

"What the hell?" he yelled. "I don't know what the fuck I'm doing."

Gurveer reached into his pockets and pulled out a .30-30 cartridge.

"Here, try shooting real ammunition instead of those blanks."

12.

The fire crackled, illuminating the base of the fire lookout with flickering orange light. The sides of the logs slowly turned to brittle carbon resembling crocodile skin, red coals, and ash. Gurveer had roasted two water snakes over a blackened spit for dinner.

Erik fidgeted with his hands

"You want something to smoke, don't you?"

Erik nodded.

Gurveer turned around and began to search his rucksack.

"I might have a little something," he said.

Erik smiled imagining himself lighting a cigarette or a cigar, or the possibility cannabis, remembering from some possibly unreliable source that Sikhs, while forbidden to indulge in intoxicants, were afforded conservative use of marijuana.

"What do you got?" Erik asked.

Gurveer pulled out half a bottle of Jamaica rum. The label was simple and peeling off the sides of the dusty bottle. The cork had been bitten several times and now permanently conformed to the contours of what Erik could only assume were Gurveer Singh's teeth.

"Here we go," he said, passing the bottle to Erik. "Have a few swigs. It's got to be fourteen years old by now."

Erik took the bottle and pursed his lips as he drank. He instantly felt the warmth in his stomach.

"I was saving the rest for another time, but perhaps there will be no other time," Gurveer said before taking the bottle back for a swig.

"I thought Sikh's couldn't drink alcohol."

"I didn't think Boers were supposed to mix with anyone else but whites."

"I'm American now," Erik said. "I never was a Boer."

"Yeah, well, I'm still Sikh, but God forgives doesn't he?"

He took another gulp.

Erik stared up the mountain, searching for the silhouette of the lookout cabin, but couldn't see it in the darkness. The forest was made empty by a starless sky. It was just him and Gurveer: two men alone beneath the void of a once attendant moon. He imagined the lightning-struck beech tree crashing into the tower and toppling across the boulders down the mountain. He could see the shrapnel falling from the cliff, or plunged into the river bottom. He snapped out of the fantasy as Gurveer handed him back the bottle. He took a sip rather than a swig this time and noticed the red cedar behind him, rippling in the wind, mimicking the light of the fire as if it were a furry, sentient creature. He passed the bottle to Gurveer who took one last swallow and wedged the cork back with the palm of his hand.

"There's a pack of red wolves here. They've were introduced only a handful of months ago."

"So I've read," Erik said.

Gurveer leaned back and stretched out his arms.

"Alright," Erik said. "How the hell did you end up out here in the middle of nowhere? You're Gurveer Singh, man. You need to be in Canada hunting bears or the Serengeti looking for the Ant-Lion. This place is nothingness. It's plagued by horrid, daily life."

Gurveer chuckled. "You're young. With time, you'll understand that everywhere is plagued by daily life. It's an inescapable plague. You might have seen more that most men your age, but you haven't quite gotten to where you need to be. It'll come to you one day on your own terms. Then you'll know why anyone is anywhere."

Erik scratched his chin through his beard. "People think you're dead out here. There are all kinds of theories.

You're like D.B. Cooper."

Gurveer grabbed the bottle of rum and plucked out the cork with his teeth.

"To the late Akal."

He tipped bottle over the fire. Yellow flames rose up, blocking his features.

"Who's that?" Erik asked.

"My son."

"I'm sorry."

"He's dead. Along with his whole family."

"He had a family too?"

"My grandson Michael and my daughter in law. Her name was Aileen. She met my son at the university in Kent. He followed her back to Knoxville. She wanted to be close to her family and he was willing to leave England. To be with her."

He tipped the bottle twice more into the fire before jamming the cork back inside.

"I followed them out here."

"You came to avenge them."

"I came to find them," he said. "They were young, interesting people. You would have liked them. They enjoyed hiking these mountains very much and had waited years until their son could keep up with them before they decided to take their first great family adventure. Akal wanted to fly to California to hike the Sierra Nevadas, but Aileen, the pragmatist, suggested they hike the Appalachian Trail. It was winter. They thought it safer to hike in the winter when the boar and black bears were hidden away. One could also see further into the distance without the leaves obstructing the view. They both took time off from work. Aileen taught primary school in Turkey Hill and Akal was a...well...he wanted to be a writer. They didn't make much money. I didn't really care. I acted like I did sometimes and…"

He paused and took a long breath.

"I should have been different. I should have been easier to talk to. They went off during the holidays and started on their way to Georgia. They were going to cover an enormous area. They never made it. Akal told me he was going to call me the night that they were going to resupply. I never got the call. I was waiting in my chair by the phone like a fool. The last time we had spoken wasn't good. It wasn't good at all. The next day I called him. He wouldn't pick up. I let it go. I started to panic. Then again, I had to think of the cell phones. Cell phones don't always work in the wilderness. They're not magic, unless I missed something. Still I kept waiting. I waited for three more days. I'll never forget those days. Aileen's parents called me to ask if I had heard anything. That day I flew here as soon as possible. I had three pictures in my pocket and showed them to everyone who might have seen them, people who worked at petrol stations, park rangers, and the police. People recognized me. They knew me from the frontier and hunting magazines. They knew my stories of Vietnam and the Congo. No one recalled seeing my son or his family. No one! Their car was still in the parking lot at the edge of the national park and no one had seen anyone driving it. The one time in the American South when a mixed race couple goes unnoticed, I mean for fuck's sake!

"I tracked them myself. I filed a missing persons report. But I was told that they were still on schedule. That there was nothing to be missing from. I sat down with the rangers–who did nothing by the way–and they showed all of the backpacking checkpoints on the trail. It took a week to find their last campsite. It was untouched. There's nothing more terrifying than a campsite without people. Nothing was out of place. It was worst thing to know they weren't there, that they took nothing with them. When I came upon the campsite, I immediately knew it was theirs. And when I called their names I imagined them running up to me and being surprised that Baba had traveled this far to join them. But there was no one. I kept wondering if they were just a few feet out of sight. Everything was askew. And the silence. That unbreakable silence. When I got to their campsite, there was still food simmering in the pot over the smoldering fire. The sleeping bags were neatly folded inside the tent. Their money was still inside one of their backpacks. I saw Michael's toys in the dirt near the bushes. That's when I could really feel it. My Adam's apple had sunk down my throat. I was choking on it. But I kept looking for clues. I thought they'd been kidnapped. Then I knew for sure. It was something I didn't want to acknowledge for so long, but I had no choice. I kept going for another day. I could see sinister faces in the tree bark as I moved. The ground was pulling at my feet. I was able to track them to a valley where I found their clothes discarded in a bramble patch. I held their torn clothes in my trembling hands for hours. I couldn't move. I couldn't think. They only emotion I had left behind my grief was blind rage. I gathered myself slowly. It felt like there was more adrenaline running through my veins than blood. I was going to kill those hill folk. I was going to carve out their hearts and smash them into the rocks. My grandson, Michael, had been dragged through the mud leaving a trail behind. Tough little guy. He had been fighting the whole way down into the valley. Then I had to think to my-self. What kind of man dragged a little boy? He could have just picked him up off the ground. Whatever had been dragging him left no prints in the ground themselves. It was winter. It was harder to make an impression into the frozen ground. But the boy dug his heels into the top layer of ice. His prints edged a narrow rivulet pouring out of a cavern burrowed into the side of a mountain. His tracks continued inside the darkness and I followed them in. I never hesitated and I never looked back."

"They were in there," Erik said.

"They were in there. Bits and pieces of hair and flesh were strewn out over the rocks. The smell was unbearable. At the bottom of the cave, I found her."

"Your daughter-in-law."

"No, I never saw my family again. But I did see the girl. The pale one. The Bardha."

"A vampire?"

"She's Albanian. I tried to remove her hearts, but she fought me off. I wouldn't allow myself to be bitten, so I retreated. That's why I've been out here for six years. I've been tracking her. But I've lost control now. She's turned countless people. The hills are filled with them, and your church only made it worse."

"It's not my church," Erik said. "And how do you know she's Albanian?"

"How familiar are you with Balkan folklore?"

"Oh, very. I keep it next to my manual on Sikh track-ers."

Gurveer didn't laugh.

"Albanian folklore, though it can be quite ridiculous, is the most accurate when it comes to understanding vampires. Cannibalism is a window into understanding their mutations. The protein synthesis that breaks down in most people doesn't faze them. Vampires are the unique few who can survive on human blood and meat. They live like parasites. There are different stages of course. The scientific allegory is often lost in other folklore. But in Albanian, things are clearer. Things are more cut and dry."

"And what the hell did you mean by 'The Barma?'"

"The Bardha. The pale one. Or, more accurately translated, the white one. She's not the same as other vampires."

"What is she a half-breed?"

"How do you now that?" Gurveer asked.

Erik widened his eyes and swallowed before saying, "Come on, Gurveer. I've been around the world a few times myself. I know the basics."

"Unfortunately, Albanian folklore is not basic. It's digressive and steeped in a mixture of Muslim mythology and conflicting Jewish stories and Pagan ideas. It is said by the Pagan books that The Bardha can move between the three stages at will unlike any other derivative vampire. The ones who are infected by her. Some of the Muslim texts tack on the caveat that such an ability puts them in league with Satan. In reality, the Muslims aren't far off. It would make her one of the first vampires to exist. This girl is the last of a bloodline. She is the descendant of the Kruja."

"Wait. That means..."

"She is thousands of years old," Gurveer said.

Erik stoked the fire with a stick. "I've seen her before."

"Yeah?"

"I was looking for a friend in Jackdaw. She was sitting

in an SUV. A cop was talking to her. I knew something was wrong. I went back out and saw that she ripped off the cops jaw. I came across her again. She was following me on the road, but I lost her. She's really thousands of years old?"

"There have always been rumors. But this is the real thing."

"Why would she be in Tennessee?"

"Who knows. It's easy perhaps. There are many places to hide, infinite directions to run: down to Mexico or up to Canada."

Erik tossed his stick into the fire.

"I know someone else who can help us."

"Can we trust them?"

"Of course."

"No offense, Erik, but you thought you could trust your mates at the church."

"She's different."

"Oh great, she's a girl too. Where is she now?"

"She's in Mexico right now, but she could be helpful."

Gurveer sighed and brushed off his knees before standing up.

"We are inebriated Mr. van de Roer. And I believe we have both said enough. Perhaps such a serious discussion is better left for the morning."

Erik smiled and said, "Can I count on weak coffee and oatmeal?"

"Without a doubt."

"Gurveer."

"Yeah?"

"I'm sorry about your son."

"Some lives take strange shapes," Gurveer said.

"Alright then."

"Adieu, Mr. van de Roer."

Gurveer began the journey down to the bunker.

"You'll make it alright?"

"I've made it alright for six years, but my time is coming. I can feel it."

13.

The trap door swung open and Gurveer rose up from the darkness.

Erik awoke, begrudgingly.

"It's got to be at least four o'clock in the morning," he said.

"Correct. It's exactly o four hundred hours. You have a gift, sir."

"What the fok do you want, man?"

"Take your gun, get your boots on, and meet me at the bottom of the lookout in three minutes," Gurveer said.

Erik stared out the windows of the fire lookout. He couldn't see anything, but he could hear the rain pouring over the black landscape.

"Alright, give me six minutes," he said.

"You'll have it done in three," Gurveer said. His teeth clamped down on a long knife. He mumbled the words, "If you know what's good you" and disappeared through the open trap door.

Erik stumbled across the lookout cabin and slipped into his boots. He grabbed the Winchester from the corner and made sure the cylinder was loaded with actual ammunition.

After getting his things, he walked down the tortured metal stairs in the heavy rain. Once again, he was doing the bidding of others, blindly following orders. His ability to diffuse responsibility to others, to an authority, real or imagined, marred his psyche like a compulsion, or an addiction. In the marines corps, he woke up in the barracks each day knowing what order to follow, knowing what the day had in store, knowing what the next year would hold for him. The only mystery was death, and he was exempt from death. Without structure, he found himself destroying the world around him. He attacked people and embarrassed himself with older women. He drank and smoked to excess. He was lost. He hated the enigma of each day as it unfolded like a soaked envelope, the ink disintegrating from the slack page. There were two sides to Erik: the rebel and the follower. If he had a choice, he would cut the rebellious, directionless part of himself off like damaged appendage, leaving only obedience. This duality was much more than a facet of his personality; it was a manifestation of his genetic makeup; the part of him that was vampire and the part of him that was human. In his darkest moments, in his most solemn reflections, he would choose to preserve the vampire over the man.

Rain pelted the metal stairs. By the time Erik reached the jeep, he was drenched.

"Here, wear this," Gurveer said, tossing him a poncho stitched from an old tarpaulin. Gurveer was already draped in a ghillie suit.

Erik threw on the poncho and sighed.

"You could have given me this before," he said.

"I had to know you were serious."

"Fokken doos," Erik muttered.

Gurveer smiled.

"Ek praat Afrikaans, Erik. Sê nie iets wat jy sal spyt,"

he said.

"I should have known," Erik said, laughing.

"Yes, you should have. Now, get in the jeep."

Erik lifted himself into the passenger's seat of the old military vehicle. The open interior was uncomfortably wet. Water pooled around the edges of the dashboard. Gurveer flipped the hood of the ghillie suit over his wet Pagh, which had shrunk to half its size, fusing to the contours of his hair and scalp. He turned the key in the ignition and switched on the headlights. The branches and twigs caught in the suspension and grille shook off like dead skin as the jeep blazed a rudimentary trail of mashed brambles and muddy imprints of tire tread.

Even with the headlights shining to their full potential, Erik could barely see the terrain before him. It was as if the jeep were scraping the precipice of an unseen cliff.

"Where are we going exactly?" Erik yelled over the engine.

"Some place dangerous."

"Great."

"That's the spirit."

Erik wrinkled his face in permanent wince to protect his eyes from the rain, while Gurveer was immune to the elements, his eyes wide open as he leaned his head above the steering wheel, concentrating on the forest floor and its obstacles. The jeep rolled over an outcrop and crashed into a bowl-shaped gulch of dead kudzu, dislodging the knotted vines from the earth as they sped forward like a rugged beast hurtling through the night; a gasping monster of steam and carbon monoxide with light pouring from its nostrils like a grotesque hybridization of a white-tusked hog and angler fish. A rhododendron branch was caught in the coil of the steel wench mounted to the grille. A fallen sycamore branch pinned itself against the axle and split like bone.

Erik glanced over at the speedometer: sixty miles per hour. To Erik, it felt as if they were going ninety. Each bush evaporated past them. Every tree trunk was sucked into their growing periphery. He kept pulling his hood over his head only for the wind to fill it like a parachute, providing no cover at all until it peeled back around his neck. Gurveer's pagh was steadily unraveling, matching the leafy fibers of the ghillie suit.

"So why are we dressed like this," Erik finally asked. "I think you owe me an explanation."

Gurveer bobbed his head back and forth, moving between the opposing trays of an invisible scale, weighing the pros and cons of his disclosure.

"You ever gone huntin'?" he asked Erik, mimicking a Tennessee accent.

"No, I ain't," Erik said.

"You are now."

Erik said nothing in response.

The jeep dropped down a steep, black gulch. Erik braced for an impact that never came, maintaining the same speed, an accelerated sensation as if the road beneath them had vanished, the jeep's vertical free fall steadily shifted to a horizontal propulsion. Gurveer drove them deeper into a void of total darkness where not even the faint blue of the night differentiated itself from the pitch black earth. Walls of shadow encapsulated the jeep's path from both sides. Erik realized they were driving in the middle of a shallow river. Tall bristles of cudweed and spiny blooms of bull thistle sprouted up around them. The water rose over the tires when Gurveer cut sharply to the right, exhausting the steaming engine into a metallic stutter, pulling them up the mucky bank. He kept driving down a treeless field. The woodland faded behind them, a monolith in the distance. Gurveer slowed the puttering jeep to a crawl and shut off the engine behind two mounds of elephant grass. The suspension fell three inches lower when the lights shut off and the hissed from exhaustion.

"It's on foot from here on out."

"Do you know where we are?" Erik asked.

Gurveer nodded and slung the Bushmaster over his shoulder.

"I've been scouting this place for weeks. It's being stalked."

Erik nodded.

"Do you believe in God, Erik?"

Erik shook his head.

"Do you believe in Satan?"

"That's a moot point if I don't believe is God isn't it?"

"No, not at all."

He patted Erik on the shoulder.

"I want you to believe in Satan for tonight. Tomorrow, if it comes, you can go back to being ignorant," he said.

"I'll do what I can."

"I'm a Sikh, a member of God's army. Tonight you're enlisted in that army as well."

"How about I stay a mercenary in God's army."

"If you're a mercenary, then you still belong to Satan and you are, ultimately, my sworn enemy."

"But not tonight," Erik said.

"Not tonight," Gurveer said as he ripped off his Pagh, letting his jet black hair fall past his shoulders.

They crouched down in the wet grass and made their way through the sloped field, their rifles hanging from their backs. The dark purview was broken in half by the ridge. They crossed it cautiously.

Everything Erik wore was soaked. He quivered in the wind.

"This must be what pneumonia feels like," he said. "If I could get it."

"Why can't you?" Gurveer asked.

Erik winced. It was a slip he regretted.

"Cause it's summer and all," he said.

"I think we'll be alright. You might get a cold if anything," Gurveer said.

A patch of wild bamboo separated the long, man-made swale from a shallow brook. Erik could hear the babbling on the far side of the dark canes. He followed Gurveer along the moss-encrusted bank to a tall quarry where he saw the remnants of a TVA mineral depot and pump shack; a hollow, stone building at the edge of the quarry. The windows were smashed, revealing an assortment of mechanized gears and electrical sockets now rusted over, the color of dried blood. They crawled up the rain-slick rock and passed the stark, white slats of a schoolhouse. The interior was overcome by weeds and knotted wood. A possum hissed at them from the inside of a chicken coop. Thin, octagonal wire had become interwoven with thorn-covered briers. A half-bent sign, caked in flecks of red clay and black soil, read "The Township of McLaughlin."

"What is this place," Erik asked.

"This is the town that Bishop's Pasture evolved from," Gurveer said. "You do believe in evolution don't you?"

"Of course," he said.

"You never know with you Boers and your horren-dous ideas and your Grensoorlags."

"You're the one who believes in God."

Gurveer winked and smiled coyly.

The blooms of a wisteria vine dangled like bunches of grapes over the collapsed front of the ghost town's five-and-dime. Erik reached up and plucked one of the violet petals before Gurveer pulled him beneath the swaying saucer of a mimosa tree and pointed to the hill. Light em-anated from the double-wide trailer which overlooked the dead scenery.

"From this point forward," Gurveer whispered. "The mission has begun."

Erik said nothing and nodded.

Gurveer held up two fingers.

"Two exits. Two entries. You go through the front, I go through the back. No one gets out of that box. We round them up and shoot. When they're down, we take this,"—he took a silver ice pick with a red wooden handle from his belt loop—"and stab them through the heart."

Erik could feel his skin burn as he stared at the glis-tening spike.

"That's silver isn't it?"

"What else would it be? Nickel? Take it."

"I don't have anything to hold it in. It's going to stab me in the side. You've had it all this time without problems. You hold it."

"Fair enough."

Gurveer slipped the ice pick back into his belt.

"You'll hear me kick open the back door first, then you barge in and take them by surprise. Just don't shoot me."

"Who is them?"

"You'll see."

"I don't appreciate the mystery. I want to know what'll be on the other side of that door."

"It's not what's on the opposite side of the door that you should worry about. It's what they have hidden underneath. You'll kick in the door and shoot three men, four if we're unlucky. That's just the start."

"Who are these guys?"

"The fallen," Gurveer said.

Erik rolled his eyes and pulled the Winchester from his back, cranking the lever.

"Are you ready?" Gurveer asked.

"Let's just go," he said.

They moved out from the combed leaves of the tree like a guerrilla unit, splitting halfway up the hill. Erik watched Gurveer disappear through the darkness of the brush and kept running toward the porch light, dropping to his knees in the soupy mud just beneath the blind covered window. He could hear a conversation between two men through the window. He slid along the vinyl siding of the trailer and crept up the waterlogged steps to the front door: a hollow square of perforated wood pulp without an eave like the opening of a tuna can. Erik hesitated outside the door. His thoughts wandered for moment. He set the barrel of the gun at angle against the brass knob and waited.

Three gunshots sounded from inside the trailer.

He pulled the trigger. A third of the door burst open. He crossed the threshold into the cramped the living room immediately overcome by the putrid smell of gasoline mingling with an even thicker chemical stench, a sickening waft of onion grease and sulfur. It hurt to take in a breath.

A man lay on the floor, his stomach burst open. A growing puddle of vicious blackberry-colored blood drenched the carpet. A toothless old man raised a black Colt and shot Erik in the shoulder. Gurveer fired the Bushmaster from the open doorway near the kitchen. Erik watched as the top half of the old man's skull broke off without sound. His ears were still ringing with an ephemeral tinnitus, which he remembered all too well from Afghanistan. He propped himself against the wall and cranked another cartridge into the chamber. A young man to his left rested an eight-gauge shotgun over the green couch. Erik shot him once in the elbow before he could fire the massive weapon. A shattered white bone emerged from his tattooed flesh. He shot him again the side of the cheek, mangling the side of his face. Bits of teeth and jaw bone spilled out from the hole near his neck.

The ringing slowly wore off.

Gurveer marched through a menagerie of two-liter bottles and plastic tubing in the kitchen. Red sludge caked the lining of Pyrex dishes. An assortment of twelve coffee grinders lined the counter beside the refrigerator.

"You're hit!" Gurveer said.

"I'll be fine," Erik said, sticking his finger into his arm.

"Don't do that you'll make it worse."

Erik plucked his red finger from his shoulder and stared at dead men in the trailer.

"These men aren't vampires," he said.

"Some would disagree with you. Have you ever seen what meth does to a man?"

"Nothing cocaine won't do, just faster and with the

worst ingredients," Erik mumbled. "Why the hell would you bring me out here if we're not killing vampires?"

"I clean up these woods. That's my job as a steward of the earth. There are more threats than just vampires."

"Fuck me," Erik said, squeezing the torn flesh of his shoulder. A thin streak of bright red blood streamed down his arm. His shoulder was already starting to heal. He hid the coagulating wound from Gurveer with his palm.

"We need to get that bullet out," Gurveer said.

"Give me your knife."

"No, no," Gurveer said. "It's too big."

Before Erik had time to react, Gurveer had taken hold his arm and plunged the silver spike into the bullet wound, wriggling the tip to pluck out the mashed metal. Erik's skin burned and swelled on contact as if it had been cauterized. He pulled from Gurveer's grasp and tripped over the dead body on the ground, falling into a puddle of blood.

Gurveer stared at him and looked back at the ice pick.

"It's a silver alloy," he said. "Mostly steel. I had it specially made in Macao. Interesting how the UV light doesn't harm you. What exactly does that mean?"

Erik swallowed. His arm sizzled from the silver burn.

"I'm a half-breed."

Gurveer held onto the spike and never broke eye contact with Erik.

Erik stood up slowly and uselessly wiped the other man's blood from his wet clothes.

"Are you going to kill me?"

Gurveer gripped the red handle of the silver spike, lowering his arm into an attack stance.

"That depends, Erik."

"Depends on what?"

Gurveer fell silent, separating his legs across the carpet, bending his knees.

Erik glanced at the Winchester on the floor. He would have to dive three feet to grab the weapon and eject the last cartridge before firing. He looked back at Gurveer.

"What does it matter if I'm a half-breed?"

"Half-breeds don't come from nowhere. What do you know about The Bardha?"

"Nothing."

"You're lying."

"I'm not."

"Then why didn't you tell me what you were before?"

"Because I didn't want you to kill me. I had nowhere else to go."

"I don't think I can trust you, Erik."

"Are you fucking kidding me? I'm the one who let you drag me out here to kill a couple of meth heads for no reason. I've done everything you asked of me."

"You hardly had anything to put on the line."

"My life can still end, Gurveer."

"I'm well aware," he said, clenching the spike.

Erik eyed the Winchester and then shifted his gaze to the eight-gauge shotgun on the couch. The shotgun was closer.

"So this is how it ends," Erik said. "I don't want to do this Gurveer."

"Grab the gun," Gurveer said, modifying his stance.

Erik looked at the eight-gauge. His shoulder stung worse from the silver than the bullet. He took an audible breath.

The young man with half a face emerged from the

narrow hallway. His tongue dangled from the open cavity of his jaw. He held a green soda bottle in his hand. Clear liquid bubbled and frothed beneath the sealed orange cap. The sides of the bottle expanded with pressure. Erik could see the alkaline catalyst strips inside the foaming liquid. The wounded young man exhausted his last bits of strength to hold the bomb. The bottle expanded further in his hand. He collapsed onto the floor, letting it roll to Erik's feet.

Erik dove over the bottle as the flames erupted. His beard and shirt caught fire.

Gurveer grabbed him by his boots and pulled him from the trailer into the rain.

Erik's skin healed quickly. He sat up in the cool downpour letting the blood and singed hair wash away.

"So...where were we?"

Gurveer patted him on the back.

"You saved my life."

"I saved you from third degree burns."

"All the same. I'll give you the pass this time, Erik. But in the future you have a choice to make."

"What kind of choice is that?"

"You'll know."

"Fokken doos."

14.

Erik awoke just before sunrise, the murky blue sky yielding a faint glimmer of morning light as if it were a dome of tarnished limestone and copper. His neck was stiff and his forehead felt strained. As the light began to win back the distant sky from the night, he went outside standing on the rusted steps as he waited for Gurveer to appear from his bunker. The old man was probably tired from their early-morning ride. The forest beneath the tree line was empty. He waited for ten minutes then went back inside the lookout. By then the morning sun was shining on the boxes and the short metal file cabinet in the corner. He shrugged and went over to take a look. The first box was full of maps, maps of Bishops Pasture and other towns. He opened another. Boxes of bullets for various guns. He worried that the next would have sticks of dynamite, which it did. The sticks looked fresh enough. They hadn't been sweating or fusing together. Carefully, he set the lid back over the box and moved to the lone file cabinet. The top cabinet was full of unorganized files. His fingers crawled along the tops of the papers, pulling out random sheets. More maps. Copies of property deeds. Another map. Something caught his attention. It was a police report and it wasn't a copy either. He was holding the original. He read the report. Two women were discovered floating in the Nolichucky River. Their bodies had bled out completely. One was missing a leg; the other had been decapitated and couldn't be identified. He pushed the paper back inside the cabinet and continued searching. There were even more police reports and flimsy, worn newspaper clippings. Everything had to do with the murders. He shut the top cabinet and checked the second. It was empty expect for three pens and a stationary kit. He laughed to himself. It was more than luck. It was fate. He had a letter to write.

15.

Cassandra walked the alleys of a strange community. Red, yellow, and blue tarps draped the nighttime stalls of the tianguis where the only light was the pale, harsh shine of the bare bulbs hanging from wires illuminating the sellers' wares. The customers moved along in anonymity, crowding the narrow street. She turned the corner onto a street that was even more crowded. Shoes dangled from the chicken-wire tops of vendors' stands. Music changed from shop to shop, inch by inch, through the crowded streets as the sound of battered radios seared holes in the night sky. *Corrido, Norteno, Banda* and *Tejano.* Dropped flowers from the Hibiscus Market bouquets, crushed paper cups, cigarette butts, wads of chicle gum, flecks of brown and green glass, used condoms, and burst firework casings scraped underfoot. Cars and pedestrians moved through the congestion at the same pace. A loud vendor with an Ecuadorian accent slapped a head scarf over her and rapidly tied the end around her chin.

"There's a *real* woman! This is Indian cloth. No one else has this in town. And you'll never get a price like this in Mexico!"

He flipped her around by the shoulders to show her off for the small crowd gathering near the stand.

"There you go, ladies and cowboys. Keep your hair safe from the wind. Keep your coiffure intact at night! It's delicate. It's pure. And it needs no maintenance. Impress the Virgin at church, but don't offend the Father!"

Two women approached the stand to touch Cassandra's head.

"Wow, it is soft," an old woman rubbing Cassandra's cheeks said.

"I've never worn Indian fabric!" another said

Delirious, Cassandra walked away from the stand when the vendor continued another rehearsed line. She cut through the market on a stone path between two residential buildings. A little boy with a soccer ball ran past her without making a sound. Overhead, a wrought-iron catwalk connected the orange adobe and framed the window boxes in a grid of chipped green paint. Bicycles were stacked atop one another. A bare clothesline divided the horizon into thirds. She moved past a festering pile of garbage bags and finally caught an unobstructed glimpse of the Mexico City sky. At night, when the smog abated slightly, she could see the moon. Tonight the crescent moon was stark and yellow, hanging over the city like a toenail clipping.

Graffiti on a nearby wall read, "If I see a thief, I'll whistle."

She realized, as she passed a small zapatería, that she was back in Barrio Bravo. Of all the places in the world she could have ended up, she thought. Walking through Tepito after dark was always a gamble, but walking through Barrio Bravo was just blatant stupidity! She checked her purse, moving the empty cigarette packs, receipts, and her keys out of the way to check on her gun, which lay at the very bottom. She stared at the wooden grip and the black steel fading into the gray lining of the purse. She would have to keep it close to her at all times, literally clenching it toward her body. There had always been rumors of expert pickpockets who could replace the contents of purses with blocks of wood and small rocks to keep the weight the same. They switched keys with rings of Coke can tabs and wallets with wads of newspaper. Many of the shopkeepers and stand vendors ran workshops behind their closed doors to teach others the trade of career theft. Being robbed, however, was the least of her worries in

Tepito. An old saying went that in Tepito everything was for sale, except dignity. Killers walked these streets with reputations to uphold. Many Cartel enforcers operated from here. Every drug known to man was bought and sold, even the stuff thought to be legend: crack, meth, powder cocaine, caballo, scopolamine for thieves and rapists, yagé, palooka, salvia for the American tourists, cannabis, choco, pascualito, tik, madrugada, ibogaine, chi-chi, LSD, mescaline, tortuga, florine, terremoto, derrumbe, molly, safron, nickel lead, and indocanto. Kidnapping and the sex trade were flourishing and had only worsened since the arrival of Eastern-European criminal syndicates. She felt the loaded gun through the outside of her purse and stepped into the shadowy alcove of a derelict building. Poster upon poster had been stapled and pasted to the walls across from her. In the heavy rains of the summer, the advertisements had begun to curl and peel off onto the pavement. La Santa Muerte had been carved into the wood in the nook where she stood. She kissed its forehead, crossed herself, and then took a breath.

Cassandra enjoyed her superstitions. It was all she had in place of a true ideology. She flipped pennies over for good luck. She wasn't sure if she believed in God, but she always found herself leaning against the image of The Virgin of Guadalupe when she felt weak. She didn't believe in all of the stories she wrote, but she knew there were malevolent forces beyond anyone's control.

Two men in white Stetsons passed the alcove without looking at her. A red pickup swerved onto the sidewalk violently cutting the corner. It wasn't safe out there, she thought. But she couldn't stay in one place too long. She pulled out her lighter and put a cigarette between her lips, leaning out into the street, looking in both directions as she lit the end. She walked toward the streetlights and heard commotion in the distance. There was light was at the end of tunnel. She just had to make it out of this block where the municipal lights had been neglected and the windows were black and vacant. She crossed a street toward a pair of rock musician. A lone guitarist played before a crowd of ten. He rested his boot on the tiny, red amp. A drummer had erected his drum set against the rough, defaced wall. They had a shoebox full of pesos and a few stray dollar bills. The guitarist's fingers lay flat on the fret board crawling through the chords of some unfamiliar malagueña while the drummer smacked the cymbal and the bottom of the paint bucket, neglecting the single tom and snare. A young boy bobbing his head to the music turned to look at her. He had on a stripped polo shirt with a popped collar. His hair was gelled solid.

"Do I know you?" he asked her.

"I don't think so," she said, tightening her grip on the pistil in her purse.

"You were on *Algo Paranormal*."

"I was on television once," she said carefully.

A TV personality could bring in a substantial ransom.

"I drove you to the station. I'm Juan."

She blew smoke out the side of her mouth and squinted.

"You don't remember me?"

"Yes I do."

She forced a laugh.

"I'm just impressed that you remember me," she said.

"I've got an awesome memory. You said that you'd never come to Tepito."

"I'm actually lost," she said.

"Where are you trying to get to?"

"I just need to get back home."

Juan tensed his lower jaw.

"You might not want to take a bus at this hour," he said.

"The sun just went down," she said.

"Anytime after dark is not a good idea."

She fought off her trepidation as best she could and smiled. "Okay....I'll figure something out."

He hesitated.

"I've got a cousin not too far from here and he's got a car that he lets me borrow from time to time. I can get you back but..."

"But?"

"I was about to get something to eat," he said.

"I'll buy you dinner if you can drive me back."

He smiled.

"That seems fair. I know a great place six blocks from here on the way to my cousins. The best migas in Tepito."

A shrill and familiar voice screamed over the street music. Cassandra and Juan turned to see the Ecuadorian salesmen pointing a stick at them.

"You!" he screamed. "You took my headscarf, you miserable thief. Give it back!"

She cast her cigarette to the ground and tore off the scarf with one hand.

"Come on," she said, grabbing Juan's hand. "Let's go."

The scarf fluttered to the sooty ground. The salesman let the wooden stick fall to the wayside as he dove toward the cloth unable to catch it before it hit the ground.

"No! It's ruined!" he screamed. "You Mexicans are

scum! You're all scum!"

The street guitarist stopped playing for a moment as the crowd stared at the salesman. He turned up the volume and started playing as his listeners encircled the salesman. Cassandra looked back. The Ecuadorian was apologizing showing everyone the dirty cloth as his excuse.

She dipped her spoon into the steaming bowl of migas and scooped up a moist chunk of French bread and grilled pork.

"We could have gone to a taco stand."

Juan shook his head.

"No, tacos are for drunks and gringos and especially drunk gringos. This is what real people eat. Real people waste nothing and weave leftovers into gold."

"You know," she said, after blowing on her spoonful of soup. "I used to work in a restaurant, a Mexican restaurant in the States. The cooks would make us all a free meal every night and they never made anything like this with the leftovers."

"That's because you never had the right ingredients in the first place. Tacos and chalupas aren't Mexican. The tortillas up there are thinner than crepes."

She took her first bite. The flavor caught her by surprise.

"Wow...that's rich."

"That's the epazote and guajillo chilies. Only in Tepito."

She took another bite.

"So, I take it this is your neighborhood."

He nodded.

"This is my neighborhood. What about you?"

"I'm from Monterrey."

"Really?"

"Yeah."

She looked around the open-air restaurant. There was very little light. She could see the old women's' expressions, but the men's' faces were covered by the shadow under the brims of their trucker caps and Stetsons. They drank Tecate and Bohemia without faces. Some wore gold chains on their exposed chests. The women were looking at her as she ate with Juan, wondering whether or not she was his mother. She had paid for the meal, a motherly gesture for sure, but he didn't really look anything like her. What did they know? She could have married a Yucatec or a Nahuatl guy. Of course, Juan wasn't really at the age when he'd be caught dead sharing a late-night meal with his mother. She realized—her time with Erik in mind–that she did prefer younger men, which made her feel worse about the way all the women were staring at her. She just wanted to get away from Tepito as soon as she could. She ate a few more bites. The soup warmed her from the chilling winds twisting through the alleys outside. She could smell the sweat of the restaurant patrons and their beers in the midst of her steaming bowl of migas and behind that something else lingered in the air, something metallic. It was going to rain.

Juan noticed the disapproving stares and whispered to her, "I think they saw you on TV."

"Yes, Juan," she flatly. "I'm sure that's it."

He looked around and smiled.

"So this is what it's like to be famous. Do you ever get tired of it?"

"I never even got used to it."

"I bet it's rough."

"I've only been on TV once, Juan," she said as she tried to eat faster.

"You're a professor or a scientist aren't you?"

"I'm not anything, but a failed journalist."

She wasn't sure why she had told him that.

"Why were you on *Algo Paranormal*?"

"Do you read much, Juan?"

"Yeah."

His dubious expression said otherwise.

"Have you read any of the Auxillo Flores series?"

"Those legend books. Yeah, I've skimmed a few of them. Not as many pictures as you'd expect in a book like that."

"I'm Auxillo Flores," she said.

"But your name's Cassandra."

She winced.

"It's a pseudonym," she said.

"So your full name is Cassandra Auxillo Flores."

"Yes, yes it is."

The overheard discussion of her name didn't make her look very motherly to the other women in the restaurant. Now, she looked like an old woman who had picked up an under-aged kid off the street.

"How old are you, Juan?"

"Eighteen."

"Oh, thank God."

A woman at the adjacent table shook her head and spoke loud enough for Cassandra to hear.

"What is this world coming to?"she said.

Cassandra and Juan ate in silence. She hadn't noticed

until halfway into the bowl that she was in need of a hearty meal. She hadn't eaten all day. Instead she had been drunk, wandering across the uncertain and unseen parts of the city. Now that there was something on her stomach, she had enough energy to move on.

"I can't believe it," Juan said.

"What can't you believe?"

"I can't believe I'm eating dinner with Auxillo Flores."

"Please keep your voice down," she said, hoping no one had heard.

"How come?"

"I don't want to attract any more attention," she said.

"Sorry."

He wiped his chin with the napkin.

"How did you get lost?"

"What do you mean? I just got lost."

"Yeah, and that might be normal for anybody. But you've written about Tepito. There were three or four chapters about Teptio in *Encrucijada mexicana*. There's even a map of the streets."

"Suddenly you're an expert?"

"Well...no...but, I thought you'd know my neighborhood better than me if you wrote a book about it."

She placed the spoon on the rim of the bowl. It slid downward and vanished into the soup.

"I'm going to have a smoke."

She fished through her purse and took out her lighter and her very last cigarette, hesitating before lighting it. She blew the initial puff, then crossed her arms and held the filter with her fingernails. There was a man on her left, near the doorway to the kitchen, drinking alone. He was fiddling with the label on his bottle, tearing it into wiry strips, when he reached up with one hand, took off his Stetson and rested it on the wooden table. His face looked older than his hands and his hair was gray but still full, rippled by wind and sweat, matted on the sides from the white hat. She didn't recognize him.

A gust of cold air took her by surprise, swiping the top layer of ash from her cigarette. Juan was scraping his bowl to finish the final dregs.

"I really appreciate everything, Juan. I really do, but I need that ride home now."

"No problem. Just let take a quick piss and we'll get out of here."

She sighed with relief.

"Thanks so much," she said.

He stood up and adjusted his jeans, then touched his head to make sure it was still spiky and solid with gel. "I'll just be a second," he said.

"I'll be here." She watched him disappear behind the wooden door.

The old man, drinking alone, sipped his beer conservatively as he studied Cassandra. She smoked her cigarette and pretended not to notice him. He was the only man without a gold necklace on his chest or rings stacked up like a totem pole to his knuckles. He looked cleaner. His shirt matched his hat. His pants, though it was difficult to tell from the strange angle of the table, were pressed and free of the remnants of the workday unlike the rest of the men whose pants were tattered and flecked with tar, paint, brick dust, flour, and mud. There was something dignified about him, which made his keen stare even more unsettling. The most dangerous types of guys were the handsome ones, she thought. They had warm eyes and knew exactly what to say next. She let him watch her. She didn't feel vulnerable. In thirty minutes, she'd be back home in her bed. Her ride was in the men's bathroom and in less time than it took her to finish a cigarette, he'd be back outside ready to go. If anything went wrong, she had the pistol.

As she returned to her seat, she wondered what had become of Claudio. He had probably shed the entire incident from his psyche as easily as he washed off his make-up. He'd go back to Omar and forget about everything, especially about getting her out of the crappy book deal. She'd still have to write a book about ghost pirates. She remembered that he had been crying when she scrambled from the nganga's apartment. Perhaps he too was wondering the streets in a dangerous malaise. Some pimp might have found him and blown handful of scopolamine in his face to boost his profit for a night. He could have been forced to work an entire night's worth of tricks and never remember a thing.

She was jolted from her thoughts when the man with the old face sat down across from her in Juan's seat. He lay down his hat beside the plastic ashtray and drummed his fingers on the table.

"Can I help you?" she asked.

"I don't know."

"What do you mean?" She cleared her throat.

He looked from side to side, a single eyebrow raised. "Who was that kid?"

"He's my nephew," she lied.

He nodded. "Your nephew. Okay."

"Is there a problem?"

She scowled at him and sucked on her cigarette.

"You don't have to try so hard picking up kids like him. They're not prepared to satisfy you the way you need. I'm in that kind of business. I've got all the kids you need."

"Excuse me?"

"Hey, let's not get out of hand, baby. You don't need more people looking at you?"

"My nephew is in the bathroom. He'll be here in a minute. You should leave."

The pimp swigged his beer and smirked.

"He's not your nephew."

"So what if he isn't?" she said.

"He's not coming back either."

"What?"

"There's no bathroom back there. It's an exit to the alley. Your date ditched you for the dinner, cheap as the soup may be. Are you willing to listen to me now?"

She dropped her cigarette to the ground and jumped up with her purse, racing through the wooden door which led her to a dark red, adobe hallway that stank of grease and burnt dough leading to a single flimsy door. He was right, there were no bathrooms. There were no toilets. She kicked open the doorway to the labyrinth of the neighborhood. Wind blew her hair back. There was a twelve foot drop off beneath her. Juan had scaled the rusted fire escape to the cobblestone streets below. She could have just clambered down the cold ladder and made her way to the Metro B Cuauhtémoc subway, but she didn't. Instead, she stood in the haphazard door frame unable to move on ward and went back through the red tunnel to the open-air restaurant. The pimp and a few other patrons recognized her look of disappointment.

"Too bad, eh?" he said.

A few old women began to laugh at her. She heard a few chuckles from the faceless men as well.

"Come sit down," the pimp said. "I'll buy you a beer. Let's talk business. I'm sure a lady like you can come to an agreement that works for the both of us."

Cassandra pulled the revolver from her purse and shot him in the chest. He winced as he fell backward in the stool. His body didn't appear to bleed until he'd been lying on the ground for a moment. An old woman crossed herself. Cassandra walked up to his body and set her foot on his chest, aiming the pistol at his face. Fire burst from the barrel. His skull collapsed. Bits of bloody skin and bone peppered Cassandra's shirt. She looked up and noticed one of the cooks struggling with a cell phone. The old men and women ran off down the street. Shudders closed and doors locked across the entire block. She fired into the kitchen above the cook's head to buy time, and then ran out into the narrow street. A lone Peugeot drove down the wrong side of the road. She jumped in front of the car and pressed the gun against the windshield.

"Get out of the car!"

The driver froze in his seat.

"Get out!"

"I don't have any money!" he said.

She tried to open the door. It was locked. She bashed on the window with the gun, screaming at the driver. A red Dino came up behind them, honking. As she looked back towards the noise, the man in the Peugeot sped away and the Dino driver stepped out into the street. His hair was gelled exactly like Juan's and he wore a leather racing jacket. He was holding an automatic revolver at his waist.

"Get the fuck out of the road, crack whore!" he yelled,

raising his gun as he strode toward her.

Cassandra fired three times. He fired his own pistol once in the air before falling on his side. He was still breathing when she took his pistol, setting it in her purse. Her hands trembled as he searched his pockets. There was a wad of American currency held together by a rubber band next to his car keys. There was no one else on the street. There weren't even police sirens in the distance. She took both and jumped inside the sports car and set the key in the ignition. The car rumbled to life and immediately jolted forward. The driver had left the stick shift in first gear. She slammed on the clutch, fighting for control. It had been years since she'd driven a stick. The front wheels raised and the vehicle swayed like a boat as she ran over the driver's body.

She drove the red 1969 Dino with the Ferrari chassis to the top of the gated parking garage across from her apartment. She checked the glove box for the registration and insurance card. The car was stolen. The name of the policy holder was Vicki Uricoechea. She walked around to the front of the car. The headlights were intact and none of the driver's blood had splattered onto the grill. The was no sign that the car had just driven over a man. She popped the trunk and found a brick of heroin, which she dumped in a trashcan beside the elevator as she exited the garage.

She crossed the two-lane road and buzzed herself into the building with her key card. Her shoes clapped against the chipped marble floor of the stairs in the silence of the building as if it had been evacuated. It was a convenient night to be covered in blood. When she got to her apartment, she tossed her keys on the counter and dropped her purse in a nearby chair.

Her landlord had slid a letter beneath the doorway along with some junk mail that had been crowding her mail slot. The magazine subscriptions and the restaurant fliers piled near the hinge side of the door but somehow the cream-colored envelope had sailed all the way to the kitchen. She stripped down in the living room and stuffed her clothes in a garbage bag. She'd burn them first thing. Then she sat on the closed toilet in her bathroom as she began to fill the tub with hot water. As the hot water filled the tub, she slumped back into the kitchen, naked, to retrieve the letter. It was addressed to her. The name of the sender was Erica de la Fusil. It had been sent from the Bishop's Pasture post office. Before opening the letter, she poured herself a tepid glass of scotch, and moved into the bathroom. She took a swig and sank her shivering, aching limbs into the water. It would take a lot of soap to wash Tepito from her body. After a few minutes of staring at the ceiling, she grabbed the expensive stationary with her pruned, moist fingers and tore it open....

16.

A teenager sat in the barbershop stool. He kept the waves in his short hair that had been cut close to the scalp and wore diamond studs in both of his earlobes. A clean, well-starched collar shot up from the salon apron around his thin neck. He pulled his phone from his pocket and began to manipulate the screen with his thumb. The barber, having already done his finest work as he did with every client for the last twenty years, stood in the hallway cradling the receiver of an old rotary telephone.

"Yeah, it ain't no good you asked me....Well he'll just have to grow up then....Shorly, I don't...Yeah, I seen it too. Alright, we'll be up there on the weekend. Okay. Thank you, Boss man...Hah, hah! I know...Bye." He hooked the receiver on the wall mount and stepped back onto the floor. His nephew, still manipulating his ephemeral shard of glass and aluminum technology, glanced at his uncle, the barber.

"Say man, when you gonna make the switch?"

"What? So I can play games with them birds on my phone all day long. Just so that I can be wrapped up in that little screen, day in and day out?"

"I got my music. I got all my family and contacts. I got the time, the weather forecast, my alarm clock, and my whole itinerary on this phone."

One of the regular patrons in the waiting area raised his head up from a magazine. "Whatchu need an itinerary for?"

"All the places I gotta be."

"Like school and the pizzeria. And home?" his uncle said, sweeping the kid's hair into the portable dust bin.

He sighed and slipped the phone back in his pocket. "You gonna see when I'm done. It helps to be organized."

"Paradin' round like you some kinda business man."

"I can't win with you old people."

The nephew paid for the haircut and passed through the glass door knocking the bell affixed to the frame. Seconds later, the bell chimed a second time. A familiar face stepped into the barber shop.

"Erik? Is that you?"

"Yup. That's me."

"You got yourself a mountain-man look these days. What's with the military getup? Don't tell me you joined one of those right-wing militias up in the hills."

Erik stroked his long beard. "You know that's not my style."

"Well, you ain't much for style now are you?"

"No, I suppose not."

The barber finished sweeping and swiveled a cushioned seat around for him. "Same old same old?"

"No, we're going to do it a little different this time."

"How different?"

"Shave it all off. Take off the beard. Take off all the hair."

"I'm a barber, Erik. Not a lawnmower."

"I'm going on a long hunting trip with an old friend. I don't want to deal with my hair. I'd rather just let it grow back evenly."

"Sound logic," he said, preparing the clippers. "What are you huntin'?"

"Albanian white-tusked boar."

"Sounds dangerous."

"Probably is."

The elderly man began shaving off Erik's red hair.

"It's gonna look funny since your face is tanned."

"It'll all be tanned soon enough," Erik said.

"Yeah, that's probably true. Now this old friend, he from the Corps?"

"Nah, South Africa."

"Ah hah. So this is the way, way back."

"Yup."

Half of Erik's hair was on the floor now. His scalp was white with pink splotches. When the beard was gone, he looked like a raccoon with a band of tanned hide across his face.

"I didn't really figure you for a hunter," the barber said.

"I'm more of a hiker, but this old friend, he insisted he needed my help. He wants to see if his African skills can go toe to toe with the American wilds."

"If you think of Tennessee as the wilds. Why not trek it out to Montana or Colorado?"

"The Albanian white-tusked boar is only found here. He wants a trophy over the mantle. What can I say?"

"Crazy white African motherfuckers."

"Yeah," Erik said, shrugging.

"So other than that, how's life treatin' you these days?"

"I can't complain. I'm getting out more. That's for sure."

"Good. I do enjoy..." He paused to shave around Erik's ears. "My morning walks round the park. Keeps the blood flowin', keeps the heart goin'."

"Gotta have blood," Erik said.

When the barber was finished with him, Erik paid and walked out of the shop.

"Odd kid," said the man reading the magazine.

"Erik's a hophead," the barber explained. "He comes in here drunk or high all the time. Makes his visit more interesting, I guess. Lord knows what he's got himself mixed up in now. Hunting trip my ass."

The reader grunted and nodded his head.

The barber swept up the ginger curls from floor. "You gonna sit there an' read my newspapers all day or you wanna cut?"

17.

Bald and beardless, Erik walked down the old Main Street in his new disguise, hoping no one from the church would recognize him. He bought a hard pack of cigarettes, a five-dollar Zippo lighter, and a ninety-nine cent banana with Gurveer's money in a Texaco that smelled of motor oil and boiled peanuts, then made his way to the post office. He might have looked like a Nazi skinhead anywhere else in the country, but in the Southeast, camouflage jackets and boots were common attire.

He had borrowed Gurveer's jeep. Singh had agreed to let him visit town in order to purchase a few provisions. Erik had pulled the jeep out of the mineshaft and followed an undulating path beside the river. He followed the back roads, the wind in his hair, whistling to himself since there was no radio to speak off. He hadn't driven anything since the church van and desperately needed the catharsis of sitting atop the roaring engine. A bluejay chased away a hawk from the forest. Buzzards rode the thermals overhead, swooping down past the tree line looking for something dead. He had looked at himself in the mirror and realized he needed to change his appearance if he was going to walk the streets where his old congregants lived.

After his cut, he headed for the center of town. He knew that the barber wouldn't mention it. They had been friends since the first time he stepped into the shop on his first day in town. A row of defunct gas lights led up to the brick building that had housed the post office since the turn of the century. Postal inspectors had rounded up bandits in the basement before the courthouse cells were erected in 1947. Six generations of county sheriffs posed for newspaper photos with confiscated whiskey stills on its steps, where the police would massacre black university students protesting segregation on the sidewalks. The aged brick had lost its color early on the way a slab of meat in the butcher's case turns brown. Rumor had it that the kids in the 1970s, imitating Paul Newman in *Cool Hand Luke*, cut off the heads of the parking meters so frequently that the town disbanded parking altogether, making the post office the only legal place to park a car for a decade. The old buildings always promoted the illusion that somehow time had less jurisdiction in the area. But Erik had come to find that any town was like a body and it too could become a corpse. Bishop's pasture wasn't there yet, but the post office served as one of several lesions of decaying flesh around town. He sat on the smooth brick steps and took his letter to Cassandra from his pockets, reading it one more time.

Dear Cassandra,

It's me Erik van de Roer from Tennessee. I could have started this letter a bit smoother but I understand that for you I'm probably the kind of guy who should announce myself with a disclaimer. You know, just out of tact in case you've forgotten.

You remember how much I loved to hike, right? Now, I get to do it every day. I've found so much solace in it. The exhaustion of hiking to the summit of the mountain wipes my brain clean of all thoughts. Once I get to the top I'm not even thinking in words or in pictures.

Anyway, I just wanted to offer you the chance to come up and visit me if you wanted a cheap trip. Oth-

erwise, I wish you all the best.

I know how you like languages, so I wrote you something in mine.

I made it clunky and easy for you.

Ek gevind hulle wat jou baba gesteel het. Jy het om hier te kom, maar wees versigtig. Dit is die kerk. Hulle is verbind tot die kerk. My probeer ombring. Ek het ook gevind iemand ons kan help. Jy weet hierdie persoon.

All the best,
Erik.

Something came over him as he was writing the Afrikaans portion. He wanted it to be simple enough for her to easily translate it. He wrote it without thinking, without taking the pen off the page as if he were taking dictation. It made him think of a scene from an old South African film. A platoon of young recruits in the Pretoria military is in training, preparing to ship out to the Bush Wars. The scene starts with their commanding officer giving them a long lecture in Afrikaans. When he's done he goes through each of their names: Van Wyk, Krenwinkel, Jobert. To which each recruit answers, "Ja, Korporal!" until he reads off the name Horne and the short Englishman says, "Yes, corporal!" The commanding officer gives him a long castigating speech until the boy replies in Afrikaans. He then goes through six different names and finally reads off Smith. The second Englishman says in Afrikaans, "Ja, Doos?" The commanding officer stares into his eyes and tells him to speak the language of the military. "Sorry, corporal. My Afrikaans isn't so good, can you repeat the question." The name of the film escaped him.

He folded the linen paper and finally sealed the envelope. The interior of the post office was plagued by the aroma of mothballs and wood rot. There was no line at this time day, and he walked up the Indian woman behind the desk.

"I'd like a ten cent stamp."

"Let me see the letter, sir."

He handed it to her and she stared at the address.

"You'll need more than a ten cent stamp if you're sending it to Mexico City."

"How much?"

She laid the letter flat on the scale.

"Express'll be about ten dollars. Normal should be about a buck seventy-two."

He peeled off two dollar bills from the roll Gurveer had given him. "Alright, there you go."

She took his money without breaking her gaze on his clothes and his freshly shaven head. Her expression lingered in the catatonic haze between amusement and a genuine impulse to call the police. Lost in unreadable thoughts, she set the money in the cash register then gave Erik the necessary stamps. He placed them on the envelope.

"You'll also need to write a return address."

"That's no problem."

"It's the law now, sir."

"Oh, okay. Do you have a pen I can use?"

She gave him a pen tied to the counter.

He started scribbling.

"What's this post office's address?"

"Do you have a P. O. Box?"

"No."

"Then you can't really use the post office as a return address."

"No, problem. I'll just make one up."

She sighed.

"Do you not live here?"

"Not anymore. "

"Then you should write your current address."

"Okay."

He signed the letter Erica de la Fusil, 1234 Looky-Loo Straat, Nowheresville, USA. The Indian woman didn't read it and set his letter in the small, international pile.

As he exited the post office, he sat in one of the many stone pavilions and checked his roll of money and deciding that he had enough for a cup of coffee at The Cricket. Starbucks had not come to Bishop's Pasture. No one to spend their money on it. The lumber-yard journeymen and the coal miners weren't going to understand a franchise like Starbucks, a company that sold an ambiance and an attitude rather than worth-while products. Even the Walmart in town became a store where people worked rather than shopped. It was people from out of town who shopped there, some driving as far as Johnson City and Picketeen. The Supercenter had rejected Erik's application twice in spite of his military service and veteran standing. McDonalds and Burger King had come to Bishop's Pasture years before the Walmart. Two of the Burger Kings had gone out of business faster than the Taco Bell and the owner, who had moved his family from Brevard, North Carolina, put up a last message on the plastic letters beneath the sign of the Main Street location, "Thanks for nothing, hillbillies." Eventually, the local Cineplex owner took down the letters from the marquee and, in the dead of night, wrote, "You're welcome, Blue-stater." The interchangeable plastic letters had been a problem from the beginning when Burger King's first message had been "Enjoy the $2 frappe." A cup of half-caf was about as lofty as it got in Bishop's Pasture. Nobody knew what a frappe was. As time went on, the second "p" fell off the billboard and someone saw their chance to steal the "f." The sign read "Enjoy the $2 rape" for three days until staff changed it to say "Try the BK Rib." McDonalds on the other hand was very popular, turning into an unofficial coffee lounge for elderly men in the mornings and a corral of young men and their jacked-up trucks and hot-rods in the evening. The Applebee's and Crackerbarrel were more or less the Friday-night institutions. Erik had wondered if a Nando would ever survive out here.

He walked across the street to The Cricket and sat in the far corner where he could light a cigarette. It had been days since he had a smoke. The nicotine slammed into his blood stream as if he had taken a deep rip off a glass bong. He was disoriented when the waitress approached his table.

"You can't smoke in here," she said.

"I always smoke in here."

"New owners changed the policy."

"Shit." There was no ashtray on the table and he rapidly stood up, his heavy boots clapping against the wooden floor, to open the window and toss out the butt. He sat back down and ordered a coffee.

"The hazelnut or the Colombian roast?"

Maybe a Starbucks was overdue after all, he thought to himself.

"I guess the hazelnut," he said.

"That accent real?"

"I'm afraid so."

"Where you from?"

"Australia."

"Long way from home."

"Tired of kangaroo meat."

"I understand that."

When the waitress returned to bring him coffee, he asked her what day it was. She gave him the day the month and the year as if she had been waiting to say it to someone all morning.

"Actually, I just wanted to know the day of the week."

She hesitated, looking around the diner for the answer. "I'll figure it out; just give a minute, all these weekdays just blend together for me."

Erik poured a single packet of cream into the coffee and said "Ja, Korporal!" to himself, smiling.

The waitress peered her head around the corner from the behind the counter and told him that it was Thursday. He raised his steaming mug in place of saying "thank you." He was lucky it wasn't Wednesday or Sunday. Now, he could go ahead with his plan. He stayed in the corner and enjoyed his coffee for another thirty minutes. He listened in on two conversations: the waitress and the new owner of The Cricket, and a pair of middle-aged mechanics. The mechanics griped about Obama setting fire to all the jobs and forcing white Southern women to receive abortions against their wishes by forcing the states to keep the clinics open. The waitress was explaining the town to the new owner who was clearly new to the Bishop's, punctuating her explanations with tidbits of folksy wisdom like, "Some of the stuff you believe about people in small towns is just as ridiculous as some of the stuff people in small towns believe."

After swallowing the last dregs of his coffee, he slapped a forty-dollar tip beneath his mug and walked out silently with a fresh cigarette lodged between his yellowing teeth.

He had one last stop to make.

In the South, one didn't have a choice when it came to dealing with churches. In every town there was sure to be more churches than bars. Sometimes there were even more churches than businesses. The church was the social club, the knitting circle, the basketball team, and the bingo hall. The only important choice one had to make when moving to a one of these small towns was to decide what church to join. And Erik had discovered a simple solution to that problem – always join the church that the mayor belonged to. In Bishop's case the mayor's church was also the criminal underground. The evangelist attitudes of the American South mirrored the Boer philosophy he had endured as a child, and he wouldn't have associated with the church if it hadn't been for Fillmore. The extra cash from the moonshine was also pretty helpful in assuaging his suspicions.

One thing about churches that Erik liked was their poor maintenance. The Reverend seldom paid the contractors, who, despite being religious themselves, steered clear of as much church-related work as financially possible. Preachers and reverends were all slow to pay, aggravatingly forgetful, and very popular with some of the roughest repo men the banks could employ, repossessing everything from church vans to the preachers' cars. Since he had helped the Reverend with his building maintenance and liquor aspirations, Erik knew everything about the Bishop's Pasture Baptist Church. He knew the codes to the safe, the doors that they forgot to lock, and the loose window latches. Breaking in was no problem.

Erik hid Gurveer's jeep behind the rotted wooden pillars used to sequester the giant AC units that churned like meat grinders. The back door to the kitchen was unlocked as usual. He entered, carrying a duffel-bag with six cans of kerosene and forty sticks of dynamite tied loosely across his back. The Beretta rested on his hip. He crept through the cold, sterile kitchen, looking at his reflection in the smudged stainless steel refrigerator doors. A lone anarchist brigade stared back. The face of revenge was always desperate, he thought to himself.

He quietly opened another door and stepped through the grassy courtyard parallel to the aluminum awning, then pushed open a flimsy window to crawl inside. He was in the main building now, where he dumped two cans of butane on the carpet in the hallway. The fluid didn't flow from the cans as easily he thought, and he ended up having to squirt the fluid out. He took a quick drink from the water fountain and passed through the vestibule to the nave, spraying fluid onto the pews and bibles. He wrapped a bundle of dynamite around the wooden cross behind the lectern then laid the fuse into a puddle of kerosene. It was no substitute for gasoline, but he wanted a chance to get out of the building without completely charring himself.

He rolled a few more sticks under the pews then returned to the hallway. He kicked in the door to the office and poured kerosene over the computers and fax machines. He went into one of the spare rooms and covered a piano, dropping a few sticks inside. He sang an old song from childhood as he emptied the rest of the kerosene, "Ag pleez Deddy won't you take us to the drive-in/ All six, seven of us, eight, nine, ten/ We wanna see a flick about Tarzan an' the Ape men/ An' when the show is over you can bring us back again." It was a miracle that his father had let him listen to the Jeremy Taylor songs. Taylor, a singer-songwriter from England, had been persecuted for the mixing of English and Afrikaans in the song, but it was the fact that an Englishmen was using Afrikaans at all that had impressed Erik's father. Of course, he never gave it a true listen until he heard the big fat "Voetsek!" at the end. He poured the rest of the liquid into the carpet between the hallway and the vestibule in the long streaks from the hip, pretending he was taking an enormous piss.

He was almost done, he just needed the moonshine. The thought forced him to recall images of him digging in the graveyard with a square shovel, tossing red clods of dirt over his shoulder. Fillmore and Jeremy had worked beside him to destroy the earth around the headstone which belonged to the missing child, a tiny Mexican Baptist whose parents, both of them orchard hands, had buried an empty casket for closure. Empty caskets weren't uncommon in a state where people constantly went missing. The Reverend, who had stood over the headstone with a white gas Coleman lantern, used to say that there was a nothing but an old, hollow box guitar buried in one of the older graves. It had belonged blues singer who had gone missing along Nolichucky River after one of his fabled morphine binges. While he had been no Charlie Patton, the Rev had always wanted to dig it up and see if the old box was worth anything.

"If you do that then the old nigger's gonna rise up from the water and find you to get his guitar back," Fillmore had told him.

"I never said the blues man was black."

"Any blues man worth a watery grave's gotta be a nigger," Fillmore had sneered.

Empty graves were also a perfect place to hide moonshine. Fillmore and the Reverend had stashed twelve jars of their homemade bourbon in the Mexican kinder coffin. It had been down there aging for two years. Erik could still hear the raindrops sizzling on the lantern, the shovels slicing into the clay, and the clods of dirt falling behind him as they accrued in a wet pile of iron-rich mud. Together they had unearthed the simple casket and cracked it open with a crowbar, marveling at the gallon jars of glistening liquid amber.

Erik had looked up at the Reverend and smiled. He had said something too. What was it? It had been morbid. He had asked someone if they had a skull to drink it out of to honor the dead boy.

He walked into the basement down the dark musty halls to the safe. The Reverend kept his special whiskey in a large green wall safe, a safe that Erik knew the combination to better than his own address. He punched in the numbers and pulled back the armored door to find that there were only seven jars left. He let a couple of them break drop to the floor. He set the rest onto the ground before opening one to take a swig for the first time. He smacked his lips and shrugged. On Fillmore's best day at the still, he could only make bottom-shelf quality whiskey. Erik took the lone jar back upstairs and threw it down across the nave of the church, shattering against the lectern, which toppled across the carpeted steps. He walked up to the edge of a puddle of stinking kerosene and lit a cigarette.

17.

The circular lights of the jeep entered the mineshaft. Erik slowed the vehicle to a crawl keeping it in line with the dim path before him. He imagined that crashing into the side would collapse the entire mine. He'd be buried alive for years, at least until he starved. Bullets, knives, explosions, fire, and thousands of the pounds of dirt couldn't kill him, but time certainly could.

He parked the jeep and pulled the tarpaulin across the top. Gurveer was hanging on the metal ladder eagerly awaiting his return.

"Welcome back to the Batcave, Robin."

"I feel more like the Punisher in these clothes."

"I don't know who that is."

"Just another superhero without powers."

"You shaved yourself."

Erik touched his bald head. "Yeah, I did." He handed Gurveer the wad of cash.

"And you spent. You spent a lot," he said, counting the wrinkled, weather-warn bills.

"Well, ammunition, coffee, a case of fruit, and six cans of lamp-fluid cost money."

"What do we need six cans of lamp fuel for?"

"We don't. I needed it to burn down the church."

"You can't burn down a building with kerosene," Gurveer said.

"Obviously. I used some of the dynamite in the fire lookout."

Erik dragged the wooden crate of supplies from the back of the jeep to the edge of the ladder.

"I spared your life, allowed you to stay here, even trusted you with my jeep and money, and you stole my dynamite!"

Erik lifted the edge of the tarp and slammed the rear door. "You can't expect me to sleep in a bunker on the floor surrounded by explosives and not find them. I'm a smoker, Gurveer, and you didn't even let me know."

"I let you stay here and you used my dynamite?"

"Letting me stay here was your decision," Erik said. "Not mine. I'm just trying help."

"You're trying to help. How? By making a shambles of the whole thing? I'm the one who found you in the forest when the church tried to kill you and gave you a place to stay, food, and a weapon. Think about the risk I took, Erik. I don't really need you. I let you in. If you really just burned down the church you have eviscerated everything I've tried to accomplish for the past six years."

Erik pulled up his pants and wiped his nose.

"Well, then that's what I just did."

Gurveer's lips parted slightly. "You're not joking are you?"

"I'm not," Erik said. "I burned down Bishop's Pasture First Baptist Church."

Gurveer sighed. "That was foolish."

"Why? If we're going to take them on, we have to give them a fatal blow don't we? Isn't that military strategy?

Dominate the high ground; take out their base of operation?"

"*We* didn't do anything. *You* acted impulsively without my knowledge and, above all else, you didn't destroy their base of operation," he said, arms crossed, massaging the bridge of the nose. "They've got the girls at a ranch west of town. Not at the church."

"Wait, they have them. The Albanian girl? I thought she was just feeding people to the ones in the mountains."

"I've been here for six years, Erik. You thought I was just sitting by the campfire with my dick in my hand!"

"How was I supposed to know?"

"Because this is my problem and my plan. Not yours. You've just gotten mixed up in it. And now they know we're after them."

"The church knows about you out here?"

"Of course, they do."

"Well for fuck's sake, Honorable Mister Singh, as far as I knew you were just a crazy old tracker shooting at bean cans. I'm the one who got betrayed by these fuckers. I trusted them. I made liquor with them. I served alongside one of them in a war. I have just as much reason to carry out this vendetta as you do. I'll take out these fokken oukies if I have to do it by myself."

Gurveer shook his head and began climbing the ladder.

"What?"

"You don't understand, Erik."

"What! What don't I get?"

He stopped climbing and stared back at Erik. "Do seriously think this is what it's about? A vendetta?"

"What else could it be?"

He laughed at him. "It's about what's right, Erik. It's about helping people. If we don't stop the church, more and more people are going to die. More people are going to suffer. I'm not driven by impulse or hatred. I'm compelled defend those who can't defend themselves."

"Then why the hell did you bother telling me the whole sob story about your son?"

"That's why I came here. Not why I stayed," Gurveer said.

"Why did you stay?"

"I stayed because I'm Sikh! I'm sworn to protect every right and every shred of innocence left on this earth! I stayed because I'm a soldier of God. A God you don't believe in."

Erik winced.

"You don't know that."

"Yes I do, Erik. I can smell the nihilism on you. It drips from your pours like the juices from rotten meat. You don't even know what you believe. You don't even know what's right and what's wrong. You just are, and at this point you've been quite lucky as to what side you've fallen on. Not me. I have something to answer to. I have purpose."

"Then show me how! Let me be a part of this. Let me help. You have to tell me the plan if you want me to follow it," Erik said.

Gurveer grabbed the case of fruit and hoisted it up the ladder, sliding it across the floor of the bunker.

"It was a war of attrition. We were going to squeeze off the church's blood supply and cripple them to their weakest point before we went in for the final blow."

"So we start by burning down the church! What's the problem?"

"The problem is that they're on the defensive now. We can't ambush them. They're going on the alert, waiting for the moment when I strike."

"When we strike."

"Now I have to rethink everything I've worked for."

"Worked for? What have you done? Let's do it now. Let's go for broke."

"Going for broke doesn't get the job done, Erik."

"Sure it does."

Part Three

1.

The ghosts of the highway, crushed by steel and glass, slammed into asphalt and stone, made their presence known by interfering with the radio static and appearing as passengers in rear view mirrors. The souls lost to the thoroughfares were not human but animal: rodents and ruminants alike fell to the bloodlust of American tread. They could be seen skirting away at the edges of the high beams, their eyes shining like floating discs of silver. Beneath them lay the remains of another silent holocaust. Thousands of miles of trees and their root had been razed, disintegrated, and permanently stunted under the steaming tarmac. The lingering consciousness of the dead continued to manipulate the direction of the road, taking precedence over all others.

Cassandra noticed the weeds tangled around the roadside crosses in the evening light. Darkness fell over the Louisiana highway. She kept her purse with the two loaded guns on the seat beside her. A road map of the Southeast and Erik's letter were flattened on the dashboard, weighted down by the bobble-headed knickknack of Señor Malverde, the patron saint of narco trafficking, which had come gratis with the stolen Dino. With one foot on the gas and the other on the clutch, she felt like she had been operating a crane until about Texas when the memories of her father's manual Fiat had kicked in. She hadn't smoked in days. She hadn't had a drink or eaten anything besides gas-station fruit either. She had saved a few carambolas and granada chinas in a plastic bag on the floor since the fruit selections would be abysmal once she crossed the border.

The desert was finally behind her but the topography was still flat and arid until she'd cut through Alabama. The mountains didn't sprout up from the ground until she took the back roads of Georgia. At that point, Bishop's Pasture was only an hour away. But she would have to endure the monotony of Mississippi. The magnolia state was the odd child in a giant Southern family, the one sibling who never did as well as the others, emulating the other children to the extent of eclipsing its own identity. There was a certain badge of courage reserved for Americans who lived in Mississippi. There the idea of living was synonymous with enduring. Those who endured Biloxi, Jackson, Oxford, or any number of the small towns were heroes for putting up with such a wasteland, yet where culture was concerned, or more accurately Southern culture, no other state could ever be considered more authentic. Not even a place like South Carolina garnered as much regional credibility. While each state in the Southeast seemed to have its own character, Mississippi was the forgotten child who might never had a job or achieved any success, but it remained far more loyal to the family values than its brother and sisters.

Louisiana was the renegade, the middle child who had just enough freedom to do what she wanted but stayed close enough to her roots to never go unnoticed. Louisiana had a supremely feminine aura. She molded her experience in and around the dangerous magic and illicit drug use.

Alabama was the hunter, the wild bushranger who chose never to conform to society's rules and pleasantries. Alabama retained its indigenous past and ate boar meat over the campfire. Its fingers were blackened with soot and its nails filled with grit. Florida was the estranged child who had taken a plane abroad, abandoning the family. It had shunned the magical and survivalist mentalities of its siblings to embrace the cuisine of Brazil, the social beliefs of Cuba, and the accent of New York. South Carolina was the runt of the litter and, faithful to the preconceptions of its tiny stature, ranted and raved with a ferocity that could have only stemmed from a Napoleonic complex. The palmetto state was the first to secede from the union to protect the principal of state's rights, state's rights to own slaves. And all big families needed twins. South Carolina would be nothing without its poorer, identical twin North Carolina. Georgia, on the other hand, served as the pampered, favored child. Doted on from birth, Georgia had an easy existence and took after each member of its family. To its north were the woods of Appalachia and to the south the spooky coastal town of Savannah pulsating with its own voodoo magic and drug-induced night sweats. Its Hispanic history paralleled Florida, and its unwillingness to part with the myopic values of the Old South could have shamed the Carolinas. Finally, there was Tennessee. In all of its rocky ambiguity, it was the South's equivalent to Colorado, but Tennessee, in Cassandra's mind, seemed to be to eldest child whose memories were paved in dirt rather than asphalt.

And she carved through the dusk air, Señor Malverde's enormous head jiggled from side to side. His black neckerchief hid the metal spring that kept his plastic body together in one piece. The saint of drug smuggling looked a bit like Clark Gable to her, a western incarnation of the famous actor from bygone days, or perhaps the subtly homosexual version of him.

Her thoughts subsided as the sky dimmed. The washed-out blue scraped the dregs of the clouds like thin bands of cigarette smoke. The purple sunset disappeared. She could see that a pit of darkness had started to grow at the end of the horizon, the final cluster of fully-formed clouds marking the beginning of the night and the Mississippi state line.

She stopped at a tiny BP gas-station and put ten dollars worth of fuel into the tank. The air smelled of gasoline and the scent of burning wood. She had expected the stench of cigarettes and spilled beer, but somewhere downwind from the brightly colored station in the Louisiana countryside a fire was raging instead. She knew that Americans had what they called "controlled burns" which meant one of two things: either the county had paid someone to set fire to their a landfill, or the park rangers were predisposing a patch of susceptible forest ablaze before the dry lighting season could ruin an even bigger area. She walked inside the musty quick-mart and headed to the cooler to search for an energy drink. Many of them were indistinguishable from the beer cans and sweetened booze to her left. She grabbed a green glass bottle with a cartoon character on the front that resembled the Shoney's Big-Boy from the 1950s. The drink was called Dr. Enuf, and its tag line was "Enuf is Enough. Since 1949". What the hell, she thought. She needed energy and the bottle appeared safer than the tall black cans of Monster with its lime-green talon tears which promised both epilepsy and tooth decay akin to smoking amphetamines. She walked over and took another look at the same bruised fruit she had seen at all her stops before paying for her drink. The cashier, a thin elderly man with a handlebar mustache from a different time, noticed the glass bottle and asked her if she wanted him to pop the top for her.

"Yeah, that'd be great," she said with enough fluidity to sound American.

He pressed the bottle against the iron claw mounted to the wall. The cap hissed and rang like a coin as it hit the ground.

"There you go, Ma'am."

"Thanks."

She took the bottle and smiled at him.

The odor of burning wood had grown stronger by the time she had returned to the Dino. She jumped inside the car and turned the key. As soon as the ignition roared to life, she raced out onto the highway.

Complete darkness had finally set in by the time she reached the state line. The road sign read, "Welcome to Mississippi. It's like coming home."

She was now comfortable enough driving the stick that she was tempted to fiddle with the radio to get it away from the silent static that had been accompanying her for a while now. Music wasn't a common passenger on the road to insanity and mayhem, but she sure appreciated it. It had taken her a day to even think about what she had done. Instead she just focused on where she was going. Still, she was a killer. It didn't really matter who she had killed. Pimps were shot everyday in Tepito, but while she had gotten away unscathed once before, now she was unclean. This time, they hadn't gotten back up. It didn't exactly feel like she had been the one who had shot him. In fact it was the same feeling she had when she shot Erik, as if some other person had taken control of her faculties. The unrecognized identity that lurked inside her. The seventeen-year-old with scissors in her stomach perhaps? The scorned journalist fighting oppression in Mexico? Carl Jung believed that each person had to come to terms with the darkest parts of their personality to become complete. Otherwise, the darker half could take precedence over a weaker individual in times of crisis.

She took a sip of the Dr. Enuf and felt her first urge for a cigarette in days. The drink didn't taste particularly foreign to her, the same as a Sprite or 7-Up.

The miracle of the jazz radio pulled the stars closer. Coltrane glided through the notes like an expert skier, leaving a soft trail of echoes behind him. She listened intently, unconsciously glancing at the radio as if it were a television as she drove. She thought for a moment. Something was wrong. The radio was playing but she hadn't switched it on. Pulling her hand away from the stick, she punched the radio knob off. A burst of insect-like static screeched from the old speakers just before the radio shut itself off. Malverde bobbed his head and laughed at her. She took another sip from the green bottle. The lights shined on the brittle reeds and buffelgrass growing around highway guard rails. Dents and twists abound. The radio came back to life. Coltrane's saxophone slithered between octaves with a risky, nasal eloquence. She turned it off again. The cartoon boy on the Enuf bottle grew a pair of fangs and his eyebrows bent inward.

She drifted into an adjacent lane, took a few deep breaths and tried to keep her eyes on the road. Consciously or unconsciously, she felt herself slowing down in the absence of other drivers. The highway was completely empty. She looked into the rear view mirror to check behind her. There were no truck lights, cars beams, nor barely visible motorcyclists.

Turning her focus back the road in front of her, the Malverde bobble-head fell to the floor. The map and the letter glided around on the passenger's seat. She reached over and did her best to fold the map with one hand. She returned her hand to the stick shift, and then looked back into the rear view mirror. A pair of bloodshot eyes stared back at her. Panicking she swerved onto the shoulder. The tires screeched to a halt surrounded by a bank of dust and exhaust fumes. The male face stared back at her from the reflection in the windshield, its features partially transparent; its eye sockets puffed with congealed blood, grinning with teeth like dried corn and stale maroon gums. Its cracked, gray skin flaked off to reveal a hollow interior like a paper wasp's nest. It was laughing at her, chuckling in a strange guttural tone as if it were belching simultaneously. Never in her life had she hallucinated something so vividly. It was not a trick of her peripheral vision or crack in her perception from exhaustion. It was right in front of her, a demonic, spectral face looking into her eyes, laughing with whatever it had left in place of a voice. And somehow her brain remained still. Madness didn't frighten her. Ghosts even less. He was just floating in her windshield, laughing. Someone who had been enjoying a normal day in a normal life might have seen this face in the windshield of a stolen car and gone insane, mumbling to themselves in a catatonic state for the rest of their heavily medicated institutionalized existence. But not her. Cassandra had been through too much. The face that was laughing at her, blood dripping from its eye sockets was nothing compared to the real horrors that Cassandra had faced, and all she could do was laugh back. She gave it good belly laugh and winked at it before taking a swing of the Enuf. She had gone to college after her unborn child had been ripped from her sliced-open stomach where only a handful of girls in her class had lost their virginity. She had been through the most traumatic life event imaginable and still dropped as much mescaline and LSD as she could find on campus. She had worked diligently at her desk at the newspaper in spite of the cartel death threats. She had built a second career from ashes and could afford an upscale apartment in Coyoácan. She had almost been raped by a posse of American teenagers half her age, and she had shot two men in cold blood since then. The last time she shot a man, she hadn't even flinched. And the worst the world could throw at her now was a scary face in her windshield?

"Fuck you, Mississippi," she said out loud, in English, and continued to laugh.

The withered face screeched like a rabid wolf and faded away. She waited a moment, sniffing the cool air, before shifting into gear and speeding back onto the road. The radio switched back on and one of Coltrane's harrowing, winding stairwell solos cranked out of the speakers. It was no longer an eerie happenstance, but a last ditch effort of a child who commits one minor act of defiance before the tantrum has run its course. Incidentally, she loved jazz. She knew more about jazz than the average individual, maybe even the average jazz lover. The only station more convenient for a demon or ghost to have landed on would have been Hispanic channel that played nothing but Chavela Vargas, Inti-Illimani, and Violetta Parra. Such a station would never have existed on the Mississippi frequencies, but a woman could dream. Speeding along the blacktop, she was suddenly bursting with confidence and probably more caffeine than a simple cup of coffee now that she was nearly halfway done with the bottled energy drink at her side.

The night dragged on and the cracked, untidy public roads packed shards of glass, metal, and grit into the sport's car's tires. The debris never seemed to end. Bottles of gin, whiskey, and Budweiser littered the bases of the concrete dividers and patches of grass between the highway shoulders and the dense, endless woods framing the gray monotony of road before her. Groupings of trees juxtaposed by an opaque night always appeared untrustworthy to Cassandra, but tonight she was overcome with confidence. The Mayhaw and Ironwood lining the road had lost their stoic powers over her, and the night was now soothing. The drive gave her time to think and reflect. Summer in Mexico City never allowed for a pure black sky. The night above her looked like shifting panels of deep blues and rundown purple smoke crawling across the naked half-moon. An unreachable horizon taunted the earth with a puppet show of interstellar beauty. The big picture was beautiful because of the constant change. The long road was an unvaried world in truth. If something was novel about the unending ribbons of pavement it must have been forgotten long ago, the experience or the idea having been rediscovered by another soul that, in the end, was the same soul over and over again. She felt safe here knowing that the flat road was endless.

Cassandra wondered how many Mexicans lived in

Mississippi. Probably not as many as in the Southwest. Mississippi was the land of conservative radio preachers and crippling poverty that lead white men to commit backyard atrocities in the land of strange fruit.

On her long trips up the U.S., Cassandra officially crossed the border at Texas, near Brownsville, but she didn't hit America till Mizz'ippa. The fate of the Mexican in America was uncertain. There were no white picket fences in the United States unless a Mexican had painted them. Then again, she thought, the true fences had been erected by cockeyed laws around the edges of the reservations and broken land trusts and the national borders. But Mexicans were good at scaling fences. Fences meant nothing to the Earth's people. The land was always theirs. Texas was Mexico. Arizona was Mexico. Wyoming was Mexico. California was Mexico. Nevada was Mexico. New Mexico was Old Mexico. Utah was Mexico. Oregon was Mexico. Washington was Mexico. Colorado was Mexico. Idaho was Mexico. Montana was Mexico. American had stolen them all. The Mexican was no immigrant, this was their home.

The car radio died suddenly killing Billie Holiday's lament. She could hear a young girl crying. It was a muffled noise that sounded like it was coming from the trunk. The sobs flowed from behind her. It was another test. A young Hispanic girl's face appeared in the rear view mirror. She was pale and bruised. Her eye sockets looked cracked and the eyelids looked black and swollen like a wasp sting. Blemishes of yellow and green cover her neck and jaw. Blood drizzled from her nose. She continued to sob uncontrollably.

"I don't know why you fuckers keep showing up in

the mirror. There's no fucking backseat in this car. What am I supposed to turn and look at," she said.

The image in the rear view mirror vomited blood and began to scream.

Cassandra ignored the noises.

Unlike the old man, the girl only appeared in the reflection in the windshield. She could speak and yelled at Cassandra, "Madre! ¿Por qué dejar que ellos me cortaron? Hace frío aquí afuera. Por favor, no me dejes solo. Ellos me están haciendo daño."

Cassandra, choosing not to engage with the spirit or the illusion before her, looked through the transparent face and focused on the road in front of her.

"¡Madre! Puedo sentir sus dientes. ¿Por qué me abandonaste?"

She calmly answered, "My daughter was dead before she was born and it's been more than twenty years. None of this scares me. Stop wasting my time!"

The face disintegrated once again and she was alone with the gentle hum of the Dino's rubber tires on the road.

2.

The bottom half of the church remained as a stump of crumbled brick, standing there like a toppled building in the midst of a wartime air raid. The roof had crashed into the charred-ash remnants of the nave and the vestibule. A few pairs of the wooden beams, blackened to a brittle crust, stuck up from the sides of a teetering, flimsy wall with skeletal unfamiliarity. A thin strip of yellow tape surrounded the perimeter, draping the frayed electrical lines, smoldering wood, and twisted aluminum like a Promenade sash fitted to a cadaver.

"I haven't a reason left in my head," the Reverend said.

Fillmore stood near the door of the van behind the scores of police cruisers and fire trucks. "I got one."

"What's that then?"

"The towelhead up on the hill."

"Guvar."

"Gurveer."

"Right. You think it was him."

"Who else would it be?"

The Reverend stroked his chin.

"Naw. He's been up and about like a mountain-man for years and never seemed to be doing much at all. I don't buy it. Give me a reason."

Fillmore threw his hands up.

"Well, then I don't know anybody else it'd be. Hell, maybe the ghosts of them Mormon boys torched the place!"

The Reverend looked around the parking lot. The cops couldn't see them. He grabbed Fillmore's throat with unexpected strength and threw him against the side of the van.

"Hey, hey, what are you doin'?" Fillmore wheezed.

The Reverend grabbed his pocket knife and set the blade in Fillmore's nostril, pulling it taut.

"You think this is a joke! My church's been burned to the ground and you're just going to lie to me. You know exactly who did this."

Fillmore did his best to shake his head without letting the blade tear his skin.

"I'll cut your fucken nose clean off. Don't think I won't."

"I don't know. I mean who else could it be?"

The Revered pulled away the pocket knife and took

his hand off Fillmore before slapping his face.

"The hell was that about?"

"You didn't kill him, did you? You son of a bitch."

Fillmore went silent.

"Erik knows everything then?"

He nodded.

"God fucken dammit!"

The Reverend grabbed him by the shirt collar and bashed his head into the warped van door.

"You stupid son of a bitch!"

"He can't die."

"What?"

"You can shoot him, slice his neck and pour liquid plumber into his applesauce, but you can't kill him. He can't fucking die!"

"Shut up."

"Honest. I'm serious. He used to drink gasoline for the battalion as a trick, but it ain't no trick. I've seen him shot and exploded before. Hell, I've shot him. Several times. He's a fucking half-breed. He's one of them."

"And the others didn't smell it on him?"

"He was too strong. He got away at the last second."

The Reverend slammed him into the door again.

"Alright, alright. I let him go. I told him to skip town and go somewhere else like he always does."

"Well, you did wrong didn't cha?"

"You ain't gotta tell me that."

Reverend stepped away and stared the brittle silhouette of the church ruins in the flashing emergency lights. Night fell fast. The commotion had died down and a few of the police officers were heading back to their cars. Enough had happened here, the police didn't need to be encouraged to ask any more questions. He couldn't hit Fillmore again. The church was still smoldering and the fire department continued to blast the hose to mat down the ashes, but the inferno and convulsing heat had subsided.

"Let me tell you something, Fillmore," the Reverend whispered, his breath hot with anger. "You gonna make right what you made wrong. As far as I care, it was you who burned it down. You got a soft disposition. Find Erik!"

"He's too powerful."

The Reverend looked back at him slowly.

"Think about it for a moment. You fucking imbecile. This burning shows that he's got a weak. He doesn't think nothin' through. Trick him. Don't let him know we figured it out. Get him to come to the ranch. Strangle him and hog tie him if he don't fall for it."

"Alright."

"Where's the old boy at?"

"I'm pretty sure he's holed up in the mountains."

"Ain't we all."

The Reverend smiled.

"You go up there and you get his ass. Were gonna see what the girls think of him. And while you are at it, if that fucking India-man doesn't help you, get rid of him too. We don't need any more embarrassments like him up in those hills."

3.

In Tennessee, summer nights sting like fall mornings. Mountain winds push back signs and twirl the opposing hands of weathervanes. Clusters of green, glowing insects dispersed into the night, some nestling in the trimmed shrubs and tall weeds on the edges of the road and the far corners of empty parking lots. There is very little God here, if any. As long as the devil made no appearance, which it seldom did, the devil in men could rest easy.

The red car pulled off the highway in the middle of the night and exited onto the empty road. The stop lights swayed on their cables and hung like strange fruit from strange vines on strange trees, holding their colors longer than usual. The Dino zoomed past the lights and pulled into the familiar brightness of the Holiday Inn parking lot. Cassandra jumped out from the lowered seat and slammed the thin side door shut. The base of her neck hurt and her knees where sore from all the driving. With her steps, it felt wonderful to finally lock them in place. She took a moment to stretch before stuffing the keys in her purse, and then she grabbed the bobble-head of Malverde and tossed it into the shrubs. The bobbling eyes hadn't glared at her since Mississippi, but something sinister remained in the drug-trafficking saint's plastic face. It could have been the soul of the drug dealer she robbed and killed, dragged along by his little plastic dashboard saint. It probably would have made more sense for him to posses the car. More than likely it was just Malverde himself watching over his evil brethren from a comfortable window seat in Hell, angry that someone like Cassandra had taken to driving the red Dino.

She walked through the two sets of glass doors to the lobby. The very same Mexican girl from last time stood behind the marbled check-in desk and, once again, addressed her in English. It was three o'clock in the morning.

"Checking in?"

"I'm afraid so."

"Just one?"

"Yes, well no."

She hesitated.

"Just one, yeah. I'm expecting someone."

"Someone to share the room?" the girl asked.

"No, just company. An old friend."

"Is he a bald guy by any chance?"

Cassandra stared at her blankly.

"No, he's bearded. I think. Thick red hair."

"Okay."

She hammered on the key board.

"There a ground floor room available. One queen-sized bed. It's smoking though."

"Smoking is fine."

"I see that you've stayed with us once before."

"I sure have."

"And it's been within the year. You're eligible for a customer-appreciation upgrade. Would you like to use it?"

"No, just a simple room would be fine. I'm very tired."

The girl handed her a room key.

"Thanks for staying with us, Ms. Jimenez."

"I haven't even given you a credit card yet."

The girl winked at her.

"You can pay cash at check out if that helps."

"Oh, I see. I'm not a prostitute you know," Cassandra said.

"Thank you for accepting your return-customer upgrade."

"You mean customer-appreciation?"

The girl's face went red and her eyes briefly shifted to the left, pointing to the security camera.

Cassandra took a deep breath to feign recognition,

though she had no idea what the girl meant. All her social interactions had become fleeting, dislocated. She took the magnetic room key and thanked the girl under her breath, then trudged through the carpeted hallway to the elevator. The pattern on the carpet moved on its own like a kaleidoscope beneath her feet. She read the room number on the keycard: 606. It was a top floor suite. She wondered how many prostitutes stayed in the hotel, how many drug-dealers peered through the keyholes with guns in their sweaty palms, how many people were alone with bibles and sleeping pills tonight. She pressed the button and the elevator door opened. She stepped inside and pressed the sixth button. The cab moved up the elevator shaft. The metal double-doors opened as if for the first time. She walked through another carpeted, wallpapered hallway, passing the ominous hum of the ice machine, waiting for the numbers to get smaller, until the correct room presented itself the way omens do in dreams. 606. She slid the card in the reader and the small LED turned from red to green. The road was still there, haunting every facet of life.

She walked into the room unafraid, shutting the door behind her. A single lamp on its lowest setting shined in the corner, painting the room a natural resin color. Erik sat beside the open window with his legs crossed. The breeze pulled in a few wayward insects and pushed her hair back.

"You're bald," she said when she saw him.

"I got a haircut."

"Back in the army?"

"No, I just needed to hide my identity. I paid the girl downstairs two-hundred dollars make sure you came here. I've only been waiting for three hours."

"How did you know I'd come here tonight?"

"I didn't."

He pulled an old bottle from the ice bucket.

"I have some Jamaica rum. Do you like rum?"

"I got your letter," she said.

"I know."

"I got it before you sent it. You spoke through a medium didn't you?"

"I might have," he said.

"Seems odd that I'd meet a Nganga in Mexico. I almost expected to see you there."

"The African Diaspora is substantial," he said. "We're literally everywhere you go."

"I killed two people and I stole money and a car to get here," she said.

"I burned down a church and spent a famous mercenary's savings for the bribe and this hotel room."

"Did you tell her I was a prostitute?"

Erik pulled the cork from the rum bottle and shook his head. "No, she invented that part herself. Don't know why."

"There are a lot of things you're not telling me," she said.

"There's a lot things that aren't worth the breathe it would take to tell them. There's only the reason you're here. Then again, there's the reason I want you here."

"Why do you want me here?"

He poured two small glasses of rum and handed her one. They drank without toasting.

"This is some of the best rum I've ever had," she said.

"It's very, very old," he said.

She sat down on the bed and took her first honest breath in a long time.

"Relax. Take your shoes off," he said.

"Is that all you want me to take off?"

Erik downed the rum and walked to the opposite side of the bed, laying parallel to her. She took off her shoes and socks then placed her folded glasses on the nightstand.

"We had a lot of fun last winter didn't we?" he asked.

"I'm not sure what you mean by fun."

"I had fun."

"Do you think this is fun?"

"No, this is a little scary."

"It was scary last time," she said.

"It was ecstasy last time."

"You were on drugs?"

"No."

"Oh."

"Yeah, I loved it. I fell asleep next to you and I woke up in your arms. It's the best thing in the world."

"I was worried about that," she said.

"Do you have a cigarette?"

"No."

"You quit?"

"I think I did," she said.

"You did or didn't you?"

"I'm not sure."

"How are you not sure? You either quit or you don't."

She shrugged.

"Obviously, I don't have much of an incentive for quitting. I can smoke a pack and run a marathon. Then again I can shoot myself in the chest and run a marathon too, but it's the little things you don't think about. I drink a lot of coffee. I've often wondered how the caffeine is actually affecting me..."

She turned to him and said, "Would you please stop talking now?"

Erik went silent.

She took off her shirt and began to kiss him.

"I've thought about you every day since you left."

"I have such an old body. Why would you find me arousing?" she asked.

He cupped one of her breasts through her bra and smelled it.

"Don't do that. I've been in the car for days. I smell terrible."

"You smell like a woman."

"I smell old. And now my breathe smells like rum."

He kissed her and unsnapped her bra to suck on her nipples. She held onto his bare scalp with one hand and reached into her underwear to touch herself with the other.

"Your head feels interesting."

"Interesting?"

She smiled a little while he took his clothes off and told him she preferred him with a beard. He rubbed his five-o'clock shadow. His hair was about the same length. She reached over and tugged at his ginger pubic hairs. They were the longest hairs on his body. His penis tightened like knot. She grabbed the base and squeezed, pushing in the blue vein, massaging it up and down subtly. Sex was life, she thought. It meant nothing on its own. He pulled off her pants and slipped her white panties down to her knees. He ran his fingers along the edges of her labia before faintly tickling her clitoral hood. She closed her eyes and felt her legs tense. He kissed her again. She could taste the cigarette tar off his teeth and the rum off his tongue. He pulled her closer to him in bed. She guided his penis inside her, resting her chin on his shoulder. She sniffled and felt a lump in her throat. Her tears trickled onto his cheek.

"Why are you crying?" he asked.

She said nothing.

4.

Fillmore fried an egg on the hotplate and ate it between two slices of sandwich bread and cold mayonnaise. In the sky, a thin band of dark blue light eventually seared into a warm copper when he started his drive up to the mountain. The world was burning to life around him. Spears of green pirouetted on thick, knotted arbors. The terrain was leafy, photogenic, surprising, and something best reserved for the glossed pages of a travel magazine.

He thought about his childhood and he thought his father. He thought of things he found significant and things he had suppressed the way a man does when he approaches death. When the earth was light and still, he set out on foot with two guns and a buck knife in tow. He knew where the mysterious man lived, the old Indian on the hill. If Erik had been seen by anyone, it would be Gurveer. Fillmore wasn't sure why, but he always thought of him as an old goat.

After a climb up to the plateau, he crossed the iron bridge where the fire lookout could be seen by the Nolichucky River. He trekked upward past the giant slanting rocks and thorn patches, until the edges of the mine appeared and he could see the warn-down cabin buried in wild vines. He removed his hat and scratched his hair. Fillmore would never go bald. He figured it was the Catawba in him. The same genetics were his excuse for his many shortcomings. His mother, a fourteen-year-old, girl from South Carolina's upcountry, had rambled through Johnson City with a white, 20-year-old TVA welder to buy a little acreage. He grew up spending nights in the barn as they fought which almost always parlayed into drunken nights in the back of police cars and musty jail cells. The military had been a logical decision, but the brutality of the training had nearly broken him.

As he moved closer to the shack he realized that he wasn't prepared. He had no idea what he was doing. He knew he should have had a coffee with his egg. His stomach curdled and hardened like a layer of sour milk. Still he trudged forward. Mud from the midnight rain caked in the worn tread of his boots stinking like dry gum, weighing him down. He left red and beige footprints as he stormed the wooden steps and looked past his own reflection in the window glass.

The cabin's interior appeared empty.

He kicked in the door. There was just enough light see. The floor creaked like a stage. Paint disintegrated and snowed from the dead walls like powder. He kept the Ruger holstered, trying to seem nonthreatening. Hopefully, the old man wouldn't shoot him down the second they found each other. Fillmore was in essence stepping into a shark tank, blindly feeling his way to a great white with a flapping vulnerable arm. He walked toward the consummate darkness of the hallway and raised his hands. A switch clicked like the cocking of a pistol. Fillmore halted in the unhealthy gleam of the UV lamp.

"Hands up!" an English voice bellowed.

"They are up."

"There you go, old sport. Now to avoid further problems, I suggest you keep them that way."

"Alright." Fillmore couldn't see him.

"Alright," Gurveer repeated. "Alright he says dutifully like a true soldier, good at taking orders. He's no idiot. He knows the stakes. He doesn't care that he can't see me or that I'm talking about him in third-person. He knows I've got a shot right between his eyes if he reaches for that fucking pistol."

Fillmore didn't move.

"What are you doing here?"

"I'm looking for Erik

"He's not here."

"I ain't stupid, Gurveer. He just burned down our church. Kinda suspicious he'd be back in town as soon as an arsonist strikes."

"How do you know he was even in town?"

"The barber seen him. He shaved his head. Had his hair in the waste bin and everything."

"One way to get caught red handed I suppose."

Fillmore laughed.

"I can tell you know where he is by your answers. You're a shitty liar."

"I don't lie. I never lie. I know exactly where Erik is, but he's not here."

"Where is he?"

"Why do you want to kill him?"

"I don't," Fillmore said.

"Then what do you want?"

"We wanna call it a truce. Just with him. This has nothing to do with you. Honest!"

Gurveer went silent for a long interval. All Fillmore

could hear now were his own panicked breaths.

"Well? What do you say?"

There was no response.

"Come on, I'm out of options. I'm out on a limb here. Can't cha see that?" He squinted in the petrifying glare of the lamp and said, "I know I've been a dog and I'm sorry about what things have come to in the past. I've shot at you. You've shot at me. I was wrong."

Gurveer said nothing.

"I'm gonna leave then. I'm backing away," he said and began to step backwards. He felt someone snatch the Ruger from his holster and unsheathe the buck knife and set it to his throat.

"Is that Erik?" he whispered.

"No, it's still me."

"How did you do that?"

"In a war situation, knowing your surroundings is key. Ultimately, it's the greatest advantage an army and the lone soldier alike can have. It's the reason the United States lost Vietnam."

"The U.S. didn't lose. We pulled out of Southeast Asia."

"No, Mr. Fillmore. *Y'all lost.* I was there. The communists won."

"If you let me go I won't come back here."

"You came to my hideout armed, even though you knew he wasn't here."

Gurveer leaned closer to whisper in his ear.

"I don't think you're a very good liar either," he said.

"You kill me; they'll just hunt you down. They'll do it legal too, get the sheriff and everybody to crash in on your little Eric Rudolph act up here. You want that?"

Gurveer dug the buck knife in deep, flattening the

blade against his jugular just as a pinprick of warm blood trickled down his sun-tanned throat. Fillmore breathed through his nose and kept his chin in the air.

"You're bargaining very poorly, Fillmore. You've brought chess pieces to a gun fight," he said.

Fillmore attempted to speak just before the flesh of his goosebumped, whiskered neck split in the wake of the sliding knife. He jumped away before Gurveer could cut deeper, tripping over a cobwebbed sofa, toppling on the merciless, bent floorboards. He gripped his profusely bleeding neck and took in a loud gasp. He wasn't sure if anything important had been severed. The Indian might have been an old man, but he was still a professional killer.

"You son of a bitch!" Fillmore screamed with a rasping throat.

Gurveer tossed the knife on the floor and the raised the Ruger to fire twice. The sofa burst in half.

"This thing's got a little kick," he said. "You're a man with good taste in his firearms."

He shot three more rounds. Two pieces of the floorboard circled up from the floor between Fillmore's legs. Dust and demolished wood surrounded him in a nauseous mist. The third shot ripped through the edge of his left hand, shattering the side. His pinky and ring finger exploded amid a searing, clenched pain. Shards of metacarpal bone stuck out from the soft gush of his blood-drenched skin. In an action that strangely required no thought, he whipped out the small black revolver from his right boot and shot Gurveer in the stomach. A crazed grin spread across the old man's face as he fell against the wall, slowing his descent with his feet. His bottom hit the ground softly. He remained in a sitting position when he pulled the trigger again. The round shrieked past Fillmore's ear and lodged into the wall behind him. His cheek stung and appeared black from red-hot metallic and powder residue delivered by the proximity of the bullet. He fired the stubby backup pistol and blasted a hole clean through Gurveer's Pagh, unsure of where his skull began and the diaphanous fabric ended. His vision blurred. Something important had been cut. He had patched and sewn hundreds of men in the corps, but had never touched his own wounds. Now, he had no choice. He dug his muddy fingers into his neck and pinched off a vein. It wasn't one of the jugulars, the anterior, exterior, or interior, but one of the bigger veins beside the exterior. He couldn't remember the name of it. The sliced bit rested between his index and thumb like a squirming filament. He looked along the rudimentary sight on the revolver at Gurveer. The former mercenary was still grinning.

"You seem like a worthy adversary. We should have fought naked," he said.

"You're crazy," Fillmore croaked.

"I know. But do you?"

"I'm not insane.

"Of course not."

Gurveer raised the massive gun and fired in one jolted motion.

The top of Fillmore's boot disappeared along with all five toes. Blood spattered on the dusty wooden floor in even streaks. He recognized the perfect whiteness of the cracked metatarsal bones tucked into a deep redness of gore, clamped together by the frayed perimeter of smoking leather and a heavy rubber sole. The shock numbed the pain. He studied the destruction of his foot without much thought about the consequences. He didn't wonder about limping or pushing a wheelchair, nor did he think about blood loss or gangrene. He aimed and shot Gurveer in the chest. The gunshot punctured a black pit in the man's breast that yielded a quick spurt of blood.

"Do you want to die here? Die like this?" Fillmore managed to choke out, red spit dripping from his lips.

"No death is above or beneath a man," Gurveer said.

Fillmore shot through the old man's eye. The back of his skull erupted, marring the wall behind him with fractured skull and brain matter. Black blood frothed from the depressed, gaping socket. The Pagh unraveled and what was left of his head drooped down to his shoulders. Fillmore tossed his gun away. He thought of crawling to a first-aid or a medical kit, but he didn't even have the energy to keep his finger pinched to the vein. He allowed his mangled hand to fall to his side. His head lay flat on the wood. A spurt of blood rose up from his neck. He could taste the iron rich hemoglobin in his mouth as he swallowed. A strange odor filled his nostrils. Onions were cooking somewhere. He could smell onions and rotten fish and shit. He could smell shit too. Immense quantities of it. His eyes felt heavy, so he closed them.

5.

"Do you know what I hate about America?" Cassandra told Erik in the dark hotel room with the sheets draped around her naked body. "I hate the emptiness."

"The emptiness?"

"The world feels like a crowded cabinet in Mexico and Europe. America feels like an empty hotel room."

"I'd rather live in an empty hotel room than a cupboard."

"Not me."

"Do you at least like the forests? I mean, it's nothing like the West but..."

"Appalachia is America's dusty photo album. It has a slight redeeming quality."

"Some people get a little zealous when they're drunk," Erik said. "But you...you're a morning-time preacher."

"My anxiety peaks at the beginning of the day. As things move forward, I calm down."

They lay in silence in the empty hotel room. She eyed the bottle of rum in the ice bucket. The ice had melted into water and the old label was now transparent, clinging to the brown-glass bottle by a tiny corner. The top was sealed by a cork rather than a screw-top.

"Where did you get that rum?" she asked.

"Gurveer Singh," Erik said.

"Seriously though, where did you get that bottle of rum?"

"Gurveer Singh."

She looked into his eyes.

"Remember my letter?"

"Yes," she said.

"He's the friend you should meet. He can help you."

"You never wrote anything about a friend."

"It was in the Afrikaans portion. You were supposed to translate it."

"Sorry, I was busy driving across the continent for you. I didn't get a chance to translate it. Besides, Gurveer Singh is dead."

"No, he's very much alive. He lives on the mountain. He's got a great hideout."

"And you think he'll help me kill the girl."

"He's a little hesitant about you, but...I think he would help. He's looking for her too."

She rubbed the crust from her eyes and grabbed Erik's testicles.

"I hope you're right."

"Okay, that actually hurts."

She tightened her grip.

"Seriously, stop that."

She mashed one of his testicles between her thumb and knuckle. Erik's face turned red as he slid of the mattress, dragging the sheets with him. His legs quivered in electric pain. She turned back over in bed and nonchalantly took the miniature carton of orange juice from the minibar, unscrewed the cap and drank.

"What the hell did you do that for?"

"I'm not sure," she said.

"You're not sure."

"Erik you need to tell me something, very honest and very important."

"What!"

She drank another gulp of orange juice.

"You have to tell me something, Erik."

He peered his head up from the floor.

"What is it?"

"How do you kill vampires?"

"Sunlight, Silver, and Time."

"Time?"

"Yeah, time. Most vampires can't live forever. They just live longer."

He shuddered from the pain in his crotch.

"The girl, though. She's been around for a while."

"Have you been alive for a while?"

"No," he said, holding his underwear. "God damn it, I think you ruptured my fucking balls."

"Why not? Why don't you get to live longer?"

"I'm a half-breed. I have a normal human lifespan."

"And yet no one can kill you."

"Other vampires can."

"And time?"

"I certainly hope so."

"Have you ever been sick?"

"I don't what sick is," he said.

"Where is she?"

"Who?"

"The girls."

"A familiar place."

"Which is?"

"The old ranch. The place where they sliced you open. She's there."

She took a breath and set the orange juice down and rummaged through her purse.

"We can get there once we rendezvous with Singh. It'll be difficult, which is why we'll need you."

Cassandra took out the Sig Sauer and shot Erik in the chest. The brass cartridge singed her naked thigh as it ejected from the gun. Erik was momentarily incapacitated. She stood up and ran to the opposite end of the bed, dragging his limp body by the arms into the bathroom. She slammed the door shut and wedged a chair under the stainless steel knob locking him in. Her clothes were piled by the bedside like a molted skin. Before putting them back on, she threw his clothes out the window. Another measure to slow him down. Finally, she adjusted her glasses and straightened her hair in the mirror and walked out of the hotel room.

6.

Somewhere on a ranch south of Monterrey, Mexico lived Cassandra's last remaining relative, Pedro Auxillo. His full name was Pedro de Jesus Auxillo Montoya and, as far as she knew, his parents were distant cousins of her father on her estranged grandmother's side. They must have been the only family her father could stand since there were at least three other families directly related to him living much closer in the city of Monterrey, people who actually had the last name Jimenez. She hadn't known everything about the calamity that was her family at the time but she did know that her father had left the church at sixteen. All of the anger and strife had something to do with his long running hatred not just for organized religion, as many parents of the new Mexican generation did, but for his specific intolerance for all spiritual symbolism. The last extension of family he felt close to where the Auxillos. Cassandra would use the name years later as the first half of her pseudonym. The last name, Flores, came from a Colombian porn star that had been raped and killed in Juarez by a cartel member and a prominent officer in Mexico City's judicial police. It was the story she covered that would cost her the newspaper position once printed. The name Auxillo Flores contained both the new and the old. It served as a bridge between who she was as who she was to become.

Pedro de Jesus Auxillo Montoya was ironically named Jesus, but then again so was her father. She remembered visiting the ranch twice a year. Once in the summer and once in the winter. It was always a several-day trip and they always slept there overnight in the cold guest room just a few feet from the stench of the barn. Her relatives usually rented out the room to Haitian and Salvadorian vagrants to whom they blindly offered temporary work. Looking back, it was odd that father was strong enough to make trips miles away from town. He died when she twenty-three, just one year before she finished at the university, and seven years after she ran away to with her boyfriend in Tennessee, a land that seemed so distant and so perfect. Her father, who was especially low-key and strangely generous for a man dying of cancer, always gave Cassandra the queen-sized bed in the guest annex while he spent the night on the fold-out cot made of canvas and wool. She would give him two or three of the dozen pillows used to garnish her bed, but always knew that a sack of corn meal would have been enough for him. Unlike her, he was a person who asked for little and gave more than he needed to. Just before she'd got bed, when he would share a drink with his family in the kitchen and laugh about days past, she would visit Pedro's room. Pedro was a homosexual. His room resembled a girl's room more than a boy's or at least Cassandra thought so at the time. She'd jump on his bed while he flipped through a magazine or his expensive American CD collection. He was good at teasing her about boys she liked and teachers she abhorred. Most of them had also taught Pedro when he briefly attended the same school.

"Mr. Cautaghenrs is the devil," he had told her. "He flunked me even though I should have gotten by with a half credit."

"No, I like Mr. Cautaghenrs."

"He's the devil."

"He is not. I think you're the devil," she protested.

"You wouldn't know the devil if you saw him," Pedro had said in such an unfeeling, truthful way, that she still remembered every word of it. .

"What do you mean?" she asked.

"The devil. The true devil," he said. "There's only one true description in the old Gnostic texts by a man who had seen him and lived."

"How do you know this?"

"I learned it in Sunday school."

"You did not."

"Yeah, they teach you this kind of stuff in class. You probably don't even know what Gnostic texts are."

"Wait," she said. "You don't go to Sunday school. My papa said so."

"I don't go anymore, not since my folks stopped going to church. I'm older now. A lot has changed."

"I still don't believe you."

"Do you want to know what the devil looks like or not?"

"My papa said there is no devil."

"Forget it kid."

"I bet you're the devil."

"Oh, leave it be."

That night she went to bed, believing that she could see demonic spirits looking back at her from undulating patterns in the adobe walls.

She wouldn't see Pedro again until his mother's funeral when she was twenty-six. He had a completely different body then. He looked thinner with a wider face somehow. His hair had gone gray. He shook her hand instead of giving her a hug when they spotted one another. She asked him what he planned to do with the farm and he told her his plans to live there and keep it running.

"Do you really think you can do it?"

"I have to."

It was the last time they spoke. Ranches had always been her inner symbol of comfort until her visit to the old Llewellyn place. Well fuck it, she thought. If her life was to be bisected by the good ranch and the bad ranch then so be it. She thought about Pedro knocking wooden posts into the desiccated earth with his maul. He had his work to do and so did she. Cassandra pressed the gas pedal of the Dino, speeding onto the forgotten roads, a shoeless horse careening back to the stable with blood on its darkened mind. I'm a killer, she thought. Fuck everybody else, I'm a killer. I'm the fuckin' devil, she thought in English. She imagined Pedro dragging the donkeys to the old tarn sheet gate in the heavy rain by a long, wizened hemp rope.

"You want to know what the devil looks like? Look at me," she whispered to herself.

The Dino rolled over a terrain never meant for its simple tires. The engine guffawed like a monster with an antimonial rib cage while the garish exhaust pipes scraped along the edges of big rocks strewn about the soot and nothingness. A low-hanging wake of settling dust marked the red car's direction.

7.

Mussolini slithered across the nicotine-yellow counter top, wriggling its girth sideways to avoid the peeling shards of Formica where the plywood was uncovered. Its head remained on a set track toward the bands of sunlight running across the half-rusted kitchen sink. The massive snake coiled its long body around the black pit of the drain and perfectly wedged its head in the ripples of scales and skin above its taught wiry muscles. Unblinking and catatonic, the sun warmed its blood as it gathered the energy to advance its mechanical existence. The Reverend looked toward the snake from the old table at the center of the room which was now littered with beer bottles and fast-food wrappers. The snake looked back at him. He grabbed a half-full bottle of beer and chucked it just above the slats in the boarded window. The clear glass shattered across all four corners of the kitchen. Mussolini didn't move. The snake was unafraid, or it hadn't accrued enough energy to slither away. The Reverend was unsure of its motives. He slammed his fists on the table, shaking a few more bottles to the floor. The world shuddered. He stood up from the table and walked through the darkened hall to the giant door where they kept the girls. The antiquated wallpaper furled upward like a veil of turgid tattooed skin revealing a void of dangerous insulation. He looked deeply into the enormous wooden monolith bolted to the flimsy wall before him. They had fortified the door with iron and oaken slats as well as chunks of silver bolted into both sides of the wood like rivets, anything to keep the girl inside. One of the other men, either Jeremy or Fillmore had scribbled a Fleur-de-lis in the center of the door. He licked his thumb and tried to erase it, but the mark remained, mirroring the damned wallpaper. The Reverend tore into his face with his fingernails and screamed in the hall.

Mussolini remained in the kitchen sink. A single bead of water dribbled atop the snake's head from the faucet. The tiny drop landed between its black, dark-matter eyes without breaking; a transparent gem atop a single scale through which the sunlight refracted rainbows onto the sink. The Reverend stared at Mussolini's reptilian face, void of sagacity, and saw the strange light appear and covered his own eyes.

"Jesus fuckin' Christ!" he yelled, slumping into the next room beside the hall where an ax was mounted on the wall, shrouded in dust and cobwebs. The Reverend plucked it off the mount and dragged it to the kitchen where he raised it over his shoulder and stepped with drunken, even footfalls to the sink. The top edge was old and rusted over, but it was still sharp and heavy enough to immediately split the giant rattlesnake's head in half and cut on through its muscular body. He kept on chopping until eight pieces of snake were scattered across the kitchen gushing blood, then took a final thrust when the metallic wedge slid off the wooden handle and hurtled into the hallway as if it were magnetically attracted to the forbidden door. The Reverend used the stick to cast a few more beer bottles into the wall. The stick dropped from his hand almost involuntarily and he collapsed to his knees amid the broken glass and chunks of rattlesnake gore. He began to hyperventilate. Bending over as if to begin vomiting, he placed one hand on the ground to break his fall and immediately cut his palm on the glass while he gripped at his chest with the other in an impotent attempt to quell his erratic heart rate.

"Jesus fuckin' Christ!" He spat to the floor trying to take in a breath. His body trembled. He remembered the dog. The calm, wolfdog peacefully walking up the flooded street in a far-off country halfway between the brothel and the derelict municipal building. He stepped out of the brothel a young army man with a gun in one hand and a bottle in the other. He saw the dog as it stopped and cocked its head to look at him. The Reverend, just a recruit at the time, looked at the dog vacantly and took a deep pull from the bottle, raised the gun and shot it between the eyes. It whimpered briefly then fell to the ground and started kicking its back legs. He couldn't remember what he had said. It must have been a joke about Old Yeller. Whatever it was, he had said something drunken and coy before taking a piss on its body. He remembered every detail about the dog, but couldn't recall the woman in the jungle later on that separate but equally horrible evening. He couldn't remember what village they had found her in and he couldn't remember how many of them where on top of her. He did remember setting her on fire. That much he remembered. It was a good solution really. He remembered eating and drinking around the fire that night. It seemed that they had burned away every trace of the act. Somewhere along the line God had forgiven him and Jesus had come into his slogged, dutiful heart. Now there was more than just Pedro Jones to atone to for. He imagined her brittle contorted face engulfed in flames and vomited on the snake blood.

Jeremy stood in the open recess between the hall and the kitchen. How long he had been standing there, the Reverend didn't know. He stood there idly, staring at the Reverend who was covered in his own wretched waste. Jeremy was the last of them: the last of the Reverend's men, the last of his posse of outlaws before the law had come down on them, the last loyal fighter standing with him in the bunker or the last rebel beside him in the firing squad after the failed coup. He looked into the Reverend' eyes with a mournful, disillusioned face and, as if to crack the stones with a final pained soliloquy laden with acrimony and guilt, he said, "I got some paper towels in the back of my truck."

The Reverend burst into tears.

"Oh, come on now," Jeremy said. "Everybody has one of those days."

"Paper towels ain't gonna fix this kind of mess."

Jeremy set his hands in his pockets and sniffled. "Well, the TV did say that they's double-quilted for extra stain fighting power. I reckon it wouldn't hurt to try."

The Reverend raised his palm to show Jeremy the gash from the broken glass. "I'm bleeding. I can't feel my chest. It's over. Don't you get it? It's over!"

"Hold your horses, now. Let me just step outside and get some stuff. We'll be okay. You just need to calm down. I think you're having a panic attack."

The Reverend clenched his chest. "I think I'm havin' a fuckin' heart attack!"

Jeremy walked through the darkness of the old ranch and approached the front door, opening up a grand excess of light from the summer day. He squinted initially and saw something bright red. The front end of the Italian sports car ramped up the steps and burst through the doorway. Jeremy's ribcage was crushed, slicing his lungs and heart, pushing blood through his eyes, ears, mouth and nostrils. The weight the vehicle dismantled pillars in the walls. The top floor sagged through the destroyed ceiling. The entire property moaned like an old ship. The back tire flattened Jeremy's face and crashed through the next wall before completely stopping. The Reverend peered through the destruction unscathed. Glass and red-hot scraps from the engine were scattered among the wreckage. The structure groaned again and the ceiling collapsed, eclipsing what he could see of the red car. A nest of wood encircled him. He waited for the dust to settle before crawling out. He dragged his body across the hot ground. He looked past his shoulder at the old Llewellyn place. It hadn't been totally destroyed. A fraction of the building drooped forward. The undulating roof curled over the front like the brim of a hat. He looked toward the field and saw a woman, tucking her head into her arms as she rolled across the ground. Every inch of her being, from her hair to her shoes, was covered in dirt.

They lay across from one another in the soil; twelve feet between them, and neither of them chose to move.

8.

Erik whistled along with the radio. Summer winds blew through the jeep. It was still dreadfully humid outside but the speed of the vehicle created the illusion of a cool breeze. He touched the rapidly healing bullet wound in his chest and rubbed the knee he had broken jumping out of the hotel room. He had forced on his clothes, which dangling from the hedges like laundry, as fast as he could before limping back to the concierge desk of the Holiday Inn to checkout and eat his complimentary breakfast. A man waiting in line for the scrambled eggs noticed Erik's bleeding chest and awkward limb.

"Are you okay, man?" he had asked. "You look like you need to go to the hospital."

"Nothing a hearty breakfast can't cure," Erik had said winking.

The sunny road led through the congested streets of Bishop's Pasture to the open farm fields, which would soon open up in September as pick-your-own apple orchards.

The mountain roads slowly changed from asphalt to gravel and from gravel to dirt and from dirt to the absence of any existing path. Erik maneuvered the jeep through a secret path between two hedges. Twigs snapped beneath his wheels. Bits of ferns caught in the grill and the mechanical wench at the front. It was only mid-day and the sun was dying. It wasn't breaking any laws of physics by setting early nor was it fading away behind a gray weather front, the sun merely appeared to have lost most of its color, shining an uninspiring fluorescent light on the mountain. Erik noticed it only unconsciously and his mood was unchanged. The jeep passed cabin that Gurveer used as a decoy. Erik slammed on the breaks. The door was wide open and part of the frame was chipped away. He shut the engine off and jumped out of the front seat. He raced up the front steps and stepped inside. The hallway glowed purple from massive UV lamp. Fillmore's hacked body lay at his feet. It took him a moment for his eyes to adjust to the darkness before his saw Gurveer's body. His face was covered in a husk of dried blood.

He found a shovel and dug two graves in the evening.

9.

As the sun, uncommitted to its earthly responsibilities, began to set, Cassandra winced in the dirt. Even from twelve feet away, she could smell the putrid odor of alcohol-vomit mixing with another stench she only vaguely recognized as blood on the Reverend. She had smelled fresh blood on many occasions in her life, sometimes it had been her own, but the reek on the Reverend was specific to reptilian blood. She knew it was reptile blood, having spent time with a Colombian butcher as a teenager who prepared iguana and snapping turtle. Consciously speaking, her only concrete thought was that she was still alive after diving out of a moving car that she crashed into the ranch house and that the Reverend lying in the dirt stank worse than an inner city dumpster.

Imaginary frogs danced in a circle around them in the field. The frogs were a brilliant pink with purple polka-dots decorating their slick amphibian skin. The frogs danced around them like a Native American tribe in peculiar, anthropomorphic strides in accordance to some lost rain dance. God spit on the earth within the next passing minutes.

The Reverend stood up, weakly. Cassandra watched him limp toward her. She raised her chin and yelled out, "Don't come any closer."

–Just do it!–he mumbled.

"Don't come closer!"

–I can't take it anymore–

His voice was inaudible.

She stood up and grabbed the revolver she had lifted from the criminal and aimed for the Reverend.

–Everything we've worked for has been for nothing. The world is against us because we've been wrong. Everything we've worked has been for symbols. I've read through the bible and only seen words thinking they meant something but words are just words and words and words and words...The symbols just stay on the wall. The wall doesn't move–

"Where's the girl?"

"The what?"

"The vampire! Where is she?"

"She's in the..."

The Reverend's head suddenly burst apart like a rotten pumpkin.

Cassandra hadn't pulled her trigger. She looked at her pistol and saw the barrel wasn't smoking. No shell had been ejected from the slide. She stood in shock, the cold gun in her hand.

The Reverend's body slowly fell to the ground, bits of brain and face slopping to the side as it hit the dirt. A single eyeball continued to stare at her.

She stood in a stunned silence. The old Llewellyn ranch beyond her was still even amid its own partial destruction. A bitter wind blew her hair to the west. She looked on, past the long field and saw Erik standing inside a jeep with a Bushmaster rifle. He sat down into the front seat and turned on the ignition, driving the military vehicle up to her.

"Thought you could get rid of me that easy, huh?"

Cassandra said nothing.

Erik set the rifle down.

"Get in. We should get out of here."

Cassandra shook her head no.

"Oh come on now, there's nothing left here."

"I'm going to kill the vampire."

"You have to let it go."

"I can't."

"You have to."

He extended his hand.

"I can't Erik. I can't let them go. It's time to kill her."

"You have no way of killing her. It's impossible. We should go. Look, there's a place, a safe place where we can plan something in the woods."

"I can't, Erik."

"Take my hand, Cassandra. Come with me."

She looked toward the ranch. "There's a basement on the ranch. I bet they're in there. There's no light in there. I know that all too well."

"Cassandra, you're in shock again. You're in shock again just like the last time. Let me help you."

"It's not the last time, Erik," she said. "This time you're not going to get back up."

"What are you saying?"

"It's you isn't it Erik?"

"What?"

"It's been you this whole time. You've been protecting her haven't you?"

Erik's hands dropped. His expression changed completely.

"I finally figured it out. That's why you wouldn't help in the first place. That's why you keep such a low profile. That's why you live here. You know her. You're protecting her."

Erik put both his hands on the steering wheel.

"So now you know."

"She's your sister," she said.

"She's my mother," he said. "That's why I spent my life searching for her, looking everywhere, West Africa, Europe. I found her here. My father found her in Albania. She's the oldest living vampire on Earth, the Bardha, and she's my mother. There you go. My supreme admission of fokken guilt. Now, what the fuck do you plan to do? Huh? It's impossible to kill her. I can't even die. That's what these fucking church maniacs have been trying to do. That's what Gurveer Singh has been trying to do. It can't be done. You can only sequester her. You can't control her.

At least I want you to live. That's all I want."

She pressed the side button on her pistol and ejected the clip, letting the slide shoot back in her hand, and then tossed the cold metal to the ground.

"Well, fuckin' great," she said. "Out of every guy I've ever been with, you're the one with an oedipal complex."

"You should go back," he said.

"Let me know just one more thing."

"Alright."

"Why did you ask me to come all this way? I could have returned to Mexico and you never would have seen me again? What am I doing here?"

Erik smiled.

"What?"

"I've already gotten what I wanted."

Cassandra pulled out the revolver Fillmore had given her and pulled the hammer back.

"Are you going to kill me again?" Erik said, smirking.

"Yes," she said and shot him in the stomach.

Erik's body swung over the side of the jeep. He collapsed face down into the dirt. Cassandra slowly walked around the jeep and, as he began to rise to his feet, shot him in the back. The force of the bullet pressed him back against the ground.

"God-damn it that hurts!"

"Imagined getting your stomach cut open and the most important thing you've ever had removed while you're still alive, still awake, still seething with perfect rage."

"You really are a writer," Erik said.

"No, I'm not. I'm a killer. I kill things from now on."

"You can't kill me," he said.

"Are you sure about that?"

Erik smiled and then winced from the pain. He tried to move but couldn't. Blood trickled down the sides of his mouth.

"Wait, did you..."

(*Now these bullets here you won't find anywhere else in the world. The maker was a small company in Transylvania, if you can believe it. Lotta nonsense up in those parts what with communism and all coming down hard and all the people flooding out of the place. But these bullets, they'as the last bullets made by this distributor. That gun you got there something else completely. I don't know where you found it, but ain't no bullets gonna fit an old thing like that lest you wanna blow the damn thing off in your hand. These'll do though. These are special. Powder's good in' em. Everything should work.*) She snapped the barrel out of the gun and loaded a few more cartridges.

"These are special bullets, Erik. These are special bullets for special people like you. They're from Romania, and, let me tell you, Romanians, like Albanians, I assume, know exactly how to take care of dhampir and vampire alike."

"You..."

"Shot you with the oldest myth in the book. Yeah, I did. I shot you with silver bullets. And know you're gonna die."

She snapped the barrel back in place and aimed for his head.

Erik raised his hand as she fired a round into his skull, splitting his brain, killing him. She unsnapped the barrel again and picked out the hot shell, then reloaded.

The frogs weren't dancing anymore. They were running away.

She walked toward the back entrance to the ranch with the gun cocked and ready, her pockets filled with shells. She didn't plan on digging any graves.

10.

The park warden closed the black, steel gate between the stone pillars, wrapping an extent of chain links around the metal edges to clip the Masterlock in place. He set his key ring back on his belt and took in the fall sunset playing out like a fire fight above the dismal rain clouds that covered most of the chaotic sky overhead. He turned back to the Welcome Center after brushing a few leaves and a smudge of chewing gum of the small wooden sign. It read, "Hours of Operation: Monday-Sunday—9:00 am to 8:00 pm."

A short walk in the twilight on the narrow trail led him to the enormous log-cabin where most of the work was done in drab cubicles behind the dark and grandiose miniature nature museum. Owls with menacing talons and austere eyes hung from the ceiling on mono-filament line. A stuffed gray wolf from an Indiana museum stood atop a varnished log behind glass in the exhibit on red wolf reintroduction, because it was illegal to kill and stuff the rare red wolf. The park warden passed all of it without thought; his legs weary from another grueling nine-hour shift. He had an expensive imported beer waiting for him in the trailer refrigerator. He had bought it at the Fresh Market six miles into town and for the past hour, it seemed to be all he could think about. He strutted past the exhibit on the importance of recycling and pushed the door open with the faded inscription, "Staff Only". One of the community service kids from the youth detention center had written "infections" in gel pen beneath the word "Staff." The park warden had a small office unlike the rest of the rangers who sat in swivel chairs behind wobbly desks which held up outdated computer monitors in their cubicles. He didn't bother sitting at his desk and instead rested his legs on the scratchy couch in the wood-paneled hallway. Miss Shirley who manned the welcome center front desk walked past him.

"What's the score?" he asked.

"Six to one."

"Already?"

"Fraid so."

"Fuck the world to death," he said with his eyes closed as he rested on the couch. The three cushions weren't long enough to accommodate his entire body and his head rested on the solid armrest.

"You can't be sleeping on the job," she said.

"I'm just dreaming about that double-chocolate stout."

"Color me six PBR's for the same price."

"Color me a Monster energy just to get through the next hour."

"Hah!" She walked down the hallway and said, "Someone left a South African Rand in the donation box, you know."

"Is it worth more than that peso from three months ago?"

"Not sure." She disappeared behind the gray wall unit.

The warden stood up in the couch and yawned, massaging his aching knees. One of the older rangers walked in from the museum with the slopping mop and bucket.

"The park is officially closed and the bathroom is officially clean."

"And I am officially tired."

The ranger pushed the bucket past him and re-marked "You want me to take Kid Florida up to the pass?"

"No you deserve to get out of here," the warden said. "You've pulled a double today didn't you?"

"Yesterday."

"Just as well. Have a good evening."

"Evening's come and gone. Now is the time to say goodnight."

"Well, then goodnight."

"And a goodnight to you too." The ranger took the mop and bucket to the special closet with the drain in the concrete floor.

The warden rubbed his knees again and slowly stood up from the scratchy couch. He still had to drive up the pass and show the new kid, a transfer from the everglades, how to take down all the nature cams. It would have been tedious work in the daytime, but it was spooky, frustrat-ing work at nights when the storage drives were full. It wouldn't even be a major task if the university hadn't asked them to do it. They were the ones compiling the footage, why couldn't they go take down the damn camer-as, he thought to himself. Then again, that's what the new kid was for. They had already sent him down the highway in Miss Shirley's mini-van to pick up a group of stranded campers who had gone too deep on a trail that apparently went all the way to Virginia.

"The trails here aren't a joke," the warden had said.

"No they are not," Miss Shirley had chimed in. She was always chiming in like the teacher's pet in the worst class of the day.

Thinking back on it, the warden wasn't sure why he

always took such a high-and-mighty tone whenever something vaguely unusual happened on the trail. In truth, he never cared too much and could easily leave work at the door of his small abode as if to wipe the entire day clean from his emotional memory, but everyone at the park believed that his work was his life, so he guess he just played along.

He walked to the back of the office area, past Miss Shirley at her computer, and stepped outside into the light drizzle. There, he saw Kid Florida smoking a cigarette near the passenger side of the state-issued pick-up truck. The small black cigarette smelled more like a cigar.

"What are you smoking?" the warden asked.

Kid Florida showed him the dark, hard pack.

"Blacks? Never heard of it."

"It's a clove-based cigarillo really." He took and enormous inhale which lit up the glowing ember as he stuffed the pack back in his jacket pocket. "We headin' up to the pass?"

"You good to drive?"

"I sure am, Sir."

"Let's get to it then, kid."

The young ranger walked around to the driver's door and jumped inside after tossing the cigarillo to the gravel just out of the warden's line of vision. The headlights illuminated the softly falling rain. The warden sat with his hands in his lap as the new kid pulled out of the gravel driveway and cruised along the dirt path toward the pass.

"A couple of winters ago," the warden said. "We had a nasty ice storm and six trees ended up falling down on this road alone. A few more on the paved street just outside the park."

"Weather gets serious out here?"

"Well let's just say Tennessee ain't Florida."

The young man scoffed.

"I'll have you know I used to work at Glacier National Park in Montana."

The warden looked at him, surprised.

"Is that so?"

"That's so. I know a thing or two about hard weather. I picked up those dipshits a week ago who got themselves lost on that trail. Well, we used to call in to have people airlifted off the trails in Glacier when a summertime thunderstorm hit."

"Helicopter and all huh?"

"Yes sir."

Their vehicle, a white pickup truck, branded on the both sides with the state park insignia, crunched along in the mud as the weather rustled the canopy. They finally reached the pass and parked on the side of the road, the truck's safety lights flashing red.

The warden stepped out of the truck and slammed the door at the same time as Kid Florida.

"You'll want to park in the same place every time and put the safety lights on just out caution. Very few people come down this road, but on that off chance a good ol'boy is hauling ass on his huntin' route, you'll wanna be seen."

"I get it."

"Good."

They walked through the rain toward the hook in the road.

"The first trail cam is just up here."

"That's fairly close to the road."

"You'd be surprised. In the daylight you can make out

bear tracks."

Kid Florida scratched his head and asked, "Just curious. How come we're not doing this in the daylight right now?"

"If you got time to take these cams down in the day, more power to you. But realistically, there are more important things to be done. Closing time's when you'll be doing this. Don't worry its only every two months."

"Great."

They crawled up the ridge through the dead leaves and unmounted the first trail camera from the bungee cord woven tightly around the thin poplar trunk. The warden loosened the cord and wrapped it around his arm like a purse.

"You can do the whole four by putting two on each arm. That way you don't have to keep taking back trips."

The young ranger looked at the canopy. "You wouldn't happen to have a flashlight on you?"

"Of course," the warden pulled the giant black flashlight off his belt and shined it on the forest ahead of them.

A pair of translucent, red eyes stared back at them.

"Jesus Fucking Christ!" the kid fell backward into the dead leaves as he yelled.

"What? What is it?" The warden offered his hand.

Kid Florida swatted it away and crawled backward.

"What the hell, son?"

"Look! Look behind you god damn it!" The kid pointed behind the warden. His hand trembled.

The warden shined the flashlight into the same area and saw the bloody eyes blink. A skeletal face darted into the darkness with reptilian speed. Both the warden and the ranger witnessed the pale, hairless torso streaked with blue arteries and a rotted exposed spinal column stink into patch of leaves. Its appendages looked human with long icteric nails.

"What the fuck is that thing?" the kid screamed.

The warden could feel his knees knotting up. He could barely move. He spoke to keep himself present. "It... It might be some kind of animal with mange."

"It looked like a fucking person! Oh, Jesus Christ! What the fuck did we just see? What the fuck did we just see?"

The kid was crying.

"Pull yourself together and get back to the truck, okay?"

The kid finally stood up without the warden's help. They moved back down the ridge with only one trail cam. Fuck it, the warden thought. They'd probably see whatever the creature was on the cam and send out a biologist. It wouldn't be him. It certainly wasn't going to be him. The university would have to put in their own fucking elbow grease.

A sharp scampering noise not unlike the rain or a muskrat gliding across the top layer of a pond caught their attention. It was coming from their left. Something was moving ahead of them, trying to flank them. The warden pulled the kid back and they crouched near a fallen trunk. They said nothing. Leaves were rustling violently around their perimeter. The warden thrust the trail cam down the ridge as stealthy as he could to confuse their direction. The kid attempted to get up and run but the warden held him back and shook his head.

Frenetic movements immediately followed the crash of the heavy plastic box but just as soon returned to the top of ridge again with lightening speed.

"There's more than one," the kid whispered.

"Seems like it."

"You got a gun?"

"Of course, not."

"There's a double-barrel in the truck," the kid said.

"The hell you doin' with a shotgun up here?"

"For shit like this. I can make a break for it and grab it."

"You make a break for the truck, what's the point of getting a damn gun?"

The noises moved in closer. The kid tried to stand up and the warden held him back once more.

"Wait for it."

"It's coming."

"Wait for it."

"But we..."

"Go!"

They jumped over the trunk slid down the ridge landing a wet gulch. The kid tried sprang up from the muck and grabbed the warden's shoulder with impressive, adrenaline-fueled strength. The warden couldn't stand on his own, collapsing back into the mud.

"I fucked up my ankle, kid. Get out of here."

The kid wasted no time, digging his hands and feet into the disintegrating walls of the gulch. He almost reached the top when the pale face of a small girl stared back at him. Her teeth where stained with blackened grooves and what looked like chips of mica and tree bark. Her body was covered in a dark soil and flecks of detritus. He fell back screaming with giant clods of earth in each hand and landed atop the warden in the puddle of rain water. Red eyes encircled the rim of the gulch.

The kid shut his eyes and screamed for help.

A withered frame clawed its way down into the center of the gulch. Steam exited its mangled nostrils, producing a faint rumbling noise that seemed not only inhuman to the warden but completely alien. Behind was something else. Another distant rumble. What was it? Something motorized was approaching them.

The alien beings stared beyond the gulch with no discernible expression of trepidation nor curiosity. Something was coming.

Kid Florida screamed for help again.

The warden lay in shock. Two circular headlights approached the gulch and filled it light. The creatures surrounding them appeared transfixed like deer. He could see the grill of a jeep and nothing else when an intense purple light behind exploded to life. Thundering gunshots ripped through the starved bodies of the creatures surrounding them. He could see a silhouette a woman before a giant UV lamp mounted to the back of the jeep. She held a large semi-automatic rifle in her arms. The bullets punctured the creatures' bodies, tearing off whole limbs. Their skin turned red in the light and bubbled like steam burns. In seconds the horde was gone except for one reddened, bony figure dragging itself uselessly up the wall of slush, burying itself at the same time to hide from the ultra-violet light. The woman calmly stepped out of the jeep and jumped inside the gulch, telling the warden and kid not to move. The warden studied her military clothes. She was holding a cross bow instead of a rifle now and, in place of an arrow, the mechanical shaft had been loaded with a fat railroad spike. The sharpened edge gleamed like polished silver. She stomped to the edge and kicked the croaking body from the mud. Its flesh boiled in the strange light. She pressed the crossbow to its heart and pulled the trigger. The spike entered the hollow chest cavity without sound. The vampire opened its bony jaws to let out a burst of air and a stinking fish-like odor before dying. She kicked the body a few times before plucking the silver spike from its chest.

"Are you alright?" she asked the kid and the warden.

The warden said nothing staring at the women. The kid pulled himself from the mud and tried to clean his face with the inside of his jacket.

"You're both in shock," she said.

The warden opened his mouth, but found it impossible to speak.

The woman shrugged and loaded the spike back into the crossbow.

"Who are you?" the kid asked.

The woman rested the bow on her shoulder and hoisted herself up from the gulch with ease, laying the bizarre weapon in the bed of the jeep. She rubbed the mud off her pants and scrapped the tread off her boots against side of the wench near the headlights.

"Who are you?"

She looked back at him and said, "I'm Amy Sue, and I'm here to avenge my death and find the heart of Pedro Jones."

Connor de Bruler was born in Indianapolis, Indiana. He grew up in Greenville, South Carolina and Nuremberg, Germany. He is 24 years old. His first novel, *Tree Black* is available from Montag Press.